"I can see there's only one way to shut you up!"

Before Alexandra could react, he grabbed her by the shoulders and swept her backward across his lap, leaving her looking up at him in open-mouthed amazement. The smile left his face and he groaned once, as if agonized, before lowering his head to hungrily claim her lips.

Her eyes squeezed closed . . . Now she was free to concentrate on the sensations caused by the movement of Nicholas's mouth on hers . . . somehow familiar, somehow even more exciting than before. To keep herself from falling (or so she told herself) she reached up and encircled his neck with her arms, an action that lifted her toward his rock-hard chest and allowed him even greater access to her body . . .

Other Avon Books by
Kasey Michaels

THE BELLIGERENT MISS BOYNTON
THE LURID LADY LOCKPORT
THE RAMBUNCTIOUS LADY ROYSTON
THE TENACIOUS MISS TAMERLANE

THE SAVAGE MISS SAXON

KASEY MICHAELS

AVON
PUBLISHERS OF BARD, CAMELOT, DISCUS AND FLARE BOOKS

AVON BOOKS
A division of
The Hearst Corporation
1790 Broadway
New York, New York 10019

First Avon Printing, August 1985

AVON TRADEMARK REG. U. S. PAT. OFF. AND IN OTHER
COUNTRIES, MARCA REGISTRADA, HECHO EN U. S. A.

Printed in the U. S. A.

WFH 10 9 8 7 6 5 4 3 2

THIS ONE'S FOR ALICE!

Prologue

IT WAS a chilly night, even for November, and there was precious little moon to ease the darkness. All the honest folk in the neighborhood had been long abed, aware that nights like these were best suited to keen-eyed owls or, as had been the case these months past, highwaymen on the lookout for any person for whom they could ease the burden of traveling the highways while hampered by quantities of cumbersome jewelry and purses heavy with gold.

Yet there were others abroad this night besides creatures of prey and their hapless victims, for in the distance could be heard the sound of male voices raised in raucous song. These voices belonged to a trio of young gentlemen who had lately quit the Bull and Feathers tavern as well as the village of Linton itself (having already been politely but purposefully ejected from two neighboring taverns) and who were now jogging arm-in-arm along the dark roadway leading away from the village.

Their song faltered and then died away completely as none of the merry trio could recollect the words to the fifteenth verse of the ditty they had been composing all that evening long (a bawdy tune whose loss to the pages of musical history could only be termed a blessing).

In silence they marched on, crisscrossing the roadway several times in the meandering gait of the happily inebriated, until they at last reached the crossroads. Once at this juncture their wine-bemused mental faculties combined with a sudden deterioration of their physical coordination, and they fortuitously sat themselves down beside the signpost before they either set off on a wrong turning or tumbled into a puddle and drowned themselves.

"Anyone know where we're at?" one of the young men asked of his companions.

"Signpost here," pointed out the second youth. "Jeremy," this one ordered the third, "your neck of the woods—tell us—are we lost?"

The one called Jeremy hauled himself upright by means of a hand over hand climbing of the signpost until he stood, rocking slightly on his heels, staring owlishly at the five fingerposts nailed to the main signpost.

After a few moments spent in fierce concentration he announced happily, "We're in England!" before collapsing to the ground in a paroxysm of giggles.

"Cup shot," the first young man observed sagely. "Well and truly corned."

"Thass no' so," Jeremy protested. "No more than a drop in the eye, Billy, thass all, no more."

The one called Billy shook his head in the negative. "Drunk as an emperor," he persisted.

"An emperor?" Jeremy questioned vaguely.

Their companion, Cuthbert Simpson, and the acknowledged leader of the trio, translated. "He means you're ten times as drunk as a lord. And, worse luck, he's right."

"Wanna go home," Jeremy retorted feebly. "Feeling dashed queer."

"Is it any wonder, my dear friend?" Cuffy, as Cuthbert was known to his friends, countered. "I *did* try to talk you out of jumping off that hen house with a chicken tucked under each arm. Any fool could have told you it wouldn't work."

Jeremy hung his head. "It should have worked. There were wings and feathers enough."

"That's true, you jingle brain," Cuffy countered, "except that even Billy here knows *chickens don't fly*. But did you listen? Oh no, not the so-smart Lord Jeremy Mannering. You were going to let those chickens fly you twice around the barn and into the second-story bedroom of the good farmer Bates's granddaughter."

Jeremy looked down at the front of his fine waistcoat and breeches, covered now with dry, caked mud acquired when his body made rude contact with the soggy farmyard, and decided to change the subject. "What say we head back to Linton Hall? But first," his eyes lit with another sterling idea, "what say we, um, *rearrange* these little finger-posts?"

As this practice had long been looked upon as an almost mandatory prank, committed by youths out on a lark for un-told generations, this idea met with near instant agreement.

Within minutes the deed was done, and the trio was about to set off again when suddenly they heard the thundering ap-proach of horses moving fast.

"Bing avast, you coves; play least in sight behind the crackmans! It's land pirates—prod your dew beaters!"

Jeremy thumped his fists against his hips. "There he goes again, Cuffy, spouting thieves' cant gibberish from that damned book. Good God. The fella reads one book in eigh-teen years and it has to be a damned dictionary of sporting language. What's he saying?"

"He says we're to go through the hedges because high-waymen are approaching. We're supposed to run away on foot—move our dew beaters," Cuffy responded rapidly, moving toward the hedges. Looking back over his shoulder, he saw that Jeremy was still standing in the middle of the road, laughing at the thought of calling feet "dew beaters." "Jeremy!" Cuffy commanded tersely. "Bing avast your arse!"

Belatedly, Jeremy moved, diving headfirst into the hedges alongside the road just before a large post chaise and four plunged to a halt at the crossroads. "A rattle and prad," announced Billy anticlimactically.

"Brilliant deduction, friend," responded Cuffy, still spit-ting leaves from his mouth thanks to his mad dash through the hedge, "if only a trifle tardy. Look—the postilion is reading the fingerposts. Now he's telling the driver, yes Billy, I mean the rattling cove, which way to go."

The post chaise lumbered off down the road, in quite the

opposite direction of its intended destination, and Cuffy saw a dark female shape outlined through the side window.

"Well, well, my lady," he murmured thoughtfully as he threw an irreverent kiss at the departing vehicle, "and whose uninvited guest shall you be this night?"

Chapter One

"WOULD you mind repeating that, Poole?" the man asked with remarkable *sang-froid.*

Poole watched nervously as his master, Nicholas Mannering, Earl of Linton, settled his long, lean torso into a chair set behind the massive desk in the Linton Hall library. His lordship then picked up a silver letter opener and began fingering its sharp tip negligently as he impaled his longtime butler with one sparkling golden eye.

It was bad enough before, thought Poole quakingly, enduring Master Nicholas's unsettlingly direct gaze, but it was doubly frightening now—almost as if the black velvet patch covering that blind left eye were capable of looking right through a person and into his soul.

"Well, um—er—yes, sir, I mean—er—*harrumph.* That is to say, sir . . ." Poole's words trailed off.

"Allow me to assist you, old friend," his lordship intervened before his flustered butler collapsed altogether. "We shall begin at the beginning, if you please. Last night I retired early with another of these cursed headaches that have plagued me since Waterloo. Am I right so far, Poole?"

Poole used one shaking finger to ease his tight collar. "That you are, sir. Powerful weary you were too, sir, if you don't mind my saying so. But before you retired I reminded you that young Master Jeremy and his friends were not as yet at home and asked if I was to let you know when they returned. Upon which, sir, you said—"

"Upon which, Poole, I said 'the man who wakes me once I finally find sleep tonight will rue the day he was born,' " Lord Linton supplied feelingly.

"Exactly so, my lord," breathed Poole, relaxing a bit. "And that's why I didn't wake you when the—er—young woman began banging on our door after midnight. Knocked so long and loud, sir, I thought King George himself was calling, I did, and that's no lie. Well, sir, when I saw it weren't Farmer George but only some dowdy dressed female—and not even an English female, if you take my meaning, sir—I told her straight that she had to leave."

Seeking to save himself from a recital of all Poole had said to the woman, Nicholas interrupted his butler again. "But she had already dismissed the post chaise that had brought her?"

Poole gave a deep sigh. "That she had, my lord. Even then I saw no great problem, as I could have had one of the stableboys run her to the Bull and Feathers, but she was having none of that, she told me. Said she *belonged* here, sir, and then—and I repeat, sir, I was *not* in my cups—this great hulking man-monster tramps into the hall carrying his weight in baggage and trunks. Oh sir, it was a sight fit to turn your hair white—this man-beast was near as wide as the doorway and twice as high. But the worst of it was his face. Coal black it was, sir—not like Molineaux, that fighter you call The Black, you know—but *painted* black and all shiny and streaked like."

Lord Linton allowed himself a small smile at the sight of the squat, chubby, middle-aged Poole trying to recreate a visual picture of the creature.

Poole saw his master's amusement and pushed on to his conclusion while, it seemed, the gods were still smiling on him. "Well sir, while the beast grumbled in some foreign tongue the woman tells me, oh so superior like, as if she *was* somebody, 'So your master's abed, is he? Well, I should hope so, man; after all, he is an ancient piece, isn't he? As a matter of fact, until Chas told me different I thought the old boy had turned up his toes long since.' *Then,* my lord, she hikes up her skirts and brushes right past me to the stairs, the beast following after her, and says she'll find her own bedroom!"

"At which point you positioned yourself at the base of the

stairs, arms outflung, and told them they would have to get past you first?'' ended Lord Linton, his one good eye twinkling at the mental image such a scene evoked.

Poole hung his balding head in shame. "I am sorry to say I did no such thing, sir. I did try to stop them, I swear on my mother's eyes—er, sorry, sir, I mean, I swear on my mother's saintly grey head—I *did* try, but the beast turned and growled at me and, well, sir, I'm not a young man anymore, you know.''

Nicholas Mannering unbent himself from his chair and rose to his full height, the early morning sun striking his black locks and highlighting them with gold. His wide mouth splitting into an amused grin, showing his even, white teeth to advantage against his deeply tanned skin, he assured his butler that he was certain he had done his best and that, indeed, no man could have done more. Then, clasping his hands together behind his back, he began pacing up and down in front of the desk. "But what about Master Jeremy and his two ramshackle school chums? Surely they could have assisted you in rousting our bizarre housebreakers?''

"Begging your pardon yet again, sir,'' Poole dared to say, "but the young master and his companions were in no fit state to be of any help, more's the pity.''

Lord Linton allowed himself a small smile. "Am I to take it then that m'brother and his guests were, perchance, inebriated?''

Poole's brow furrowed in confusion. "If in-ineb—er—if that word you said means were they falling down drunk, then I must sadly say, yes, my lord, they were.''

"And would you also say that to rout this same hapless trio out of their snug little beds at the ungodly hour of eight in the morning could only be deemed cruel and inhuman treatment, when anybody of any sense knows being forced to confront the inevitably painful results of an evening of deep drinking even a moment before noon, at the very earliest, could easily convince those same afflicted persons that death was not only imminent but to be eagerly anticipated?'' his lordship prodded.

Poole grinned his widest grin. "Powerful cruel, sir," he concurred happily.

Lord Linton shrugged his shoulders in patently mock sorrow. "Yet I fear I must ask you to send servants to do just that, Poole. If we are to deal with this uninvited guest and her great beastie, I would prefer to do it with my brother at my side—and his erstwhile friends as well, as long as they are in residence anyway. See that they join me within the next half hour, please." As Poole turned to relay his lordship's order to the footman in the hall, barely hiding his glee over this golden opportunity for revenge on the youths who were so patently useless last night when the man had been sorely in need of advice and assistance, Lord Linton added, "And have a pot of coffee sent in here—a large pot, as strong as Cook can brew it."

Drat you, Jeremy, Nicholas thought to himself after the butler had departed. How much longer are you going to indulge in these hey-go-mad starts of yours? If it's my attention you desire, brother, you certainly have it!

While waiting for his brother and his friends to put in their appearance, the Earl, his unknown house guests temporarily dismissed from his mind, reflected yet again on Jeremy's recent behavior.

His brother, now eighteen, seemed to be attempting to throw over the traces in a bid for independence—that, and displaying a strong desire to be at home at Linton Hall where he could "take care of you, Nick, I owe it to you."

A series of minor infractions had given rise to an almost constant correspondence between Nicholas and Jeremy's headmaster, but even the Earl's most eloquent entreaties could not keep Jeremy from being sent down for the rest of the term when the lad, in a fit of pique, tossed his dinner at an annoying fly. The fly providentially escaped the missile that finally landed, very improvidentially, square in the face of the hall proctor.

When Cuffy Simpson and his cousin Billy Bingham, Jeremy's best cronies, immediately followed their friend's lead by tossing their own suppers at two of their tablemates who were unfortunate enough to be sitting-duck targets, a veritable free-for-all of vegetable flinging and mutton tossing broke out throughout the dining hall—with predictable results.

Since Billy was an orphan and lived with Cuffy's parents, and since those parents were visiting in Ireland until after the Christmas holidays, Jeremy decided there was nothing for it but to bring his friends home with him.

That was three weeks ago—three long, trying weeks for Nicholas and, it now seemed more than obvious, Poole as well. It was now November 1, 1815, and before the first day of 1816 dawned some two months hence, Nicholas was sure he would be able to look back on June and the horrors of Waterloo as only a pale reflection of the epic battle that was bound to burst around his ears if he could not find a way to control the three hellions now under his roof before they set the whole of the neighborhood at war against them.

Now, just to add to his problems, there was this business of some unknown female barging into his home, badgering his butler, and then barricading herself inside his late mother's bedchamber, some black-faced wild man—her husband perhaps—with her.

He stepped back to allow Poole to push the serving cart in front of the sofa, took the steaming cup of coffee the butler offered him, and then went to stand at the window embrasure, sipping from his cup while conjuring up and then discarding several theories about the unknown female.

He had been standing there for some minutes when his thoughts, which had been remarkable for their lack of profundity or productivity, were interrupted by an aggrieved voice coming from the doorway. "Do you know what time it is? It's 8:30!"

Mannering turned slowly to face the newcomer to the room. "My congratulations, Jeremy. Whoever said you don't pay attention to your lessons? Why you've only been at school this last decade or more and already you have learned how to read a clock. I cannot help but feel your enormous school fees have not been paid in vain. Tell me, have you learned anything else of import you wish to impress me with this morning? For instance, a snappy recitation of your

15

sums, or perhaps a short dissertation on the rule of Charles I? Or shall we dispense with these edifying transports of wisdom and discuss more mundane matters? Such as— where did you and your madcap partners in crime go last night? Which of my neighbors is to come calling today carrying either a bill for damages or a horsewhip he wishes to take to your hide? Or last but most certainly not least, do you by any chance have even the foggiest notion what a strange woman and her hulking male companion are doing in our mother's bedchamber?''

Throughout this long, deceptively soft-spoken diatribe, young Jeremy Mannering had been visibly shrinking before his brother's sharp-eyed gaze, but at Nicholas's last words the boy straightened up, looking momentarily blank, then seemed to become suddenly enlightened. A vivid red flush ran up his neck and into his cheeks.

His brother saw all these easily read clues to Jeremy's probable guilt and ventured, "Do you wish to tell me the whole of it now, or do you choose to wait for reinforcements?''

Instead of giving an immediate answer, Jeremy lurched across the room to pour himself a cup of coffee, his badly shaking hands putting him in danger of scalding himself. He took several quick small sips of the steaming liquid in an effort to gain some control over his baser instincts (which were telling him to take to his heels just as fast as he could), and in the hope the coffee would have the double-barreled effect of easing the pounding in his head while making his mouth feel less like it was lined in uncombed wool.

The entrance of his two friends caused him to sigh in relief. Surely Nicholas wouldn't cut up too stiff with guests in the house.

Cuffy Simpson was the first to enter the room, his trim figure and blond good looks seemingly unaffected by his night of cheerful debauchery. His cousin, however, was another matter. Billy Bingham, blessed with neither his relative's physique or looks, had also missed out on the family strong stomach. His chubby body fairly dragged itself across the carpet, striving to reach the restorative coffee in an effort to stave off a complete collapse, and his normally sallow complexion looked positively green beneath his thatch of muddy brown hair.

While Billy kept a two-handed death grip on his cup, drinking from it noisily like a large dog lapping up water, Cuffy, already reclining on the sofa, meticulously spread a napkin over one knee, took one or two delicate sips of his own coffee, and said amicably, "Beautiful morning, isn't it? Sunshine, a blue sky, what more could one ask for in a morning? Does anyone care to go for a ride?"

Nicholas, who had been watching all this little play with varying degrees of interest, humor, and disbelief, questioned Cuffy: "Tell me, if you were to ride out this morning, oh, let's say as far as the crossroads, and then momentarily lose your way—in which direction would the fingerpost for Linton Hall be pointing?"

Billy looked at Jeremy, whose face was just then a very painful red, nudged his cousin in the ribs, pointed to their friend, and pronounced, "The cull is leaky, and cackles."

"Translate, Cuffy," the Earl ordered, well accustomed to Billy's propensity toward cant language.

"A cull is a man—Jeremy—and Billy says he's leaky, apt to blab, which," Cuffy's eyes turned accusingly on Jeremy, "he obviously has done, cackling just like a barnyard hen."

"I did not!" Jeremy protested hotly. "I never said a word. Nicholas guessed it, that's all. I don't know how, but he did."

His brother came over and draped a commiserating arm about his shoulder. "You aren't 'leaky,' Jeremy," he soothed him, "but then again I shouldn't play at cards if I had your face—it speaks for you without your ever saying a word. Besides, do you think you three invented changing fingerposts as a lark? It was only a lucky guess on my part."

"Devilish acute, ain't he?" Billy stage-whispered to his cousin, who hissed back at him to shut his trap and give his tongue a holiday.

Nicholas was on the verge of forgiving the three boys, all now looking suitably repentant—even Cuffy—when Billy, who was still harboring the fear his drink induced miseries might yet prove fatal, felt his heart drop to his toes as he realized he was nearing the final stages of the death throes—he had begun to hallucinate!

It had to be an hallucination. There could be no other explanation for the sight he now saw framed in the doorway. The apparition was, first of all, *huge,* being at least six and a half feet tall (though it could have been twelve and a half feet, Billy wasn't sure), all of it made up of very solid-looking muscle for a figment of one's imagination.

There were beaded slippers of some sort on the creature's feet, five-inch-long fringe hung from the outer side seams for the entire length of a pair of buckskin leggings, and a huge cape constructed of some dark brown animal fur was slung about a fine set of brawny bare shoulders. Atop the large head, a mop of long, coarse, black hair was banded about the forehead with a thin leather thong. But it was the apparition's face that took and held Billy's incredulous eyes. The face was painted coal black!

"I'll never touch another drop, Lord, I swear it," Billy babbled, completely forgetting his stylish slang in his agitation. "Just, please Lord, *make it go away!*"

At Billy's exclamation the other occupants turned toward the door.

"Oh, I say!" exclaimed Cuffy, for once nonplussed.

"I think I'm going to be sick," Jeremy added forlornly.

Only Lord Linton appeared unmoved by the presence of a demon in his library, as he took three paces forward and said, "Good morning, sir. Care for a cup of coffee?"

The demon spread his feet more firmly apart, folded his massive arms across his equally massive chest, and replied, *"N'gattósomi."*

By now Cuffy had recovered his composure. Grinning wickedly, he turned to Billy and asked, "Care to translate, coz? No? Well then, at least close your mouth—or as you'd prefer to say—dub yer mummer."

Jeremy began to dance around the room, one finger pointing at the man in the doorway. "I know what he is, Nick—he's a wild *Indian!*" he exclaimed triumphantly.

"So it would seem," his brother returned. "Now all we

18

have to do is ascertain whether that gibberish he was spouting means he's thirsty or that he intends to remove all our scalps with that wicked-looking rib sticker hanging on his belt before going merrily off on his way.''

"It means he's thirsty," a feminine voice announced from behind the Indian. "If it was your scalps he was after I'd currently be addressing a roomful of hairless corpses." With that, the owner of the voice stepped out from behind her companion and strode confidently to the center of the room, thereby allowing everyone to get a good look at her.

And look they did, drinking in the sight of a tall, slimly built young female of about nineteen or twenty dressed in clothing that had been out of style in England for at least five years. But, as clothes never quite made the man, her clothes could not unmake her, for she was undeniably one of the most strikingly beautiful women this part of the country had ever seen.

Hair that resembled shimmering blue-black silk hung in an unbroken fall down to her waist and a little beyond, with not a single tendril or wisp of curl cluttering up the purity of her strong high cheekbones, smooth rounded forehead, classically aristocratic straight nose, or finely carved chin. Framed by a thick fringe of long black curled lashes, her huge black eyes appeared to slant upward at the outer edges, like a cat's, and although there was a slight pinkish bloom to her cheeks and her full wide mouth was enchantingly rose-kissed, her clear complexion was colored by a golden-all-over tan. She was, in a word, exotic.

"*Two* Indians!" Jeremy shouted before Nicholas could quell him with a stern look.

The Earl could see the girl was trying to suppress a grin. Obviously the chit was enjoying herself hugely at their expense.

"*Mattapewíwak nik schwannakwak,*" she told her companion, causing him to grunt and nod his head.

"What did you say to him?" Cuffy dared to ask.

The woman turned to the lad, smiled (thereby showing off a full set of startlingly white, even teeth), and informed

19

him demurely, "I said, loosely interpreting, of course, 'The white people are a rascally set of beings.' "

The young men stared at her in awe, but Mannering had reached the limit of his endurance. Their unwelcome overnight guest and her black-faced shadow had some explaining to do and it was time and enough to make a beginning. So thinking, he approached the female and asked baldly, "By what right, madam, did you come barging into this house last night, bully a valued family retainer, and then take up residence for the night?"

The Indian growled something evil-sounding under his breath but a motion from the girl silenced him.

With unhurried movements the girl poured herself a cup of coffee, laced it liberally with sugar, and sat herself down, of all places, in Nicholas's own chair behind his desk.

"I see I have some explaining to do," she said, eyeing the other occupants of the room one by one. "I'm here in answer to Chas's—that's my father—dying wish. Frankly, left to my own devices I wouldn't come to England if I were to be offered the throne. For all Chas was English, *I* was born an American and I'm proud of it, but there's no denying deathbed promises, now is there?"

She took a gulp of coffee, grimaced at its sweetness, and went on, "Chas told me the whole sordid tale before he passed on, you see—how he ran afoul of my grandfather and was cast out of house and home. Not that it mattered much, as he was a younger son anyway, but I could tell his pride was still hurt even at the end. Anyway, once he was sure I was to be left alone in the world, he made me promise to come here to see my grandfather. I guess Chas hoped the old curmudgeon, or Chas's older brother if the old man was already dead, would take me in."

She stopped for breath and looked Nicholas in the eye. "Now, who are *you?* You're too young to be my uncle, and it's certain you're nobody's grandfather. How do you fit in the family?"

The Earl rubbed absently at his left temple, which was beginning to throb. "Young lady, I have not understood a single word you have said. However, I do believe we can begin to unravel this muddle once I tell you that these three over here," he pointed an accusing finger at the trio, "amused themselves last night by rearranging all the finger-posts at the crossroads outside Linton. You may think you know where you are at, but you are probably several miles distant from your intended destination.

"This, madam, is Linton Hall. I am Nicholas Mannering, Earl of Linton, and that shamefaced redhead is my brother Jeremy."

"So sorry, ma'am," Jeremy muttered weakly.

Mannering continued: "The other two are friends of Jeremy. The aspiring dandy over there, the despair of his afflicted parents I might add, is Cuffy Simpson, while that humble, slightly vacuous-looking youth is his cousin, Billy Simpson. Now," he prompted, "if we could know *your* name . . ."

The girl did not, as Nicholas had assumed, nay, even hoped, look the least disconcerted to learn that she had spent last night, not in the bosom of her family, as she had supposed, but in a house full of strangers—and *male* strangers at that.

"Certainly, my lord," she responded readily enough. "As I was named for my grandfather—Chas's way of hoping some soft spot in his papa's heart over that bit of sentimentality would assure me a place at the old man's table —telling you my name may assist you in directing me to my intended destination. My name, gentlemen, is Alexandra Saxon."

The silence in the Linton library once Miss Saxon had finished speaking was positively deafening.

"That's impossible!" the Earl exploded, at last breaking the uncomfortable silence.

Miss Saxon quickly directed her attention solely on Lord Linton, although the sight of the three young men all staring at her bug-eyed, their mouths agape, was a very diverting attraction. "Impossible, my lord? Surely not. Improbable, maybe. Incredible, most assuredly. But *impossible?* Why, my lord—have you not heard of the birds and the bees?"

His lordship had the good grace to color under his tan, but

he recovered himself neatly. "I am not so ignorant as to be unaware of the mechanics of conception, madam," he informed her coldly, trying (in vain) to disconcert her, "but I do admit to a grey area when it comes to the reproductive capabilities of a *corpse!*"

In answer, Miss Saxon gave a gay laugh that succeeded in turning Mannering's blush into an angry flush. "Oh ho," she said cheerfully, "is that the way of it then? Chas said it might be."

"Then Charles Saxon did not die just months after leaving home under a cloud over twenty years ago?" Jeremy broke in.

"He most assuredly did not," Miss Saxon told him, "and I am proof of that, now, aren't I?" Turning back to Lord Linton she pressed him, "Tell me, please, sir—as I am interested to hear in what manner Chas was supposed to have met his Maker—how did my grandfather explain the death? I assume Grandfather left himself a loophole in case poor Chas had a change of heart and one day showed up on the family doorstep."

"I believe, if memory serves, your father was lost in a shipwreck," Lord Linton put in dryly.

"Oh, of course," Miss Saxon gurgled, clearly delighted. "Then would come the rescue at sea, unfortunately by pirates whom he luckily escaped some years later. Or perhaps he had a convenient loss of memory—that returned miraculously one sunny day. Then, *voilà*, the prodigal returneth!" She shook her head in amazement. "A crafty old soul, my grandfather, wouldn't you say?"

"Why did your father leave in the first place?" Cuffy broke in, clearly quite interested in the proceedings.

"I'm not quite sure," Alexandra answered. "Chas was never too clear on that point, although I believe it had something to do with his being a younger son, with no say in running the estate. Anyway, he sailed to America, settled in Philadelphia, met my mother, and remained in the city until his death."

At these last words the Indian, long since forgotten by everyone but Billy—who was still staring at the man as

22

though he might either disappear or attack at any moment—began a low rumbling moan deep in his chest. The sound grew louder as it rose in pitch to become a high, strident wail. The men in the room felt a shiver of apprehension run down their spines at the sound, but then, just as abruptly as it had begun, the wailing stopped.

Alexandra apologized hastily, "I beg your pardon, sirs. He *will* do that every time I mention Chas and d-e-a-t-h in the same sentence. They were quite devoted companions, you know," she ended, as if that explained anything, which it didn't, at least not to Lord Linton.

Now his lordship skewered the girl with his one good eye. He was beginning to experience an uncomfortable, anxious feeling deep inside him and decided it profitable to clear up any lingering misunderstandings as quickly as possible. This anxiety may have been responsible for the crudity with which he put his next question. "Are you, madam, I earnestly pray, born outside legal wedlock?"

"Oh, I say!" interjected Jeremy, purely aghast at his brother's question.

Now it was Miss Saxon's turn to cast daggers at his lordship with her two black, flashing eyes—much more disconcerting than Linton's one-eyed version of such a look, or so thought the observant Jeremy. "It makes a difference?" she questioned from between tightly clenched teeth.

" 'Course it does. Only stands to reason. By-blows of no account. A gentry mort's a whole different kettle of fish. Right, mates?" This sterling little piece of information came from Billy, whose bright smile quickly withered under his companions' hard stares.

"You large-mouthed baboon!" Cuffy hissed.

"Always said he was short of a sheet," Jeremy apologized desperately to his brother. "Nary a hint of a furnished toploft."

As they all shuffled and gabbled in their discomfort, the Indian, noticing Miss Saxon's rigid posture, slid silently into the room to take up a menacing stance behind her, one hand on her shoulder, the other on the hilt of his knife.

Lord Linton quickly took charge, explaining, in great detail, the reason for his rude question. It was one thing to have the illegitimate offspring of a peer under his all-male roof—but quite another to have the dear, and only, granddaughter of Sir Alexander Saxon compromised by inadvertently spending the night in that same all-male household.

"In that case, sir," Alexandra replied, beginning to enjoy herself mightily, "you may consider me compromised."

"Oh, lord, it's pistols for two, sure as check!" Jeremy cried fatalistically. He knew how monstrous disagreeable old man Saxon could be—and that was on his good days. There was just no telling the sort of rumpus he would kick up over *this* little bit of news.

It only took a few seconds for Cuffy to realize that Miss Saxon's presence in this "all-male residence" was in no small part due to the prank of the night before, and he hastened to whisper to Billy, "I suggest we best toddle off now, coz."

"Yes, you'd best do that," Nicholas agreed, overhearing Cuffy. "As I am feeling a strong desire to lay violent hands on someone it might be prudent of you to absent yourselves with some haste. *Not you!*" he concluded in a stern voice as his brother made to quit the room hard on his friends' heels.

Once Jeremy was again settled in a chair, Mannering, hands again clasped behind his back in a well-known gesture of deep contemplation, began to pace up and down the carpet, giving voice to his thoughts.

"Sir Alexander will not take kindly to our sad misuse of his granddaughter. With both his sons dead, and without issue until you showed up, madam, he cannot but feel quite protective of you. It is already too late to remove you to an inn and pretend ignorance of your existence. By now, thanks to my servants, I am sure all the world and his wife knows, if not precisely *who* you are, at least enough to place us all well and truly, as Billy might say, in the suds.

"No, madam, I confess I can see no way out of our dilemma save one." Turning to bow deeply from the waist in her direction, he ended flatly, "Miss Saxon, from this moment on you are to consider yourself my affianced bride."

The Earl's words at last seemed to score a direct hit on

24

Miss Saxon's composure. Jumping at once to her feet she shrieked, "Are you daft, man?"

Mannering took a twig from Miss Saxon's tree. "Daft, madam? Surely not. Dismayed, maybe. Depressed, most assuredly. But *daft?* Why, Miss Saxon, have you not heard of honor among gentlemen?"

"But—but," Alexandra blustered, "that's totally medieval!"

"And that, madam, describes your grandfather to a cow's thumb—medieval. Other than to fall on my sword in the home wood, I see no other way out of our dilemma but an immediate marriage. No less would satisfy your grandfather."

"Er—um—*I* could marry her, Nick," Jeremy offered weakly.

At this, Mannering's lips twitched appreciatively. "Why, Jeremy, that is very noble of you, truly it is. But I think not."

"Oh, thank you, Nick, *thank you!*" his brother exhaled gratefully. Then at Nicholas's arch look, he turned to Alexandra and tried to redeem himself in her eyes. "Not—not that it wouldn't have been my honor, my very *great* honor, to have wed you, ma'am. It's just that I'm only down from school because of some minor fracas and I'm due back right after the holidays. So you can see how that would be quite difficult to manage were I leg-shackled—er—*married* to you. It wouldn't really *do,* don't you know. Besides," he added lamely as his brother began to chuckle, "I ain't really in the petticoat line."

"Calm yourself, infant, I have no doubt you mean well, but your every word digs the pit around you deeper, and I fear much more shoveling on your part would put you completely underground. Besides, I don't believe your sacrifice would be acceptable to Sir Alexander. It's the head of the house he'll seek satisfaction from on this one."

"He can shoot the pips out of a playing card at twenty paces, old as he is," Jeremy added sorrowfully to Alexandra. "Wouldn't do to set him up in the boughs."

Now Alexandra began to pace, her dark curtain of hair

flowing behind her as she fairly stomped about the room. Clearly she was incensed. "Now look here," she stated at last, "this is all a tempest in a teapot. I'm only here because I promised Chas I'd come see the old curmudgeon. I never said I was planning to *settle* in this benighted country. I'm an American, I've neither the desire nor the need to live under my grandfather's roof. Besides," she added heatedly, "no one tells me what to do. Not my mother when she was alive, not Chas, not m'grandfather, and sir, most assuredly, *not you!*"

There came the sound of one pair of hands clapping. "That was a splendid show of 'Yankee spunk,' Miss Saxon," Mannering drawled wryly, "but I, alas, do not for a minute believe a word of it. Chas, as you persist in calling your late father, would not have deemed it necessary to send you here at all if you were well situated in Philadelphia."

Alexandra let out her pent up breath in a frustrated sigh. "All right, lord smarty-pants, you win. If my grandfather refuses to own me, I'll be spending the night under the hedgerows for I am completely without funds. That in itself is bad enough. But to have to beg charity is one thing; to be forced into marriage for the sake of someone's ridiculous sense of honor is just too much. I'd rather starve!"

Taking in the lady's militant stance (not to mention the Indian's menacing glare), Linton decided to pour a little judicious oil on the troubled waters. God knew he was no happier about the situation than was Miss Saxon, but once in her grandfather's presence the chit might be made to see that marriage was the only solution to their problem.

Once he had presented the idea that they immediately adjourn to Saxon Hall, Alexandra agreed to that plan of action with alacrity. "But Harold comes along. Chas was adamant that he never leave my side," she said emphatically.

"Harold?" Jeremy spluttered, aghast. "Your Indian's name is *Harold?* Oh, never say so, ma'am, it's just too altogether ordinary to be borne."

The black-faced man-mountain took three quick steps in the young scoffer's direction before Jeremy fairly bolted from the room, promising to have Nicholas's carriage brought round directly.

Chapter Two

ONCE they were settled in the carriage—Miss Saxon and Lord Linton sitting across from each other on the squabs maintaining an uneasy peace, and Harold sitting up behind the horses, massive arms crossed over his chest, coolly eyeing one truly nervous Linton coachman—Nicholas gave the order to drive on.

Miss Saxon showed her distaste for conversation by keeping her head averted, shamming instead an extraordinary interest in the bare November landscape, while Lord Linton assessed her yet again with his discerning eye. Quite a looker, he admitted to himself reluctantly, not that her physical appearance lessened or heightened the chit's degree of compromise a whit—but at least the next generation of Mannerings need not fear going through life with humped noses or the curse of a decided squint.

It is amazing, he reflected as he watched the thin sunlight set off answering glimmers in Miss Saxon's truly glorious mane of hair, how I could go to bed one night a dedicated bachelor and find myself committed to marriage before luncheon of the following day. Ah well, so much for resolutions. I might beat dear Helene to the altar after all—I wonder if it is socially acceptable to marry before the woman who jilted you can sweep her way down the aisle of St. George's?

This self-satisfying thought caused a small smile to come to his lips, and feeling a bit more charitable toward the young woman just then staring out the off-window with an intensity that would make a person believe she had never seen an apple orchard before, he decided to make an attempt at polite conversation.

As to a topic, Nicholas had no need to stretch his imagination—the estimable Harold certainly would do for a start. So thinking, he cleared his throat and ventured, "Miss Saxon? I hope I do not intrude on some profound thought, but I admit to a small curiosity about your traveling companion. Do you feel you could perhaps satisfy this unseemly indulgence of nosiness?"

Alexandra, although she would never admit to it, had been feeling more and more apprehensive with each turn of the carriage wheels that brought her closer to her initial meeting with her grandfather. What if he turned her away from his door without so much as a hearing? It was bad enough when she only had to consider how well he would accept her existence. To be handed a further blow to the family escutcheon in the form of her being so feather-brained as to make her presence known in the area by sleeping in entirely the wrong bed was certainly pushing her luck.

So if Lord Linton wanted to pass the time with idle conversation—conversation that just possibly could keep her mind off her troubles—she was more than happy to oblige him. "What is it about Harold that you wish to know, my lord?" she asked sweetly, acting as if her black-faced companion was come from a variety of species as common to England as turnips.

Nicholas smiled, reading her tongue-in-cheek response quite clearly. "For openers, I'd say an explanation of how he comes to be in your life at all might prove enough to capture my attention. After all, although I am not that familiar with your country, I do believe Philadelphia to have been fairly free of Indian attack for quite a few years now. And an Indian named Harold? Those I imagine to be as scarce as hen's teeth most anywhere in America. You realize, of course, that m'brother's sense of high adventure was dealt a mighty blow when first he heard Harold's name. I am sure he had been banking on some appellation a bit more, shall we say, *exotic.*"

"Harold," Alexandra admitted, "*is* quite singular—even

in America—although I have become accustomed to him, seeing that he has been about ever since I was a child. Chas—my father, if you remember—was a particular patron of the museum Charles Wilson Peale set up in Philadelphia in, oh, about 1790 I think it was. This museum was devoted to displays of tomahawks, wampum, scalps, and other sundry Indian artifacts—all set against a suitably realistic background designed to resemble a forest. It was quite an impressive spectacle, I assure you. Chas was quite proud of his association with the scheme. Well," she expanded, "as part of this display they had caused to be set up a miniature version of an Indian village, complete with a full-size wigwam. One day it was merely a stage setting depicting an Indian residence, and the next it was occupied by friend Harold.

"Chas said he never did figure out where Harold came from or how he discovered the museum. All they know is that one morning when they opened the museum there he was, sitting cross-legged in front of the wigwam and making himself at home. Chas and Mr. Peale saw no harm in it, and it did serve to bring a good deal of people to view the exhibits, so Harold was allowed to stay—not that I believe anyone could have budged him a jot if they wanted to."

"That explains the man's presence, I suppose," the Earl returned. "I can even push my imagination enough to encourage it to expand to include a friendship developing between this Indian and your father. But, *Harold?* Really, Miss Saxon, that little bit of nonsense is carrying things just an imagining or two too far."

"Not for Harold's tribe," she informed him. "The Delaware take their mother's name as their own. Harold was the result of a liaison between a chief's son and a settler's daughter—a quite *willing* maiden if Harold is to be believed. Her last name was Harold—it is Norse, I think. From his father he took the name Sachema, which means king. I do hope that clears things up a bit for you?"

The Earl gave a short snort. "Madam, it does not begin to scratch the surface. For instance, why does the man paint his face black?"

Alexandra could see that his lordship would not be satisfied with anything less than a full explanation. "As I have already said, Harold is of the Delaware Nation, or at least he is half-Delaware—although I would not give you two pennies for your chances of living out the day if you dared to call him a half-breed—and a member of the Turtle Clan called simply, the Lenni Lenape. Although the tribe disappeared from the area many years ago, somehow Harold managed to stay in Philadelphia, and he holds doggedly to all the Lenape traditions.

"One of those is to paint their faces for different reasons. Red means power and success, blue is for defeat or a time of trouble, yellow announces bravery, white signifies peace, and black, as you may have deduced for yourself by now, means death. Harold truly loved Chas. Therefore he will wear this outward sign of mourning for one full year. Luckily, it is already half over.

"As to his dress—in case you were about to ask—he wears the traditional winter dress of the Lenape, fringed buckskins and a bearskin draped over his shoulders. It is rather an impressive sight, you're probably thinking, but then you have never sat in a closed coach with Harold after he's been caught in one of your miserable English downpours. I assure you, sir, the smell of wet skins and fur, combined with the rancid perfume of clarified bear fat with which he greases himself periodically, is not pleasant. But it is his summer attire that may set the neighborhood ladies to swooning, as it consists of moccasins, a breechclout, a few strings of wampum, and little else."

By now they were more than halfway to Saxon Hall. "That is very interesting, Miss Saxon. And now, thanks to your father's death, Harold is—um—your responsibility?"

Alexandra laughed a bit at this misreading of the situation. "Gracious, no. Don't let Harold hear you say that. It is quite the opposite—Harold has set himself up as *my* guardian. He is, I must add, quite disappointed in his charge, however, for I am nearly of legal age and still unmarried. Indian maidens, you understand, wed no later than at the age of thirteen or fourteen. Harold considers me quite the old

31

maid.'' Alexandra's expression clouded as she was brought sharply back to the present by means of Lord Linton's knowingly raised eyebrow. "Oh yes," she ended lamely, "I had quite forgot that for a few moments there. Harold must be beside himself with glee, don't you think?" Then, with a bit of returning courage she ventured, "You won't object if he insists on giving the bride away, will you, my lord? You should see him in ceremonial dress—he really is a wonder to behold."

So much for diversionary tactics, Mannering told himself ruefully. It had worked for a while, during which time he had learned more than he really cared to know about the estimable Harold, but now they were neatly back to square one—their coming meeting with Sir Alexander Saxon, a man whose ferocity could make Harold seem no more threatening a figure than an innocent babe in leading strings.

"Ah, yes," he sighed now, "we come again to the subject of marriage. I refuse to enter into a discussion of the yeas or nays of the subject—I leave the convincing you of its importance to Sir Alexander, who will doubtless make his reasons for immediate nuptials between us crystal clear—but I do believe we should talk a bit about the man himself. Sort of in the way of preparation, shall we say?"

"There was no great love lost between him and Chas, if that's what you mean to tell me," Alexandra volunteered. "He may have been a bit close-mouthed on the subject, but Chas certainly lit no candles in front of a portrait of his sire. No, I expect no grand welcome—only a roof over my head until such time as I can make other arrangements for myself, arrangements that take me back across the ocean as governess to some traveling family or some such thing. This damp island of yours holds no great appeal for me."

"Your oft-repeated low opinion of this country will no doubt endear you to your grandfather," the Earl put in sarcastically. Before Alexandra could launch a rebuttal, he went on, "Sir Alexander is a firm believer in the greatness of 'this damp island.' Indeed, his world begins and ends with this country—the far-flung colonies of the Empire being barely tolerated by the man. As for America—that ungrateful bag of malcontents who dared to throw us over—well, your father could hardly have picked a better way to insult his father than by settling there."

"I see. Perhaps, then, it is why Chas chose it. Is there any other subject I should avoid if I don't wish to be shoved outside my grandfather's door before I've so much as tasted his porridge?"

Now Nicholas laughed outright. "Madam, I fear we should have to travel in this carriage all the way from John O'Groats to Land's End to give us enough time to cover all your grandfather's dislikes, quirks, and the like. We do, however, have barely enough time for me to give you a short primer on the man. To begin with, he has refused to recognize what century we are in, holding fast to the time of masters and vassals and the like. His domicile will more than show you what I mean so I'll leave that for a while.

"As to the man's personal eccentricities—they are many and varied. Not unlike many Englishmen, he hates and despises anyone who has not been so fortunate as to be born an Englishman. That is not to say he loves his fellow countrymen—on the contrary, it is England he loves, not Englishmen. It's just that he condescends to tolerate us.

"As to his personal habits, with which you would do well to become familiar if you are to spend any time at all under his roof, he much resembles many English peers in the respect that he drinks like the proverbial fish. In Sir Alexander's case, it is gin that he favors—morning, noon, and night. Also, and it would be wise to remember this, he despises anyone who will not stand up to him, while at the same time he will tear a strip off your hide if you ever dare raise your voice in his presence. It is contradictory, I know, but nevertheless true.

"He also worships land and money. These are his gods. He won't care a rap if you are smart as a whip or talented beyond the normal—if you have no money you are worthless."

"It would seem then that I should not be expecting the man to fall on my neck, overcome with joy, when I arrive at his door nearly penniless," Alexandra cut in with a bit of

33

temper evident in her voice. "Perhaps it would be best if you just told your coachman to turn the horses about and have an easy end to all of it. I can slink away and none will be the wiser. It certainly would save your bacon for you nicely," she pointed out.

"It's too late for that, more's the pity," his lordship shot back rather nastily, "as Harold alone under my roof was enough to set the household servants buzzing around the village for a fortnight. Now that they know who you are—and let me assure you they do, as servants seem to know everything—there is no way I can dispose of you without someone thinking I have two bodies hidden under my azalea bushes."

This last exchange served to put an end to all talk between the two, and the inside of the carriage was once more reduced to a tense silence. It is possible this would have been the case for the remainder of the journey, except that as the carriage rounded a bend in the road that brought them for a few moments into a clearing where the view was not obstructed, Alexandra, who was once again staring out the off-window, caught sight of something that caused her to blink, stare, and then blink yet again.

"If I didn't know better, I'd say I just saw a castle," she muttered under her breath. She was not so stupid as to think there were no castles left in England. In fact, she was sure there were dozens and dozens of them spread across the island. But this castle looked different from any of the others she had seen along her drive from the docks at Falmouth. As she caught another look at the building when they passed an opening in the trees, she realized what had struck her about this particular castle—all the other castles either had been in ruins or had been altered by additions or other improvements that had brought the buildings more in line with the nineteenth century. "It looks like something straight out of the Middle Ages!" she remarked, a bit of excitement in her voice.

"I take it you have just caught sight of Saxon Hall," Lord Linton observed matter-of-factly from his corner of the carriage.

"It's beautiful—simply beautiful!" Alexandra breathed, her dark eyes shining. "I would not be surprised to see the drawbridge come down and a knight in shining armor ride out to meet us. Oh, Chas never told me his home was a castle. A real *castle!* How could he have ever brought himself to leave it?"

"I'd reserve judgment on Chas's reasons if I were you," Mannering broke in smoothly. "At least until you've had occasion to use the plumbing. It too is straight out of the Middle Ages."

Alexandra threw him a fulminating glance and was about to make some cutting remark when a loud blast on a yard of tin made her clap her hands over her ears. "What in thunder was that?" she yelled as the sound of the horn died away.

"That bansheelike trumpeting is *de rigueur* when approaching Saxon Hall, madam. How else would Sir Alexander's servants—I mean vassals—know to lower the drawbridge?"

Alexandra allowed the Earl's sarcasm to flow right over her head as she was at once caught up in the romance of having her arrival at Saxon Hall heralded by trumpets—or at least one trumpet. Leaning so far out the window she had hurriedly rolled down as to give Nicholas a much appreciated view of her rounded derrière and more than three inches of exposed ankle, she watched enraptured as the massive wooden drawbridge began its slow descent across a moat filled with some very green-looking water.

Instantly, the sound made moments before by the coachman's yard of tin was turned into a pleasant memory, as the ancient chains that held the drawbridge set up an earsplitting noise that sent shivers down her spine and made all the little hairs on her arms stand bolt-upright. She rapidly drew her head back inside the carriage, once more pressing her hands to her ears to block out all sound.

"Did I forget to mention the fact that Sir Alexander has never been known as a stickler for upkeep?" Nicholas shouted above the din.

"Oh, shut up!" Miss Saxon yelled back at him, and then she made the grand gesture of removing her hands from her ears and sitting up straight on her seat, her teeth clenched together tightly as she willed herself not to flinch even once for the remainder of the time it took to get that dratted drawbridge lowered.

Once peace had again returned to the countryside (although it was doubtful the birds would return to the vicinity any time soon), Alexandra remarked with studied calm, "A bit of judiciously applied grease should remedy that little problem. I do not for a minute believe such a small problem to make much of a statement against such a beautiful place as this."

"Ha!" the Earl exploded. "If the drawbridge is to be considered a *small statement*, one can only wonder what you will call the remainder of Saxon Hall's little inconveniences—*The Complete Works of Shakespeare*, perhaps?"

The carriage had once again been set in motion, its wheels bumping heavily as they rattled across the drawbridge, and soon the coachman had halted the horses in the courtyard. Alexandra had the door open before Nicholas could move, and Harold had lifted her lightly down on the flagstones before the coachman could lower the steps. It was left to the Earl to follow as conventionally or unconventionally as he cared to do, and nodding his servant away, he vaulted to the ground without aid of the steps, landing lightly just inches from Alexandra.

"Quaint American custom—this being lifted down from carriages. I really can't see why we English ever bothered to invent carriage steps. But then not all of us have giant Indians to assist us to the ground or ankles strong enough to take the pressure of leaping about like demented frogs."

Alexandra was too nervous to reply to Mannering's teasing. Now that she was actually here, within shouting distance of her grandfather, she was more nervous about the meeting than she cared to let the Earl know. There had to be a good reason why Chas left home more than a quarter of a century before and never once made a move to return. Had he really left of his own volition, or had he been tossed out on his ear by his father?

She wiped her suddenly moist palms on her grey traveling

cloak, a movement that did not go unobserved by Nicholas. She straightened her collar, pushed a time or two at her hair—just now blowing about her face in the wind—and took one or two deep, steadying breaths. "Let's get it over with, shall we?" she said, her voice cracking just a little bit.

Mannering looked down at her, for although she was fairly tall, he towered over her by a good head and a half, and suddenly his emotions were touched by her plight. She really had been having a hard time of it lately, he thought to himself. First her father dies, then she travels halfway across the world to keep a deathbed promise, not knowing what sort of reception she will receive at the end of her long journey. And then, just as though she hadn't already enough on her plate, there was the final blow—her compromise under his roof last night.

The Earl held out his arm to her and said, almost gently, "Let's have at it then. And remember, barking dogs rarely bite. Just keep that adorable chin tilted in precisely that confident manner, let me do the talking, and perhaps we shall just brush through this without any permanent injuries."

Alexandra lifted her face and gifted Lord Linton with an absolutely dazzling smile—a smile that did something very strange to a small area somewhere near the pit of his stomach. "Thank you, my lord," she told him earnestly.

The Earl swallowed hard before replying, "Please, as we are soon to be married, I believe you may call me Nicholas."

The smile that had so nearly bewitched him disappeared, leaving him with the feeling that the sun had suddenly slipped behind a cloud. "We are not soon—or *ever,* for that matter—going to be married, Nicholas. I maintain that I fail to see the harm of spending a night in one of your bedchambers while Harold was on the scene as chaperone," she shot back testily before just a small bit of the smile returned and she ended more softly, "but you may call me Alix." Once more the Earl's insides were sent topsy-turvy.

Heedless of Mannering's emotional ups and downs, Alexandra began looking around the courtyard where they were now standing. Nicholas explained that this was called

37

the inner bailey, the carriage having already passed through the outer bailey—which was the name given to the courtyard that lay just inside the high curtain wall that surrounded the whole of the castle grounds. Along this curtain wall were placed several round towers with turretlike roofs—once employed as lookouts—he continued as she murmured her approval.

Within these walls, he went on, and surrounded by the lower stone wall that made up the inner bailey, lay the donjon—or castle keep. What had from a distance looked to her to be a grand, sprawling pile was, in reality, she now saw, just a lot of stone and empty spaces surrounded by more stone. The donjon itself was not nearly so romantic a sight when viewed head-on. Oh yes, it did rise a majestic seventy feet or more into the air, but its ancient blackened stone and scarcity of windows made it much more opposing than welcoming. It did not even have a door on its ground floor! Chas's birthplace could scarcely be called cozy.

While Alexandra looked vainly about for an entrance, Nicholas instructed the coachman to walk the horses and motioned to Harold to follow him as he walked round the corner to where a wizened-looking old man dressed in green velvet livery was laboriously limping his way toward them. "Nutter, old fellow," the Earl called out in way of greeting, "don't exert yourself so. We would have made our way to you in time. Rest a moment, won't you, and then be so good as to take my friend here to the kitchens and give him something to gnaw on. As far as I know, he hasn't broken his fast yet from last night, and with a body that size, I'd hate to be anywhere around if he decides to swoon."

By now Alexandra, her neck already stiff from craning it up at the donjon looking for some sort of entrance, had joined their little group and she added, "Something for me too, Nicholas, if you please. I can't remember when last I ate. Your English food—at least that offered at the posting inns where we stopped—is so bland as to put me almost totally off my feed. Tell me, do you English boil *everything?*"

At Nutter's offended look, Nicholas turned to Alexandra

and observed mildly, "You certainly do know how to make a good first impression, Miss Saxon. You'll have Nutter here fairly eating out of your hand if you keep up this flattery."

Alexandra turned to apologize to the servant, but the old man was already limping away, muttering under his breath. Harold walked at his side, leaning down and nodding as if in full agreement with everything the man had to say.

"It would seem your Harold is a bit of a diplomat," Mannering observed dryly. "It would be a pity to tell Nutter his companion doesn't understand a word he's saying."

Alexandra's mouth opened as if she were about to say something, but suddenly thinking better of it, she hesitated before finally saying, "Nutter seems singularly unimpressed with Harold. You'd think he saw Indians every day of the week."

"Nutter sees barely anything, Alix," Nicholas informed her. "To him Harold is nothing but a large shape. That's why I was so quick to approach him—he knows me by voice, and I wanted to assure him as to who I was. But never fear—he is a capable servant for all his nearsightedness. He knows every stone in this great pile, having lived here with your grandfather for all his life."

Mention of her grandfather brought Alexandra back to the business at hand. "How do we get inside this 'pile of stones'?" she asked, hands on hips as if she were formulating a plan of attack.

Mannering captured one of those hands in his, noticed how chilled it was, whether from cold or fear he did not know, and led her around the corner behind which Nutter and Harold had disappeared. There, abutting one entire side of the donjon, was a stone building much shorter and squarer than the tower. "This is the forebuilding," he told her. "It is the only way you can enter the donjon, and even this way is secured by means of visitors having to climb this great staircase before really being able to say they have at last arrived safely inside."

The top of the steps finally reached, Mannering opened a heavy oak door and stood back to let Alexandra enter before him. She was met by yet another green-liveried old man, who bowed creakily as she approached. The servant was kept from toppling over onto his face only by clinging desperately to the large, painted lance he was employing as a cane. "Who wishes to see the Master?" the old man croaked.

"It is I, Nicholas Mannering, Earl of Linton, who begs audience with your master," Nicholas intoned solemnly, evoking a quick glance from Alexandra, who was astounded at his formality with this servant after his familiarity with Nutter minutes before. "Also," the Earl went on, "I have with me this lowly female, who, if your master pleases, craves to plead her case before him, asking only that he not judge her too harshly for her sins."

That did it! "What in bloody blue blazes are you spouting about! I never heard such drivel. Lowly female, indeed! Judged for my sins! What sins?"

The servant took no heed of Alexandra's outburst but merely bowed again before plodding out of the room. Once he was gone, Nicholas let out his pent-up breath and began to laugh. "Whew!" he said once he could breathe normally. "As often as I do this I never fail to feel like the world's greatest fool the entire time."

"*That* I can understand," Alexandra threw back cuttingly. "But how dare you call me a lowly female? I'm beginning to feel like stepping through that door has catapulted me backward in time a century or two."

"Oh, further back than that, my dear, I assure you. Look, if you think you can't go through with this, just let me know and you can stay out here while I go in alone to talk to your grandfather. After all, if you think outbursts like the one you treated that servant to will be condoned once we're inside the Great Hall, you have another thought or two coming. You'd be out on your ear before you knew what hit you—if the old man didn't decide to have you flogged on the spot."

Before Alexandra had a chance to reply, the servant took two steps back into the room, banged the heel of his lance on the stone floor three times, and announced that an audience had been granted. This time, instead of preceding Nicholas,

Alexandra hung back a few paces, hiding a bit behind his large form as they entered the Great Hall.

At first sight the Hall seemed bare and gloomy. At second sight it seemed even more so. There were, Alexandra counted, only two deep-set windows to light the entire large room. There was no real fireplace at all, only a large hearth in the middle of the floor, the smoke coming from its fire swirling mistily about the room in its search to exit through the windows and chinks in the walls.

The walls themselves were whitewashed, although the grime hanging on them showed this bit of housekeeping to be a frequent necessity. As to furniture, that commodity was noticeable only for its absence. Except for a few rude trestle tables, a large iron-hinged cupboard, and several long wooden backless benches, the room was devoid of the stuff.

It was only after a few moments—once her eyes had adjusted to the dimness and the smoke—that Alexandra thought she could make out, standing atop a low platform against one wall, a pair of high-backed wooden chairs—one of them occupied by a reincarnation of Henry VIII!

Dressed in deep burgundy velvet interspliced with rusty-looking cloth of gold, his neck encircled by a sooty grey ruching of lace and his ample legs encased in faded red stockings that made it look like he had two fat sausages in place of the usual lower appendages, the man fairly sprawled in his chair, a greasy half-eaten chicken leg dangling from one beringed, dimpled hand. His fully bearded face was as big and round as a dinner plate, his two dark eyes looking like berries peeking out of a pastry tart. Topping all this off was a burgundy velvet many-pointed slouch hat that tipped precariously to one side, its lone ratty-looking feather curling rather desultorily in the air.

"Good God!" Alexandra hissed under her breath to Nicholas. "I don't believe my own eyes. And you acted like Harold was an oddity—this character makes my black-faced Indian look like a sober Quaker! Why—"

Nicholas cut her off before her voice rose any higher. "Dub yer mummer," he whispered, taking a leaf from Billy's book of cant sayings. "Be quiet and let me do the

41

talking." Leaving Alexandra where she stood—and she stood like a statue frozen in marble—he approached the raised platform and bowed deeply from the waist. "Good morrow, Sir Alexander. I regret the intrusion, but I have come on behalf of this damsel here—this damsel in distress, might I add."

Sir Alexander nodded his head once in acknowledgment and then lifted the chicken leg to his mouth to take another satisfying bite. Suddenly the food fell from his hand and he leapt up—no mean feat for one of his girth—demanding in what could only be described as a bellow: *"Who in thunder are you?"*

Nicholas took an involuntary step backward at this unexpected happening, which was lucky for him, as Sir Alexander would have mowed him down in his haste to get a closer look at this female, who was just now drawing herself up in an attitude of belligerence.

"Answer me, girl!" Sir Alexander commanded yet again. "By Jupiter, I'll have an answer if I have to wring it out of you!"

Alexandra's momentary fright had soon given way to temper—after all, although it was only just gone noon she had already had a perfectly frightful day. Raising herself up to her full height—that "adorable" chin Mannering had remarked on tilted at a pugnacious angle—she replied steadily, "My name is Alexandra Saxon and I am Chas's daughter. His *legal* daughter," she added, making sure she was not to be treated to another barrage of questions as to which side of the blanket her mother had been lying on when she had conceived.

This speech halted Sir Alexander in his tracks and his florid face paled behind his beard. "Charles's daughter. You're the picture of your grandmother. The very picture." His voice trailed off as he shook his head sadly. "Charles must be dead then. It's the only reason you're here now—he swore he'd never set foot in Saxon Hall again."

Alexandra's heart was touched, and she laid a hand on her grandfather's shoulder, as he was not a tall man for all his commanding air. "Chas died more than six months ago in Philadelphia," she informed him quietly.

Nicholas watched with some amazement as a variety of emotions flitted across Sir Alexander's face, before finally settling itself into an angry mass. "Dead, is it—confound him, that profligate—"

"Have a care, old man," Alexandra warned tightly, "that profligate was my father."

Alexandra may have looked like her grandmother, Mannering thought randomly, but it was obvious where she got her sweet temper. Stepping in between the two Saxons he soothed, "Now, now, let's not descend into old quarrels. Sir Alexander, your sons may both be dead now, but at least the Saxon name lives on through this girl here."

The old man cocked his head to one side at that thought. "That's true enough, Linton, I suppose, although only the blood line will go on. The name dies with me."

Here it comes, Nicholas thought gloomily. Here's where I either save the day or end up getting a firsthand look at the infamous Saxon dungeons. "How fortunate for you to bring up the subject, Sir Alexander—the subject of marriage, that is," the Earl began staunchly. He paused for a moment to run a finger under his suddenly tight collar. "You see, sir—"

"Oh give over, you idiot," Alexandra broke in. "Lord knows what you have to say won't improve any with keeping." Turning to her grandfather she told him baldly, "This fool here says I have to marry him."

"By thunder!" Sir Alexander bellowed, and turned to peer very hard at his lordship.

Nicholas returned the man's look with a lopsided smile. "I imagine you can ascertain from the lady's tone that she ain't mad for the notion. Perhaps if we all sat down, I could explain everything for you."

"Married?" Sir Alexander thundered again. "Explain, you say? This calls for some serious discussion. Nutter!" he shouted, his voice echoing in the high rafters. "Fetch us some sustenance—and bring me my Hollands."

At Alexandra's questioning look Nicholas leaned down to

43

whisper in her ear, "Hollands is a sort of gin. It may look like the old boy's drinking water, but I assure you no mere glass of water packs the punch of Sir Alexander's Hollands."

They adjourned to one of the trestle tables, Nicholas and Alexandra sharing a bench on one side while Sir Alexander arranged his ample behind on another bench across the table from them.

An uneasy silence was maintained until Nutter and the other servant deposited a tray of strange-looking meat and a decanter of Hollands in front of their master. There were glasses enough for three, but it seemed they were all to share the same bowl of meat, as Sir Alexander demonstrated by picking out one greasy-looking morsel and popping it into his mouth before pushing the bowl in their direction and waving a hand over it in a move that said, "Help yourselves."

Nicholas had eaten at Saxon Hall before—which explained his sudden loss of appetite. Alexandra was not so forewarned. She dipped her fingers into the bowl and lifted out a large chunk of meat, putting the entire piece into her mouth at one time. Mannering watched her face in amusement as he waited for her reaction. It was not long in coming. First her dark eyes widened. Then her throat began to work convulsively. As he looked more closely, he could have sworn he saw little beads of perspiration break out beneath her eyes.

Before he could put out a hand to stop her, she grabbed the goblet in front of her and took a large gulp of Hollands in hopes of putting out the fire in her mouth. It didn't—it merely added fuel to the flames. As she broke into paroxysms of coughing and sputtering, Mannering helpfully pounded on her back, trying his best not to ruin the effect of his solicitude by dissolving into laughter.

"Nutter," he asked the servant once Alexandra had regained some control over herself, "tell me—do you *boil* this meat?"

"Boil it, my lord? No sir, it weren't boiled. I jist cooked it like alwas, rollin' the pork first in salt, then in ginger, galingole, cloves, and two kinds of pepper. The master likes ta know when he's got sumthin in his mouth, so he alwas says."

"You knew that would happen," Alexandra charged Mannering angrily as she wiped her tears on the sleeve of her dress. "How dare you not warn me? Oh, for two pins I'd dump the whole of that poisonous dish smack down on top of your insufferable head!"

"The devil you will, gel!" Sir Alexander exploded, wiping his hands on his chest. "By Jupiter, only Charles could sire such a bad-mannered female. Six of the best with the birch rod, Linton—that's what this one needs."

"I'll keep it in mind, sir," Nicholas answered, grinning broadly at the still fuming Alexandra. "But I must tell you that your granddaughter has little reason to love me. You see, sir, she hasn't exactly had an easy time of it since she set foot on her homeland."

"It is not my homeland, and you know it," Alexandra interrupted.

"Sit still and keep your mouth shut!" her grandfather commanded in a voice that shook the gin goblets. "Linton—carry on."

"Yes—er—yes, sir. Well, as I was saying, Alexandra has had quite a time of it. Traveling by post chaise is never comfortable, and from her few confidences it would seem her journey was more uncomfortable than most. Possibly this explains the extreme fatigue that led her to take herself off to a bedchamber last night without first making quite sure she was—er—precisely where she thought she was. You see, sir," and now Mannering measured each word carefully, "she thought she had arrived at Saxon Hall when in reality she was somewhere else altogether. As a result, she spent the night under the roof of an all-male residence, unwittingly compromising herself quite thoroughly."

Sir Alexander bounded to his feet, the bench he had been sitting on toppling over onto the stone floor. "By Jupiter, I never before heard the like. Whose roof was she under?" he asked, leaning his hands on the table and peering into Linton's face.

45

Nicholas swallowed hard. "In point of fact, sir, it was *my* roof."

Here it comes at last, Alexandra thought smugly. Now this insufferable, one-eyed simpleton will get his comeuppance. Go on, grandfather, she urged silently, tear a strip off his hide. Her satisfied smirk faded before it ever really had much of a chance to begin, however, when Sir Alexander boomed, "Confound it, lad, that's a splendid piece of news! I had thought you had taken one look at the gel here and fallen arsy-varsy in love with the chit like I did with her grandmother. Stands to reason, don't it, for she is a fetching piece. But this is even better—compromised her, did you? Splendid! Never could abide those long-drawn-out engagements. With any luck I should have a great-grandson to dandy on my knee before the first snowfall next winter."

Now it was Alexandra's turn to hop to her feet. "Well if that don't beat the Dutch!" she charged. "My own grandfather pushing me into marriage within an hour of learning of my existence. Well, let me tell you, old man, I'll be having none of it. Harold! *Harold!*" she yelled in the direction of the kitchens, *"N'dellemúske! Wischiksik!"*

For once Sir Alexander was nonplussed. He looked from his granddaughter to Lord Linton in bewilderment before at last asking, "Who is Harold? Why's she spouting gibberish?"

The huge Indian had heard Alexandra call to him that she was leaving and wished him to come quickly. Such a command was not to be taken lightly, he knew, and he took one last bite of the greasy meat he had been throwing down his gullet with as little notice to its spicy flavoring as if it were no more seasoned than a bit of brown bread before running soundlessly up the stairs and into the Great Hall.

"I said—who is Harold?" some strange-looking fat man dressed up like a wild turkey was asking as the Indian entered.

Drawing himself up to his full height, Harold strode kinglike into the Hall, not stopping until he was breathing straight down into Sir Alexander's face. *"Lennápe n'hackey,"* he pronounced in regal tones—telling Sir Alexander he was a Lenape—whereupon the old man took three paces backward and, tripping over the raised platform, plunked rudely rump down on the boards. "By Jupiter!" he breathed in awed tones. "By bloody damn Jupiter . . ."

Chapter Three

ALIX wearily dragged herself up the steep spiral stone staircase that led from just outside the Great Hall to her own sleeping chamber, her feet treading soundlessly in the moccasins Harold had sewn for her the previous summer. As she climbed, she began working at undoing the dozens of buttons that closed the front of her heavy worsted gown, wishing yet again that she had the daring to wear the fringed, knee-length buckskin dress that had also been a gift from the Indian—it certainly wasn't as cumbersome as this gown. But Sir Alexander had been put out enough over the moccasins—saying they were instruments of the devil—all because they had made her approach so silent that her "Good morning" had caused him to jump, spilling his goblet of "gripe water."

Gripe water, she grimaced, as she sank down on a chair and rubbed at the back of her neck. Hollands, that's what it was—and at ten in the morning no less! Alix gave a cynical half-smile as she thought of the different names her grandfather gave to his gin. Geneva, The Last Shift, colic water, Cobbler's Punch, Crank, Diddle, Heart's Ease—even Frog's wine—and just once when he thought she was out of earshot, Strip Me Naked! He had a different name for every occasion, every time of day, but the contents of his goblet remained the same—potent gin.

She had her work cut out for her, that much was sure, if she intended to break her grandfather of his drinking habit. Not that this was the least of her worries. Oh no. It was only a small part of the budget of woe she had to deal with before her conscience would free her to leave this accursed island and return to Philadelphia.

Dressed at last in her nightgown, Alix turned down the heavy quilt on the only bright spot on her heavily clouded horizon—the massive feather bed that welcomed her each night like an old friend. When she had first seen the bed—a large, curtained affair set on a heavy wooden frame laced with ropes and topped by a huge, thick mattress—she had thought she'd died and gone to heaven. The mattress was stuffed full with duck feathers and down, a filling that molded itself around her slim body and was as welcome a refuge as a mother's embrace. With the coverlet tucked up under her chin it was almost easy to believe that a night spent in such a paradise could only be a foretaste of a glorious day to follow. Such however, was not the case, as she had found out in no uncertain terms on that first inglorious morning. It had taken only one trip to the garderobe—the small latrine that served as the only water closet for the donjon—to disabuse her of the notion that she had indeed died during the night and gone to her reward.

It wasn't that she was a female overused to luxury—Chas had never been rich—but never before had she realized how spoiled for creature comforts she was as when she had first spied out the small, cold room with no amenities save a low, stone slab with a hole in its center. No wonder the knights were forever going on crusades—she thought evilly—they were probably searching for an alternative to that icy slab on cold winter mornings! Drat Nicholas Mannering anyway—for wasn't it he who had first mentioned the plumbing at the castle?

Yes, Alix thought meanly as she punched at her feather cocoon, drat that Nicholas Mannering. She would never forgive him for the way he had acted when Harold's appearance in the Great Hall that first day had served to give her grandfather such a turn. It was bad enough he had offered not a single word of explanation to the man, but she could have brought herself to forgive him this lapse if he hadn't taken it into his stupid head just then to plunk himself down on the trestle table and howl like a delighted half-wit.

While Sir Alexander had stuttered and stared, Harold had growled and stared back, and Nicholas had rolled about giggling like the village idiot, it had been left to Alix to try to sort some sense out of the muddle. It hadn't been easy, she recollected, wrinkling up her nose. Only after Harold had been convinced to leave the room and return to his meal could Alix find time to calm her grandfather before he could be taken off in an apoplexy, all thoughts of her departure abandoned.

"You scoundrel," she'd then accused the Earl. "And you said you would help me."

Nicholas had just then been busy wiping at his streaming eyes with his handkerchief—lifting the black velvet patch slightly to dab underneath it. "I *am* trying, honestly I am," he had protested before going off into another round of giggles.

Putting her hands on her hips, Alix then had struck a quite menacing pose. "Oh aren't you just," she had sneered back at him before pointing a finger at the door. "Go home, Nicholas," she had ordered him. "You've become dreadfully in the way."

"Now, Alix," Nicholas had parried, trying manfully to control his hilarity at seeing the usually overbearing Sir Alexander reduced to blubbering insensibility, "don't poker up on me. Remember, we are betrothed."

"In a pig's eye, we are," she had denied hotly, this last finally succeeding in getting through her grandfather's shock at seeing Harold and bringing him smartly to his feet.

"Linton," the old man had challenged the Earl hastily, "don't listen to the gel; she's got no say in the matter. She's just like her grandmother—a damned handsome, obstinate woman. But never fret, she'll come round. In the meantime, sir, I'm holding you to your bargain." Harold may have temporarily muddled Sir Alexander's senses, but that didn't mean he'd entirely lost his wits. It was a splendid match— the wedding of two ancient, honored names in the district. He'd be damned if he'd let Chas's one good deed— providing him with a granddaughter—slip through his fingers without first making good use of her.

Mannering, now fully recovered, had made a deep bow from his waist in Sir Alexander's direction. "On the contrary, sir, I need no arm-twisting to make me realize that a marriage between your granddaughter and myself should take place as soon as may be contrived. It is that compromised granddaughter who seems ready to back out of our agreement."

"What agreement? I made no such agreement," Alexandra had interrupted.

Alix wriggled and squirmed in her bed as she recalled Nicholas's next words. Turning to pierce her armor of bravado with one cutting look, he had returned in a voice coated in ice, "Of course you did not, my dear. This is a *gentleman's agreement,* your wishes on the matter being neither sought nor relevant. However, if you wish to be disobliging—"

"I do," Alexandra had cut in nastily, before her grandfather put a stop to all argument by ordering Linton to withdraw and present himself at Saxon Hall in seven days to report on his progress in arranging the nuptials.

The week that followed this truly inauspicious beginning of their acquaintance had been fraught with arguments and minor confrontations as grandfather and granddaughter vied for supremacy in their battle of wills. The marriage was not discussed at all, both thinking they had settled that particular matter to their satisfaction (and both of them wrong, but then who was around to set them straight—Nutter? Harold?—Not likely).

High on the list of subjects upon which they disagreed stood the black-faced Harold. Alexandra wanted him treated like one of the family. Sir Alexander wanted him transported posthaste to Botany Bay. The Indian, oblivious to the furor, spent most of his time sitting cross-legged in front of a rude wigwam he had set up near the open hearth in the Great Hall, smoking his pipe and muttering a lot.

Alexandra squirmed again in her bed as she recalled her grandfather's reaction to her statement one day that she was only in England because Chas had made her promise to take care of the "old man."

"By Jupiter!" he had exploded. "If it was revenge Charles was after, he certainly chose his weapon well. I can think of no worse fate than to allow another managing female inside Saxon Hall, rest your sainted grandmother. Confound it! Why was I so cursed? My firstborn a flaming muckworm of a son—a total milksop, girl, I tell you—and my second the most ungrateful puppy ever whelped. I wanted him to have it all—nothing's entailed you see—but would Charles hear of it? No, he wouldn't do that to his older brother—as if that bluestocking would have cared, for such a bookworm twit you've yet to meet."

Sir Alexander had downed a half-goblet of Geneva in one angry gulp. "And what did all my generosity get me, I ask you? The muckworm turns up his toes—walked straight into the roadway reading a flaming book and got knocked into horsetails by a carter's wagon, you know—and the runaway sends me a female *keeper!* Oh, I've been paid out in full, I have. *Nutter!* Bring me more Heart's Ease!"

At least Alexandra now knew the real reason Chas had bolted. He didn't want to usurp his brother at Saxon Hall. It sounded very noble, she mused, until one thought about how totally unsuited Chas would have been to becoming lord of the manor. With his hey-go-mad schemes and bizarre interests, he would have had Saxon Hall mortgaged all the way up to the top of its battlements within a fortnight—if he hadn't turned the whole place into a home for a passel of wayward young females, that is.

But no matter how Sir Alexander fussed and fumed, and no matter how uncomfortable she was under his roof, Alexandra had made a promise to Chas and she was darned well going to keep it. Twenty-four hours after setting foot inside Saxon Hall she had begun a one-woman campaign to bring some semblance of order into her grandfather's household.

Sir Alexander had admitted that the place "could do with a wash and a brush-up," as Nutter and the rest were getting "a bit beyond it."

Sniffing disdainfully, Alexandra had replied, "A wash and brush-up? *Hummph,* I should just about think so. And as for your 'vassals' as you call them, Nutter is two years older than the flood, and he's naught but a boy beside the rest. What do you do with them at night, Grandfather—roll them up like the ancient pieces of parchment they are and stack them on shelves in the dungeon? In round words, Grandfather, your vassals are a shag-bag lot and your castle is an uninhabitable mess. But it's not to worry, I promise to set it to rights.''

For six days Alexandra had done just that—working her fingers to the bone all the day long just trying to make a small dent in the grime that had taken decades to accumulate over every surface in the Great Hall and adjoining rooms. The servants helped as much as they could, Nutter being the best of the bunch, but between their creaking joints and poor eyesight they were more of a hindrance than a help.

Yet already she had turned out the solar—Sir Alexander's private hideaway—as well as a small chamber that was located behind it. Today had seen the completion of her work in the Great Hall itself, except for the small room cut right into the thickness of the wall of the Hall, a vaultlike room called the treasury, and this she would tackle first thing in the morning. So thinking, she closed her eyes and was soon fast asleep.

When she awoke, it was to see the dawn of what seemed to be another damp, rainy English day. Sorely tempted to tug the covers back up over her head, she nevertheless rose from her comfortable haven and began plaiting her hair into a long ebony rope that would keep it out of her way as she cleaned. "No sense glooming all day in my chamber," she told her distorted reflection in the rusted and spotty slice of metal that served as her mirror, before she made her way first to the hated garderobe and then on to the Great Hall.

"Oh ho! There she is, Nutter," her grandfather exclaimed when he caught sight of her. "All right, girl, give over," he demanded, advancing on her, his great expanse of belly swinging before him with every step. "Where is it? By Jupiter, girl, I'll not be having this. I want it—give it back, I say!''

Alexandra was under no misapprehension as to just what

her grandfather was referring. During the course of the last week her housecleaning had succeeded in ferreting out more than two dozen well-hidden bottles of Hollands secreted around the donjon. Having put the kitchen supply of gin under lock and key the very first day she was in residence, she had been more than a little surprised at the old man's resourcefulness, but she now imagined that he had checked all his hidey-holes without finding a single bottle of his cache.

"And a good morrow to you too, Grandfather," she said now, adding pleasantly enough, "You're looking quite oppressed, you know, you old fidget. Could be it's nothing but a natural bit of early morning crustiness, but then I could be mistaken, couldn't I?"

"I'll give you early morning crustiness, you child of the devil!" Sir Alexander flung back at her. "Look'ee here, girl, I know what you're about. You think you've got me, but I'm up to all your rigs. Give me back my Geneva, I'm telling you!"

Alexandra lifted her determined chin. "You're not telling me anything of the kind, old man. Left on your own you'd drink yourself right into the grave, but you'll not put that on *my* conscience. I promised Chas—"

"Damn Charles! Damn your conscience and damn your promises!" Sir Alexander ranted, waving his arms excitedly as he charged back and forth in front of her in high dudgeon. Then suddenly his tactics changed. He sank onto a nearby bench and raised one pudgy, beringed hand to his chest. "It's sick I am, sick as a horse. I need my Heart's Ease, girl," he whined piteously. "Have pity on an old man."

It almost worked. Alexandra had opened her mouth to tell Nutter to bring a small goblet before she saw her grandfather peeking up at her from under his supposedly closed lids, a fleeting smirk of satisfaction turning up the corners of his mouth. "That was very good, Grandfather," she crooned silkily. "You nearly had me fooled. Too bad you let me see the triumph on your face. Forget it," she warned as he began once more to moan, now both hands clasped to his breast. "You'll get your normal ration of gripe water at luncheon and again at dinner and that's the end of it."

"Just like your grandmother, that's what you are," her grandfather groaned. "Flaming tartar she was too." Yet he did not push the matter, much to Alexandra's surprise, but only shook his head and retired to the privacy of his solar. Well, she thought smugly, he'd find no gin there either—she had taken care of that yesterday. So thinking, she followed Nutter down to the kitchens, where she greeted Harold and ate a quick breakfast.

Alexandra had been off target when she thought Sir Alexander was heading for another cache of gin—not that he wouldn't have welcomed a dram or two at the moment. On the contrary though, he had retired in order to wipe a tear from the corner of his eye—a show of emotion he did not choose to let his granddaughter see. It had been a long time since anyone had cared enough about him to see that he didn't drink himself senseless—not since his beloved wife had passed away some thirty years earlier as a matter of fact, and he found he rather liked it. It was a shame she'd be leaving his castle soon to become Lady Linton, but he knew his reward would come in the form of the great-grandson he was already looking forward to with greedy anticipation. Besides, Nutter was no match for him—he'd then have his gin supply back up to full measure or he wasn't half the man he thought himself to be!

Alexandra had just closed the lid on yet another great chest stuffed to the top with silver cups, dishes, and candlesticks—all now neatly polished—when she was called from her task by Nutter.

"Lord Linton to see you, miss," he told her as she rose from her knees on the dusty stones of the treasury and wiped a none-too-clean hand across her brow, leaving a smudge behind.

"Indeed," Alexandra replied testily, upset with herself over the slight fluttering the mention of his lordship's name had set up in her stomach. "Then don't keep him standing about needlessly, Nutter. Tell him I'm not receiving visitors this morning.''

How dare he call on her uninvited, she thought angrily. Yes, the seven days her grandfather had mentioned were up this morning, but who would have thought the man would be so obtuse as to think he actually expected him to put his nose back in her business after she had so flatly told him to take it out? Besides, she looked a fright, and there was no way for her to get to her room and put herself to rights without first passing through the Great Hall and exposing herself to Linton's bound to be supercilious scrutiny.

Thinking herself safe from further interruption, she turned to the cabinet that held Sir Alexander's best wine, her intention being to wipe the bottles free of the dust that lay over them in thick coats. As she reached for the first one, she was halted by a voice that warned, ''If you're planning on disturbing those bottles, I'd think twice if I were you. They don't rest on their sides in those racks by accident you know.''

Nicholas! Anger fought with the undeniable thrill of hearing his slightly amused drawl as Alexandra struggled to remain calm. Anger won. ''How dare you barge in here after I told Nutter to send you away?'' she demanded, her dark eyes sparkling in the dim light.

''If it's being alone with me in here that bothers you, Alix, I must say it's a little late for you to become so moral—seeing as how we've already slept together,'' he answered her.

''Slept together?'' she shrieked, setting up an echo in the stone room. ''Slept together!'' she hissed again, carefully keeping her voice lowered so Nutter, whose hearing far outclassed his eyesight, could not overhear. ''I did not sleep with you. I slept in one of your bedrooms. Besides, it was Harold who shared my chamber, not you.''

Nicholas's head turned slightly as he peered at her provokingly with his good eye. ''Harold, you say? Was it interesting?''

''You know darn well Harold is sixty if he's a day, and that he slept on the floor just inside the chamber door,'' said

Alexandra tightly, hauling back mightily on the reins of her temper. "Oh, why must you be so provoking?"

Nicholas took a snow white handkerchief from his pocket and busied himself with wiping at the smudge on Alexandra's forehead. "I don't really know, my dear. Perhaps because it's so lamentably easy to provoke you. Rather unsporting of me, d'ya think?" He finished wiping her forehead and replaced the handkerchief in his pocket. Stepping back a pace, he examined his work and declared, "There you are, all right and tight. Do you wish to give me a kiss in thanks?"

"You must be stark, staring mad," she told him before she turned her back on him entirely.

"What ho!" came Sir Alexander's exclamation from the doorway to the treasury. "Have I tripped across a case of April and May amid the wine bottles? Well, no matter. After all, you are betrothed now, aren't you."

Alexandra could have cheerfully strangled her grinning grandfather, but at Nicholas's next words, her anger became redirected.

"Ah, Sir Alexander, you've well and truly caught us out, haven't you. But never fear, the arrangements for the marriage are already well in train. I promise you, I have been nothing if not thorough. The ceremony takes place just after the new year—any more haste would be unseemly, don't you think?"

"How enterprising of you," Alexandra gritted while inwardly jumping up and down with glee. Not until after the new year, was it? she thought happily. Little do these two jolly connivers know I reach my twenty-first birthday New Year's Day. What a fine pair of fools they'll look when they find I am come of age and not bound to obey any man!

While Alexandra had been thinking her private thoughts, the Earl had been telling Sir Alexander that, since the weather had cleared so nicely after the gloom of the morning, he had had the happy notion of taking Alexandra out for a ride in his curricle. Knowing her absence from the Hall for a few hours would make any search for gin bottles that much easier, Sir Alexander hastily gave his blessing to the outing, and before she knew how it had happened, Alexandra found herself changed into her driving outfit and up alongside Linton as he tooled his matched pair of greys down the hill outside Saxon Hall.

"Congratulations," he said by way of opening the conversation. "I could not help but notice that the drawbridge now operates with nary a squeak."

Alexandra only shrugged.

"The whole castle, as a matter of fact, already reflects your good housekeeping," he pressed her, refusing to succumb to her bad mood.

"It was no great feat, I assure you," was all she answered.

This was not going well, Lord Linton told himself. Pinning on his most winning smile, he said, "The boys all send their best. They have been champing at the bit to come pay you a visit—or should I say, pay friend Harold a visit. I believe they mentioned something about viewing what they sincerely hope is his extensive collection of scalps."

Alexandra could not hide her smile. "They seemed to be nice boys."

Nicholas gave a bark of laughter. "Nice, is it? They're all next door to yahoos, that's what they are. Cuffy, that Master Jackanapes, was born to be hanged, while friend Billy has an attic that positively crawls with maggots. Jeremy, my dear brother, like Billy is not remarkable for his quick wit, but he is at heart a good boy. I guess all three of them are, but sometimes their antics tend to make me question that fact. I'm happy, though, to hear you don't bear them any ill will. After all, it was their prank that landed you in this muddle."

"It's not them I blame for this 'muddle,' " she told him now. "It was you who made such a fuss and then dragged me off to tell my grandfather the whole. I still say the whole thing could have been neatly brushed under the rug with none the wiser."

"Then obviously you do not know England, Alix," he returned with maddening calm. "Besides, now that the deed is done, I've my own reputation to consider, you know. I don't wish it bruited about that Lord Linton has been jilted *twice*."

Alexandra couldn't help noticing a touch of bitter self-mockery in Nicholas's voice. "So that's it," she accused him, turning in her seat to face him head-on. "Already left at the gate once, your pride can't stand the thought of another bride getting away. Well, you should have thought of that before you dragged me into your plans. I'll not be used to revenge yourself on some wayward fiancée."

"Is that what you think? That I'm using you?"

Alexandra took the time to look—really look—at Nicholas. What a handsome specimen he was, with his dark hair and dangerously romantic eyepatch. Certainly if it were only a bride he was seeking, he would have had no trouble finding one. So why had he picked on her? Could it be that he had not been planning to beat his erstwhile bride to the altar and that he truly believed her compromised and was just doing the honorable thing? Yes, she mused, it was possible.

Or perhaps he was suffering from an incurable wound of the heart and looked upon marriage to a near stranger as a fitting way to continue his line without running the risk of having some love-struck bride disturbing his mourning for his lost fiancée? If so, she had certainly fallen into his hands like a ripe plum.

"Why did she jilt you?" she found herself asking.

Now it was Nicholas's turn to be silent. This girl was no milk and water miss to be turned off with some farradiddle or other. No, she was devilishly acute, Miss Alexandra Saxon was, and none but the truth would satisfy her.

"It was the eyepatch," he told her at last. "I went off to Waterloo without the patch and came back without the eye. She took one look and went screaming from the room in high hysterics." There, see what she makes of that! he thought, daring her to look him in his remaining eye.

Alexandra swallowed hard once or twice before saying, "Well if that isn't above all things stupid! You're well rid of her, Nicholas."

Mannering could have chosen from among a dozen rejoinders she might have given him, but her actual answer truly jolted him. He opened his mouth to—was it to thank her?—when suddenly three riders broke from the trees, sending his greys to plunging and dancing as he worked to get them under control. *"Stand and deliver!"* one of the highwaymen yelled over the din.

"Like bloody hell I will!" Mannering hollered back, controlling his pair with superhuman effort before snaking the whip out over their backs, urging them into an immediate gallop.

Alexandra held onto the side rail with one hand as with her other she squashed her hat firmly down on her head. *"Go it!"* she shouted in Mannering's ear, obviously enjoying herself immensely, earning herself a wide grin from his lordship.

They were on a fairly flat stretch of countryside, luckily, and Nicholas knew there was little fear of the curricle hitting a rut and overturning. Later, once he had had a chance to reflect on his actions, he would probably be amazed that he had dared such a potentially dangerous maneuver with Alexandra up beside him, but for the moment he was too full of the thrill of the chase to think of anything but the sport of the thing.

On and on they raced, the horsemen slowly fading, for their broken-in-the-wind plugs were no match for the Earl of Linton's matched greys. Looking over her shoulder at the thieves, Alexandra laughed at the trio bouncing up and down on their horses' backs like bobbing corks—obviously none of them great riders.

Just then an imp of mischief tapped her on the shoulder, and she quite readily gave in to impulse. Releasing her hold on her hat she cupped her fingers around her mouth, took a deep breath, and gave out with a remarkable imitation of the spine-tingling, high-pitched Lenape alarm whoop Harold had taught her long ago. *"Y-i-i-i-i-e-e-e-e-e-i-i-e-e-y-ip-yip-yip!"*

It was a good thing Lord Linton was such a top-o'-the-trees sawyer, for not only did Alexandra's yell send the thieves' horses to bucking and shying, it also served to nearly unstring the high-blooded greys, who laid back their ears and ran like the wind in an effort to remove themselves from the vicinity as well as from the dying echoes of that blood-curdling scream.

They had covered almost another full mile before Mannering could draw the curricle to a halt, pulling the horses off the path and directing them to a spot under a tree in the meadow. Only then did he turn to look at Alexandra, taking in her high color and glittering eyes and acknowledging to himself that she was far and away the most handsome woman he had ever clapped eyes—eye, he amended mentally—on.

She was also, he soon recollected, thinking of her recently demonstrated propensity for hoydenism, probably the most infuriating, provoking, unsettling—*interesting*—woman he could ever meet, should he live five lifetimes.

Slowly, oh, so slowly, one side of his chiseled mouth slid upward in a closemouthed smile, causing the skin around his good eye to crinkle up in laugh lines and setting off a deep, slashing dimple in his cheek. Obviously he was still caught up in the spirit of the chase. "Come here, woman," he commanded huskily, slipping an arm around Alexandra's waist.

He pulled her to within an inch of his face, their mouths almost touching, before his grin faded. Then he whispered, "My little savage," and closed the gap.

Alexandra hung there, her arms hanging bonelessly at her sides, while Nicholas's hand held her unresistingly against his chest. She was incapable of pulling away, incapable of protest, incapable of anything, in fact, but feeling—feeling the warm firmness of his lips as they moved against hers.

It wasn't as if she hadn't been kissed before; after all, she wasn't that young. But this kiss was whole universes away from the quick, clumsy kisses her swains had pressed on her occasionally at some party or other. This kiss was a revelation. No one had told her how the mere meeting of two pairs of lips could make her feel as if her entire body had just been plunged into warm, scented rose water—her limbs going all soft and mushy while a white-hot heat burned in the pit of her stomach.

She moaned, she couldn't help herself, and Nicholas took advantage of her parted lips to deepen the kiss, a move that succeeded in setting her entire body aflame. Her hands crept up to grasp his shoulders, as she was suddenly desperately in need of something solid to hold on to, and nothing could have been more solid than Nicholas's broad shoulders.

Yet they weren't solid, although they had been until he felt the touch of her hands, at which time they shuddered involuntarily, and his heart, which had been pounding heavily in his chest, skipped a beat or two before setting off again at a pace that would have far outdistanced his fastest horse. He indulged himself in these unaccustomed glorious feelings for a moment longer—as he might as well be hung for a sheep as a lamb—before firmly putting Alexandra from him.

"You will," he paused to take a deep, steadying breath, "you will permit me to say that any further disclaimers of my compromising you into marriage shall be unnecessary."

Alexandra had been looking at him from behind a rosy haze of utter contentment, all animosity quite forgotten, but at his words she blinked hard, dispelling the fog and suddenly seeing everything with, his lordship was to think later, rather a bit too much clarity.

"Kiluwa mamalachgook!" Alexandra gritted, her eyes narrowed into angry slits. And then she hit him.

Now, Nicholas would have been the first to say that perhaps he deserved a slap on the cheek. Indeed, he had already begun mentally preparing for the feel of Alexandra's open palm on the side of his face. It was only to be expected after what he had said—what he had done. What he was not prepared for was the solid thump of Alexandra's balled fist landing smack in his midsection, and he doubled over, all his wind knocked out of him.

When he could at last raise his head, it was to see his attacker once more facing front on the seat, every hair in place, her gown and pelisse returned to their former order, and the girl herself looking remarkably unlike the scintillating creature he had so lately felt come alive in his arms. In fact, if anything, she looked prim, almost plain.

"Who—who taught you that?" he was forced to ask, still tenderly massaging his sore ribs.

"Harold," she returned calmly, smoothing down a crease in the skirt of her gown. "He always said the best way to defeat the enemy is to do the unexpected, catch him off his guard. You expected a slap, don't deny it. Next time, if I should ever be so unfortunate as to cross paths with you again, you will expect a punch in the stomach. You will, alas, be disappointed. That too Harold taught me—never try the same trick twice on the same person."

"Bully for Harold," Mannering grumbled into his cravat as he turned the horses toward Saxon Hall. "I suppose you were also cursing at me in his heathen tongue?"

Lifting her chin and looking off to the side of the road away from the Earl, she sniffed disdainfully, "Indians don't curse, at least not in the vulgar way you *Yengees*—English—do. When you've been cursed by a Lenape, you'll know it, for I shall be happy to translate. I merely called you a spotted snake. It seemed to fit at the time." She turned her head to look him up and down, a sneer in her eyes. "It still does."

Mannering made no further attempts at conversation, feeling himself best served by keeping his thoughts to himself. Within a quarter of an hour he had deposited Alexandra just inside the outer bailey and driven off toward Linton Hall. This journey was not so silent, although Linton rode alone, for he passed the time by calling himself every kind of fool he could think of and inventing new ones as he went along.

Harold would have been very proud of him.

Chapter Four

HOPING to work out her anger at Nicholas by means of a frenzied bout of housekeeping, Alexandra spent the remainder of the day deep in the dingy Saxon Hall kitchens. Alas, her efforts, consisting as they did of prodigious amounts of determined pot bangings and violent cabinet door slammings—prompting the servants to hastily recall pressing duties elsewhere in the castle—proved to be a lamentably unsatisfying substitute for beating the insufferable Lord Linton into a quivering pulp (they didn't do the kitchens any great whacking lot of good either, but then what were a few more dents in a passel of pots that were so ancient they had probably landed on the island in the train of William the Conqueror?).

Yet what alternative did she have? Certainly, flying to her grandfather with the news that his only granddaughter had been nearly ravished by the lecherous Nicholas Mannering would be the very pinnacle of folly. She could see Sir Alexander now—rigged out in his rusty medieval armor and perhaps even sporting her favor on his sleeve, prancing back and forth on his trusty steed outside Linton Hall—demanding in a loud voice that Mannering come out and fight.

Alexandra smiled a bit at the picture her thoughts conjured up before sobering again. Her grandfather wouldn't go pelting off to Linton Hall to avenge her honor. He considered Nicholas to be her fiancé—or her betrothed, as the old man termed it. No, he'd probably just laugh, wink, poke her a time or two in the ribs with his elbow, and make some embarrassing remark about his dreamed-of great-grandson.

She could tell Harold, she thought evilly. Even though

the Indian was pleased to think there was yet a single man left in this world fool enough to wed an over-the-hill spinster of twenty, he would not take kindly to having his charge pawed about like some common tavern wench. Surely Harold would take it upon himself to paint one of his wampum belts red and deliver it to Nicholas—the Lenape method of declaring war on their enemies. Alexandra's eyes glittered nastily as she tried to envision Nicholas minus his crop of coal black hair. *That* would surely show him a thing or two!

But once again her glee was short-lived. Harold was an Indian all right, but he was only *one* Indian, and an old one at that. His warrior days were far in the past, if indeed he had ever trod a warpath at all—which was highly unlikely she reminded herself, since the last battles near Philadelphia took place when Harold was only about ten years of age.

The Indian couldn't fight for her, and confiding in him would force him to fight, only to end up injured or, even worse, made into a figure of fun by Nicholas and the others at Linton Hall. Much as she ached for revenge, much as she longed for a comforting shoulder to lean on, this was one battle she had to fight alone.

So far she was outclassed, outmanned, and outgunned. What she needed, Alexandra decided, was a weapon— something that would shift the advantage away from Mannering and in her direction.

Long into the night she tossed and turned, cudgeling her brain to think of just the right weapon she would need to bring Nicholas to his knees, at last falling into an uneasy sleep colored by dreams in which she was searching, endlessly searching for a weapon.

"Venison, chickens, geese, capons, herrings, cod, plaice—whatever that is—bacon, porpoises. *Porpoises!* Good heavens, whoever would have thought m'ancestors dined on porpoises!"

Alexandra had been busy in the treasury since rising early—after spending a restless night—and was by mid-morning knee-deep in piles of ancient records and household accounts she had found in a large chest in the storage room. There was no real need to keep any of the documents, she realized, but figuring some future Saxons might wish a peek at how their forefathers lived, she carefully sorted and stacked them all and replaced them neatly in their oil cloth wrappings.

Sitting back on her haunches, she pressed a hand to the small of her back, which had begun to ache abominably from her enforced bending to reach the deepest depths of the chest. From the Great Hall just outside the half-open door of the treasury she could hear her grandfather going over the rules to his favorite card game while Harold made appropriate grunts every now and then.

"Good God," she said aloud to herself, "as if it weren't bad enough, that the man forces Nutter to play with him—cheating the half-blind fellow all hollow—now he must try to fleece Harold as well." She leaned back some more in order to peek out through the crack in the door to see her grandfather sitting across from Harold at one of the trestle tables. Sir Alexander sported a cunning grin while the Indian, who was having a great deal of difficulty holding the cards that made up his hand, listened to yet another spur-of-the-moment rule that assured Sir Alexander of having the winning hand.

As Harold pushed another small wampum belt across the table, where it was at once snatched up and examined by the old gentleman, Alexandra noticed a large goblet at the Indian's elbow. Gin! Now her grandfather was plying Harold with gin. It was the outside of enough! Everyone knew an Indian had no head for spirits. She shook her head disgustedly and made to get up and put a stop to this nonsense once and for all.

Just as she had almost gained her feet, her eyes spotted another document stuck in the corner of the tattered lining of the chest lid. Oh well, she thought, it's just one more absurdly huge order for sea salt or a listing of the alms the lady of the household doled out to the poor. She might as well add it to the rest.

Alexandra tugged gently at the yellowed parchment and realized at once that this was no ordinary document—the

66

quality of the paper was quite superior to any of the others she had come across. Soon she had it in her hands, unrolling it to find the whole sheet to be covered in fine script and encrusted with more than a half-dozen official-looking signatures and wax seals.

Carrying it over to the candelabra to take advantage of the increased light, she held the document close to her face as she worked to decipher the Old English script. Slowly, as the words she was reading began to make an impression on her mind, a small grin replaced the frown of concentration, until at last she clutched the parchment to her breast, threw back her head, and gave out with a mighty yell.

"Wheeeeeee-ooo!" she shouted, her voice coming back to her again and again from the thick stone walls.

Two benches crashed noisily to the floor in the Great Hall as the startled men dropped their cards and sprang to their feet—Harold reaching for his knife and Sir Alexander searching blindly for his goblet of Blue Ruin.

"What in thunder is it, gel?" her grandfather blustered as soon as he'd gotten his breath. "If it's naught but a silly mouse has run across your toes, I'll have your missish hide. Knocked my goblet over, I have, and I'll not forgive *that* lightly."

Alexandra came bounding into the Great Hall, a wide, silly grin nearly splitting her face in two. Going over to Harold, she caught the Indian's hands and danced him about in a circle chanting, "I've found it! I've found it! I needed it and I found it!"

Sir Alexander could see nothing but a moldy old piece of paper squashed in the girl's fist as she persisted in holding on to the Indian and capering about like a chicken who's just lost its head.

"What have you there?" he shouted over the din. "What have you found?"

Alexandra stopped in midwhirl and skipped up to her grandfather to wave the parchment under the man's rosy-red nose. "What have I found, Grandfather?" she chortled. "I have found release. I have found revenge. I have found the fairy pot at the end of the rainbow, King Solomon's mines, buried pirate treasure! I have found what I have been searching for! *I have found a weapon!''*

Running toward the spiral staircase, she called over her shoulder to the two men who were just then looking at her as if she had suddenly taken leave of her wits, ''Don't just stand there like statues. Give me five minutes to change and we'll be off.''

Thinking his granddaughter was already more than a little ''off,'' Sir Alexander yelled, ''Where are we bound, you widget?''

Alexandra whirled and spread her skirts as she dropped into a deep curtsy. ''Why, we're off to pay a call on my *betrothed,* wherever else?''

Sir Alexander turned to the Indian and remarked, ''Chas didn't marry until he hit America, as I recall. Never did ask about the woman. Should have. Do you suppose insanity runs in the family?'' At Harold's blank stare Sir Alexander cursed a time or two and said disgustedly, ''Why do I waste my time talking to a heathen who cannot even remember what is trumps? Maybe this insanity thing is catching.'' He drew himself up to his full height, which wasn't all that impressive when viewed beside Harold's imposing stature, tucked a few inches of ''excess baggage'' under his wide belt, and announced, ''Well, you black rascal, don't just stand there, get that mangy fur of yours and let's get going. We're calling on Linton Hall, you know.''

Harold bowed his head slightly and replied, *''N'mauwi pihm, geptschat,''* which translated, meant ''I am going to take a sweat, fool,'' and went off toward the kitchens, leaving behind an angry but, fortunately, uncomprehending Sir Alexander.

Meanwhile, a few miles away at Linton Hall, Nicholas Mannering had made a discovery of his own. That this discovery did not cause him to shout with joy or dance about with happiness came as a bit of a surprise to Jeremy, as he had convinced himself that his brother would be delighted to find that Helene Anselm—once Nicholas's fiancée—had unexpectedly dropped in for a visit.

Not that Jeremy held a very high opinion of Miss Anselm—acknowledging that the girl had an unusual beauty while still aware that it scarcely made up for her sad lack of wit. Add to that one positive gorgon of a mother (who seemed to come along with Helene as sort of a combination deal) and one perfect twit of a brother named Rupert, and Miss Anselm's appeal dipped even further.

But Nicholas had been smitten with the chit the moment he laid eyes on her in town and had somehow cut out all her other admirers to the point where their engagement had been posted in the *Gazette* just before Nicholas took off for Brussels and somehow landed himself in the thick of things at Waterloo.

Jeremy would never forgive the heartless chit for tossing his brother over upon his return, saying his scar and eyepatch were too much for a person of her delicate sensibilities to tolerate. When Nicholas then hied himself off posthaste for Linton Hall, forgoing all the post-Waterloo balls and fetes, Jeremy was thoroughly convinced his brother was heading for a sad decline—ergo Jeremy's decision to have himself booted out of school for a space in order to keep his brother company.

Now Helene was back—or so it surely seemed, if the amount of baggage currently stacked in the foyer could be taken as an indication of her intended length of stay—and Jeremy supposed Nicholas to be immediately thrown into ecstasy.

He couldn't have been more wrong.

While Jeremy was closeted with his friends discussing this latest turn of events—and wondering aloud what good old Nick was to do when he finally recollected that he now had *two* affianced brides underfoot—the Earl was pacing back and forth in his dressing room, cursing a blue streak while his hapless valet tried in vain to convince him to remain still long enough to have his cravat tied properly.

"Damn and blast!" his lordship swore, not for the first time. "Everything was running along so smoothly, and now *she* has to pop back into my life like some half-forgotten nightmare. And to tote that dragon-mother and brainless boob brother of hers along with her is just laying it on a bit too thick and rare. Well, maybe I was fool enough to fall for a pretty face and well-turned ankle once, but no Mannering makes a cake of himself twice—at least not with the same chit! What are you about, man? You're choking me, you know.''

"Beg pardon, milord," the servant quailed, "but if you was but ta plant yerself for a space—er—I means, sir, if you was but to stand still for a moment."

"I'm sorry, Bates," his lordship apologized, "planting myself for a moment would be a pleasure. Perhaps I shall be able to think better in a stationary position."

While the valet finished his work, first asking his lordship to kindly raise his leg so that he could have his boot slipped on—then begging his lordship's pardon, but would his lordship prefer the aquamarine or the plain gold signet ring with this jacket?—the Earl concentrated on just precisely what would be his best approach to the dilemma now awaiting him downstairs in the morning room in the shape of three encroaching Anselms.

Contrary to what his brother believed, Nicholas had been far from heartbroken when Helene ended their engagement. Indeed, he was only halfway to Brussels when he had first begun to regret his precipitate proposal, brought on, he was sure, by a combination of heady perfume, a starlit night, and rather too much vintage brandy after dinner. Helene Anselm was a pretty piece, there was no doubt of that, but he no more loved her than he loved the opera dancer he'd had under protection that last twelvemonth or more—that fact was brought home to him by the realization that he was able to part from both of them with nary a bit of regret as he went off to deliver the Ministry message that had given him the excuse to travel to Brussels in the first place.

Not that it was worth the loss of his eye, and the resultant headaches that, thank goodness, were at long last showing signs of fading, but if Helene had not called off the engagement he would have found some way to call a halt to the marriage—if it meant he'd have had to ship out to India under an assumed name.

70

Just then another thought struck him and he jumped up from his chair, knocking Bates off balance just as he was about to carefully wipe a small smudge off his lordship's shining Hessians, and exclaimed, "My God—*Alix!* I've got to get shed of these Anselms before she catches wind of them, or there'll be the devil to pay for sure."

He slammed out of the dressing room while Bates watched him go, wringing his hands as he spied out a three-inch-long string hanging from his lordship's coattails. The Earl bounded down the long curving staircase, passing by his grinning brother and cutting short his sibling's sarcastic remarks with an abrupt "Stow it, brat," before crossing the foyer on determined feet and throwing open the doors of the morning room.

"Ladies, Rupert old man," he began as he walked into the room, "how nice it is of you to stop by for a visit on your way to—um—it seems I am in ignorance of your final destination. Where is it you are bound for?"

Miss Anselm, a vision in robin's egg blue muslin, just now seated in Nicholas's favorite chair as if it were her right, giggled delightfully at his lordship's *faux pas.* "We are bound for Linton Hall, silly," she trilled in her light (and, the Earl now noticed for the first time, rather gratingly *high)* voice. "We were at loose ends after Brighton became thin of company, and since our estate is in the midst of redecoration, so tedious you know, we were at a loss as to where we might situate ourselves for a space. That is, we were until Mama remembered your many kind invitations for us to come to Linton Hall any time we pleased."

Those invitations were extended while Helene and Nicholas were engaged, which the Earl opened his mouth to point out, but before he could utter a word Mrs. Anselm piped up, "Now, Helene, sweetums, you must remember that an unfortunate misunderstanding between the Earl and yourself might have altered that invitation." While "sweetums" busied herself trying to pout and look pretty at the same time, Mrs. Anselm turned to Nicholas and went on smoothly, "Not that the hysterical words of a lovestruck young girl can be taken with any degree of credulity. So overset, so

71

racked with grief was she when first she saw your sad, sad wound. Ah, my lord, you must understand how overcome my little lamb was at the time and disregard that unfortunate scene. She," here she spared a loving glance in her daughter's direction, "has had a multitude of time to reflect on her folly and realize that True Love overcomes all obstacles. And that," the woman sighed dramatically, "is the bald truth and the real reason we are here, even if my daughter cannot yet find it in herself to unburden her heart to you while her mother and brother are present."

Well done, his lordship acknowledged to himself. The woman is a real master both at lying through her teeth and improvising on that lie as she goes along. And she was up-front about things—at least, she was as up-front as she was capable. Nicholas could almost find it in himself to be amused if it weren't for the fact that should Alix catch wind of the Anselms being under his roof she would cry off from their engagement quicker than the cat could lick her ear.

If Alix were not on the scene, if the boredom he had been feeling as winter came on and there were so few activities either socially or on the estate to engage his mind had not been totally dissipated by Alix's arrival, perhaps he might have found it enjoyable to play along with Mrs. Anselm's little game for a while, if only to see exactly what rig the old dragon was up to this time.

But Alix *was* on the scene and he would have to forgo this little bit of sport and then shove their carcasses out the door posthaste. He was just about to deflate Mrs. Anselm's pretensions with a few well chosen home truths when Poole entered the room and announced rather distractedly, "Sir Alexander Saxon and Miss Alexandra Saxon have arrived, my lord, and wish to have speech with you." More quietly, he added so only the Earl could hear, "The young miss seems to be in quite a state, sir. Perhaps you'll be wanting me to put them in the library away from—well, you know who?"

Actually, his lordship would rather Poole could put his latest visitors elsewhere—preferably in some distant county—until he had settled things with the Anselms, but he knew that to be impossible. Oh well, he thought, shrugging his broad shoulders, in for a penny in for a pound, and he asked Poole to please show his visitors into the morning room and told him tea and refreshments would be required in half an hour.

Poole withdrew, slowly shaking his head at his master's folly, returning shortly with the Saxons in tow. Sir Alexander had taken no more than two steps into the room when he stopped in his tracks and exclaimed in his gruff voice, "Well, sink me if it ain't Matilda Anselm. And who are these two with her? The chit looks passable. But the boy? An effeminate twiddlepoop if ever I've seen one. Do you have the dressing of him, Matilda? Looks like a Gunther ice all tricked out for dessert. Just goes to show the folly of petticoat power when there's no man about to keep her in check. By Jupiter, woman, it's really too bad of you, you know. Husband's probably twirling in his grave iffen he knows of this piece of work."

While Alexandra and Nicholas avoided each other's eyes for fear they would set each other off in paroxysms of laughter, the lad called Rupert flushed so deeply pink as to exactly match his satin waistcoat, while Helene—not known for her brain power—gifted Sir Alexander with an inane smile. It was left to Mrs. Anselm to rescue the moment, which she did rather well, by saying, "Ah, Sir Alexander, we meet again. Tell me sir, how long has it been? Twenty years, I wager, and you're still an abominable tease. Pray sit down here next to me and I'll call for some refreshment more suitable than tea. Was it canary you favored? No, I don't think so. It was gin, wasn't it? Of course it was. No wonder you are so out of sorts. Here it is almost noon and I'll wager you've had nary a drop to sustain you. Well, never fear, Matilda will remedy that oversight forthwith!"

Sir Alexander was immediately mollified. He still believed Matilda to be the most totty-headed female he'd ever met, but there was one thing about her he'd always liked— she always remembered just what a man favored by way of liquid refreshment. Within the space of a minute he was sitting beside the woman on the sofa happily sipping from the crystal goblet Poole had placed before him—still not knowing why he was at Linton Hall, but suddenly in no great hurry to find out.

Alexandra wasn't so easily settled. Nicholas watched her closely as he effected the introductions, his toes curling in his boots as he realized she was under no misapprehension as to the identity of Miss Anselm.

"I could not help but notice a large amount of baggage in the entrance hall, Miss Anselm," Alix remarked conversationally as she sat down near Helene. "You have come for a visit, I suppose? Tell me, are you related to the Mannerings?"

Helene blushed prettily beneath her auburn curls and replied coquettishly, "You might say that, Miss Saxon. Nicholas and I were once engaged to be married, and if it were not for an unfortunate misunderstanding, I would already be mistress of this household."

Oh, I doubt that, Alix thought to herself. You might have been in residence, my dear, but it's your mama who would have the running of things unless I miss my guess. Aloud she only offered sweetly, "And now this misunderstanding is all cleared up and you are once again betrothed?"

"If Mama has anything to say on the subject, it is," came a voice from the corner of the room. Rupert Anselm had made his presence known.

"Rupert, *darling*, I do believe I saw young Jeremy pass by the doorway. You were once school chums, were you not? Why don't you run along and see if you can find him, hmm?" Mrs. Anselm's smiling face hardened a fraction. *"Now, Rupert!"*

Rupert, his small burst of independent thought neatly scotched, bowed his head, mumbled, "Yes, Ma'am," and slipped swiftly from the room just as Sir Alexander exploded, "By Jupiter, Mannering, did you hear what that lad said? Said this chit here is your betrothed. What wild work is this?"

Alexandra turned twinkling eyes on his lordship, tilted her head to one side—making herself look for all the world like a puppy just given an undeserved swat on the behind—

74

and asked, "I do not understand, Nicholas. Have you had second thoughts?"

Yes! the Earl wished to shout, I've had second thoughts—thoughts that tell me I would have been better served to have lost my neck at Waterloo, seeming now to have saved it only to have it thoroughly wrung by Sir Alexander! But he refrained from airing his feelings. Instead he just smiled, shook his head, and told his audience, "It seems we have a bit of a muddle here, ladies and gentlemen."

Hmm, thought Alexandra nastily, it would seem our friend Nicholas is a master of understatement. A muddle, indeed. One cannot help but wonder how he would describe the war of 1812—as a "slight skirmish" perhaps? Her own mission shelved for the moment in the light of this newest development, she was content to sit back and watch the fun from the sidelines—throwing in little comments from time to time to keep things lively.

"It is true," Mannering began, nodding in Mrs. Anselm's direction, "that I was once engaged to wed your daughter. But is it not also true that it was Helene who called off the wedding?"

Mrs. Anselm waved away such nonsense with a dismissing sweep of one hand. "A momentary overset of sensibilities, not to be taken seriously," she sniffed.

The Earl allowed one eloquent eyebrow to raise in astonishment. "Momentary, madam? More than five months have passed—surely more than a fair amount of time."

"Time be damned!" Sir Alexander interrupted angrily. "It's my granddaughter you're to wed, Linton. I've had your word on it."

The fair Helene, beginning to feel something just might be amiss, looked nervously in the Earl's direction. "Is this true, Nicholas, dearest?" she lisped nervously.

Sir Alexander, not remarkable for his tact, answered Helene's question by baldly announcing, "It's fact all right. Compromised her, that's what he did."

Mrs. Anselm turned narrowed eyes on Alexandra. "How very *enterprising* of you, dear," she cooed.

"Enterprising, my foot!" Alexandra burst out, jumping

to her feet. "A case of damned bad luck is more like it. Besides, *I* have never given my agreement to the match."

"*Aha!*" breathed Mrs. Anselm, her smile growing wide once more.

While most men would have been brought to a standstill by the formidable problem now facing Nicholas, he was somehow beginning to see a bit of ironic humor in the situation. Here he was, with one woman—who had earlier spurned him—trying to renew their engagement, and another woman—whom he had compromised not once but twice—fighting hammer and tongs to be shed of him. He didn't know whether he should be flattered or insulted. Either way, he found it was not all that unenjoyable being fought over by two beautiful females (not to mention one matchmaking mama and one outraged grandfather). After a few moments of thought, Nicholas chose to be neither flattered nor insulted—he chose, rather, to just sit back and wait for further developments.

These were not long in coming. While in one corner of the room grandfather and granddaughter exchanged bitter words concerning just exactly who was in charge of that granddaughter's future, Mama and offspring were conversing furiously in another, Mama doing the majority of the talking.

The more Mrs. Anselm talked, the smaller Helene appeared to grow, until finally she seemed almost to disappear entirely—which she did in fact presently do when she fainted dead away behind the brocade sofa.

"Oh my poor baby!" Mrs. Anselm shrieked theatrically, putting a quick period to the whispered argument at the opposite end of the room. Helene's mother dropped to her knees beside her stricken daughter, chaffing at one limp hand while telling all who would listen that her daughter must be put to bed immediately as her tender constitution had been dealt a severe, if not a near mortal, blow.

Alexandra, from her position standing just behind Helene's head, could not help noticing that the girl's eyelids fluttered once or twice before Nicholas bent down to ungently hoist her slight form into his arms. She's bamming, Alexandra deduced quickly—most probably on orders from her mother.

Unknown to Alexandra, Nicholas was thinking the same thing, but there was precious little he could do about it other than pinching Helene into giving herself away (which he owned he had given a bit of thought). As he trod up the staircase, the limp Helene dangling gracefully in his arms, Mrs. Anselm followed close behind on his heels, barking orders to Poole to have all their luggage sent upstairs as she was sure her poor baby would not be able to travel any more that day.

"Blister me," Sir Alexander commented from his position at the bottom of the stairwell, "Matilda would have made a great general. Now she's taken possession, it will be nigh impossible to nudge her out again."

"You think it's all a hum too, Grandfather?" Alexandra asked.

"Sink me, of course it is," he shot back testily, "and sure as check Linton knows it too. I cannot understand why he allowed it unless he's running some rig of his own."

Alexandra looked up toward the now empty landing, a thoughtful frown puckering her brow. "Do you think he means to make me jealous? If so, the man's more of a fool than I thought him to be. If you ask me, I think he doesn't want either one of us and only hopes we will kill each other off fighting over him and leave him in peace. Not that I give a tinker's curse if he does marry the chit—although he's much too good for that brainless widget—but he knows you'll try to hold him to your bargain."

"I by damn will! Let the Anselm woman take the young sprout—it's the Earl for you, my girl," Sir Alexander blustered, blithely settling the fate of both the Mannering men.

"Jeremy?" Alexandra questioned, taken aback. "But he's just a child. That odious Anselm woman would serve him up for dinner. Besides, if ever I saw a person out for the main chance, it is Mrs. Anselm. No," she shook her head thoughtfully, "it's Linton himself she's after. Something must have happened to make her rethink the engagement."

Sir Alexander gave a disdainful snort. "Something happened all right. The daughter ran out of *beaux* and the mother ran out of funds.'' He laughed aloud. ''What she didn't count on was Nicholas's finding himself another bride.''

''Who wants no part of him,'' Alexandra added mendaciously. ''Don't forget *that*, Grandfather.''

''Blast it, gel, how can I forget it, with you blabbering it about constantly for all to hear? Matilda saw her chance and took it, no thanks to you. Now that she's got the girl entrenched upstairs, it will take an earthquake to shift her. And stop grinning like the village idiot. Anyone would think whistling Earls down the wind was no more than a lark to you.''

From his position at the head of the stairs, Nicholas could not help overhearing the conversation taking place below him. The plan that had begun to glimmer in his brain just before Helene had enacted her dramatic swoon was now rapidly taking shape. He would pretend to play along with Mrs. Anselm's little game—keeping Helene on the scene—and try to use the girl's presence to his own advantage. Alix may not think she wants to marry me, he told himself, but her reaction to my kiss was not one of repugnance—not by a long chalk.

No, Alix wasn't as adverse to him as she pretended to be, he was sure. Perhaps a gentle nudge in the right direction was all that she needed.

Not that he was in love with her, he clarified mentally. He had tried that emotion once and found it fleeting, fickle, and decidedly unreliable. After all, he had for a time truly believed he was in love with Helene—an outstanding example of why men should choose their mates with their heads rather than their hearts if ever there was one.

Alexandra suited him. She was beautiful, intelligent, and spirited—not to mention heir to all Sir Alexander's considerable worldly goods. It was true the Saxon and Mannering holdings did not, as the saying went, ''march together,'' but they were close enough as to make no difference and went a long way toward sweetening the pot—although Nicholas wasn't by nature a mercenary man.

He might not have planned to marry so soon after his lucky escape from Helene's clutches, but now his reasons for pushing Alexandra into matrimony seemed even more valid. At first he had only wrestled with his sense of honor, and being a gentleman (and in no little awe of Sir Alexander's power to make his life a living hell if he refused to do the honorable thing), he had quickly seen the good sense of offering Alexandra the protection of his name.

Also weighing in favor of the match was Jeremy's nerve-shredding, mother-hen protectiveness ever since Helene's defection—clearly the boy wouldn't rest until his big brother was, in Jeremy's mind at least, happily ensnared in parson's mousetrap. If it came to a choice between wedding Alexandra or putting up with Cuffy and Billy forevermore underfoot, besides having Jeremy hanging around him as if he were about to put a period to his existence as a result of his sad disappointment, Alexandra won hands down.

Of course—the Earl was honest enough to admit to himself at least—marrying a beauty like Alexandra, rich or poor, wasn't exactly a hardship. Bedding her, in fact, should prove to be a true joy.

Nicholas looked down the staircase and sighed. Alexandra herself was proving the one real fly in the ointment—stubborn little baggage that she was showing herself to be.

If only he had already sent the notice of their engagement to the *Gazette*. But no, he had thought it might look more than a shade havey-cavey—the girl having only arrived in England a sennight earlier. A quiet wedding right after the New Year, that was the ticket, with a vaguely worded announcement inserted in the papers after the fact. Besides, Alexandra was proving difficult with her oft-repeated refusals to behave like a sensible puss and accept his offer gracefully. *Two* retractions in the *Gazette* in less than a year just might serve to really send him into a sad decline.

He had thought he was wearing down her resistance—he and Sir Alexander—but even earlier today in the morning room (and in front of the Anselms, no less) she had repudiated him yet again.

Helene's presence at Linton Hall did make things deuced

awkward, but her visit just might be worked to advantage by a man clever enough to correctly play the cards dealt him, Nicholas mused as he continued to watch Alexandra. Before giving himself any time to reflect overmuch on what he was about to do, he descended the staircase to have a few words with his recalcitrant fiancée.

"You'll be happy to hear that all seems to be under control upstairs. Helene is resting comfortably with a cloth dampened in *eau de cologne* bathing her forehead whilst her dear mother has requisitioned three chambers for herself and her offspring and is at this very moment giving my poor staff fits with her orders," he told them.

"By Jupiter, you're in for it now, my boy," Sir Alexander warned, stabbing a pudgy finger at Linton's chest. "Mark my words—you'll not budge that one 'til spring now she's got her carcass upstairs. A conniving, devious woman if ever one was made, that Matilda, as was her mother before her. German, you know," he added as if this explained everything. "Came over from Hanover with the first George, took one gander at our fair island, and never looked back. Greedy buggers too, all of 'em—went back to Hanover for their brides just to keep the money in the family.

"Matilda's father-in-law liked the cards though, and nearly ran them all aground with his gaming debts. It's my guess Matilda used up the last of the blunt to try and marry herself a new fortune with that widget of a daughter. Her own kind don't seem to want her, now that she's pockets to let." The old man shook his head in disgust. "Looks like you're it, lad, since the gel couldn't bring down any bigger game. But Matilda's been outfoxed this time, by Jupiter, because it's my granddaughter you'll be wedding, not Widow Anselm's die-away daughter."

Seeing a militant look registering again on Alexandra's face, Nicholas decided it was time to throw out a lure or two and see if his "fish" would take the bait. Arranging his face into a suitably sorrowful expression, he told Sir Alexander, "I doubt even my fortune is inducement enough to bring Helene to the altar, no matter what her mother intends. She threw me over once you know—on account of my," he paused and hung his head before sighing, "my *disfigurement.*"

Manfully trying to hide his very obvious distress, he went on mournfully, "Just now, upstairs, Helene chanced to open her eyes as I was reaching out my hand to touch her forehead—only to ascertain whether or not she was feverish, you understand—and she—she *flinched* away from my hand. The poor child was clearly frightened half out of her wits."

"Why that miserable, unfeeling, insensitive—" Alexandra struggled to find a suitable word, finally settling on *"ninnyhammer!* How dare she do such a thing?" Even if Nicholas didn't care a rap for Miss Anselm, it still must be painful to have someone be so obviously repelled by his patch. She lifted the hem of her skirt in preparation of ascending the staircase to give Miss Helene Anselm a piece of her mind before Nicholas stopped her cold with his next words.

"Don't be so harsh on her, Alix," Nicholas intoned fatalistically. "It's no different with you. Oh, I know you say you don't believe yourself compromised—although you know all your disclaimers to be nothing more than self-deception—but I am cognizant of your true reason. You can't stand the sight of me either. You're just too kindhearted to say so."

Alexandra whirled back to confront this calumny. "How dare you? *How dare you!* I could stand in this spot from now until noon tomorrow cataloging the multitude of things I dislike about you, Nicholas Mannering, and all without ever once repeating myself, but your wound has absolutely nothing to do with it. Besides," her voice softened marginally, "personally, I think it makes you look rather dashing, although I am sure it is quite an inconvenience and must even pain you at times. Still, it's not as if you had lost an arm or a leg like so many others have done."

"Well put, by Gadfrey," her grandfather commended, gifting her with a hearty slap on the back that nearly sent her cannoning smack into Nicholas's broad chest.

"Your granddaughter does have a way with words, sir, but the fact remains that I am in a sad dilemma. Helene probably would bring herself to go through with the marriage, now that I think on it, as her fear of her mother outstrips even her repugnance at my appearance. But what kind of life would that be, I ask you, to have a wife who recoils from my slightest touch? On the other hand," he said, pressing home his advantage, "I have offered myself to your granddaughter here, who also rebuffs me. Although," he added facetiously, "we have heard it from her own lips that she does not find my *appearance* repulsive—only the rest of me.

"Much as you may demand it, and much as I agree with you, Alix refuses to become my wife. With no other avenue left open to me, I fear Mrs. Anselm will yet get me in the end. I am a sad case indeed, and I despair of finding a solution to my problem any time soon."

Sir Alexander, uncomfortable in the face of Linton's show of emotion, coughed and blustered but said little of anything to the point in the way of furnishing aid or comfort to the dejected Earl. While Sir Alexander allowed his tongue to tie itself into knots, Mannering kept his gaze glued on the black-and-white tiled floor of the entrance hall and wondered if his hasty plan was to prove brilliant or merely a waste of his theatrical talents. He had shot his bolt and was now relying on Alexandra to come to the only conclusion he had left open for a woman of sensitivity to make. Yet she remained silent.

Just as Nicholas was about to drop his lost soul posture and have an end to the farce, Alexandra finally spoke. "I think I have an idea, Nicholas," she began slowly. "If Grandfather is correct, and since he knows Mrs. Anselm I can only suppose he is, it will take drastic measures to remove her from Linton Hall as long as she believes there's any chance she can get you and Helene to the altar. Therefore, the only solution I can see," she sighed in submission, "is for us to formally announce our engagement—only here at the Hall, mind you, as none of us will wish to go through the retraction later in the newspapers."

Nicholas ruthlessly overrode an almost overpowering urge to throw back his head and crow his delight. His plan had succeeded exactly as he had envisioned it, with Alexandra reacting just as he had hoped she would!

"Thanks to my rather violent disclaimer earlier in the morning room," Alexandra went on hurriedly, in the way of someone wishing to get over rough ground as quickly as possible, "I believe we cannot make even this quiet announcement immediately—not, that is, with any hope of being believed. I suggest we wait until a few days have passed, during which time we will supposedly have made up our little differences."

Ah, Nicholas could not help complimenting himself, it is just as Shakespeare said. I had only to "Bait the hook well: this fish will bite." Savoring his advantage, he giddily pushed for even greater leverage. "A mere announcement won't be enough for Mrs. Anselm, Alix. I'm afraid we'll have to act the loving couple for at least a week or more before that determined lady admits defeat and departs."

Alexandra sighed again and raised her eyes heavenward in exasperation before voicing her reluctant agreement (denying herself a glimpse at Nicholas's face and its unable to be suppressed although rapidly erased expression of irrepressible glee). "A week only, Nicholas," she added warningly, "and not a minute longer. This scheme had just better work."

"Never fear for my end, Alix, my dear, as I tell you now I plan to put on a very convincing performance. It is my doubts of *your* abilities at play acting that make me wonder about the dependability of your scheme, no matter if you wish it to go on for a week or a month—knowing as I do how thoroughly you dislike me. Besides," he added with a hint of sadness once again creeping into his voice, "if truth be served, I still am of the opinion my patch offends you."

"Oh, cut line," Alexandra demanded hotly. "You don't appear to me to be going into any major decline because of that damned patch. You'll not cozen me with those die-away airs and deep sighs. Really, Nicholas, did you think that for one minute I *fell* for that ridiculous claptrap you've been spouting? It just amused me to see how far you would go. You had a lucky escape once from Miss Anselm, and now you're using her to your own ends—else you'd have sent her packing an hour ago. Please, don't go laboring under the delusion I am helping you out of the goodness of my heart!

"I have my own reasons for helping you to dislodge your ex-fiancée from her bolt-hole upstairs, and pity for your physical and emotional states certainly isn't one of them.

"Oh no, Nicholas," she laughed rather menacingly, "you have no reason to fear I won't play my part well. But then you'll also have little time for rejoicing once I have got you shed of the so encroaching Anselms, for then I shall have cleared the field and will feel free to wage war in my own defense. And you will not like it, Nicholas; you will not like it one little bit."

Turning to Sir Alexander (who had been hard pressed to follow the conversation these last minutes and who was just then looking about him for some liquid refreshment), Alexandra said, "Come, Grandfather, we mustn't outstay our welcome."

"But—but I don't understand. Did you talk to Nicholas about whatever it was that was so all-fired urgent that you dragged me away from my card game to come over here with you?" her grandfather asked in confusion just before his temper finally got the best of him. "Plague take you, gel, don't shake your head 'no' at me! You're enough to drive a man to drink, do you know that? What in blue blazes was I supposed to hear once we got to Linton Hall?"

"Yes," Nicholas prompted, belatedly realizing that Alexandra would never pay him a purely social call and she must have had some definite mission in mind, "why did you come, Alix—not that you and Sir Alexander aren't always welcome."

Alexandra looked back and forth between the two men before telling them with a smile, "It'll keep, gentlemen, it'll keep. Now come on, Grandfather, before the Widow Anselm comes to her senses and realizes there's another eligible bachelor down here for her to try to scoop up into her net."

"Who'd that be?" he asked blankly before raising his bushy eyebrows in alarm. *"Me?* Oh no! She'll not get this sly old dog, by thunder! Come on, gel," he shouted, already bounding heavily toward the door, "it's back to Saxon Hall for us—and we'll have Nutter lock up the drawbridge once we're safe inside."

Alexandra's ploy had safely diverted her grandfather, who soon forgot everything else as he wiled away the rest of the afternoon happily fleecing Harold of twelve shillings, three arrowheads, and a small string of discolored beads—royally cheating at cards as the two stole surreptitious swigs from the bottle he had badgered Nutter into fetching behind his granddaughter's back.

Alexandra allowed Sir Alexander to believe he had hoodwinked her for two reasons. One, she had a lot on her mind, and at least her grandfather was keeping occupied and unlikely to badger her about her pretend engagement or ask her yet again exactly what was written on the piece of parchment she had waved under his nose so triumphantly that morning. And two, she had liberally watered the bottle of gin before placing it in the open where Nutter could find it and carry it to his master.

While Alexandra walked back and forth in the courtyard of the inner bailey, her breath making little clouds in the cold air as she paced and thought, Nicholas was out riding his fields on his favorite stallion, mulling over Alix's last words.

"Wage a war on me, will she, Saber," he remarked to his only audience—his horse. "It would seem the arrival of the Anselms has brought about only a temporary truce as, unless I am mightily mistaken, Alix's opening salvo was to have been fired upon me today. 'It'll keep,' she said. It must be a formidable weapon she has, Saber, but for the life of me I cannot come up with a single clue as to what it is. Whatever it is, though, it is obvious she wants a clear field in front of her before she attacks, and that is the main reason she has offered to participate in this engagement—much as I'd like to believe my playacting alone convinced her."

He shrugged his shoulders and dismissed Alexandra's

strategy from his mind. "No matter. Whatever it is, I shall soon spike her guns with my impassioned assault on her tender affections. With any luck I shall have her head over ears in love with me well within the specified week. After all, my patch don't put her off—she said as much, and more than once too. My Alix may be a pigheaded little savage, Saber, but she's an *honest* little savage. As for disliking the rest of me—she likes my kisses tolerably well, and that's enough to go on with for now.

"Besides, women are not cut out to be soldiers, Saber my friend—their emotions tend to get in the way of their already lopsided logic. Miss Alexandra Saxon is no exception to that rule, no matter what she believes.

"Actually, it is all working out quite famously," he reflected immodestly. "I'm rather pleased with myself over the way I'm handling the entire situation if I must say so myself. By the time the New Year has arrived," he projected optimistically, "I shall have gotten shed of the Anselms once and for all." (Nicholas was not, as he might well have done, seeking revenge—he only wanted them *gone.*) "Jeremy," he glibly prophesied further, "will be safely back at school, happy in the knowledge that I am cured of my depression and no longer in need of his companionship—and taking with him his ramshackle friends, thus giving all the countryside around Linton cause for rejoicing. And lastly, of course, but by no means less importantly, Miss Alexandra Saxon will be my bride—my *willing* bride—satisfying Sir Alexander, preserving my honor, and," he paused to chuckle at his own wit, "warming my bed.

"Ah, Saber," he shouted joyously into the raw November wind, "isn't it wonderful when a plan executes so flawlessly? Come on, boy, let's have us a gallop!"

As Saber took off across the fields, his hooves throwing up mighty clumps of dirt behind him, his master gave himself over to the heady exhilaration that comes from believing oneself to be totally in charge of one's own life, in complete control of one's own future, and absolutely certain of one's own destiny.

While it was true, as Nicholas had quoted to himself

earlier, that Shakespeare had written that a fish would bite a well-baited hook, perhaps Lord Nicholas Mannering, Earl of Linton, should have spent some little time pondering another of the immortal Bard's observations: "Lord, what fools these mortals be!"

Chapter Five

"VISITORS, miss."

Alexandra raised her chin from its resting place in her cupped right hand and regarded Nutter absently. She had, ever since arising that morning, been reading and rereading the parchment she had found the day before in the treasury and it still had her feeling a bit bemused.

"Visitors, Nutter?" she queried. "As in more than one?" After Nicholas's warning—which was how she thought of his spoken intention to outwardly court her—she would not have been surprised to have him show his face at Saxon Hall today. But to have brought along *witnesses*—most probably in the form of one or more of the Anselms—was doing it just a little too brown, even for him.

Rising from her seat in the deep window embrasure of the solar, she shook out her skirts and motioned for Nutter to lead the way into the Great Hall. "Raise the curtain, Nutter," she whispered angrily under her breath, "the play is about to begin."

But when Alexandra entered the Great Hall, it was not to see Nicholas and Company, but rather, to her immeasurable relief, to greet Jeremy and his two friends.

"Well, isn't this a pleasant surprise!" she exclaimed, holding out her hands in greeting.

"See, Cuffy," Billy whispered loudly, "told you she was a prime 'un. Glad to see us, she is, even tippin' us her daddles."

"Just because a woman offers you her hands don't mean she's happy to see you—just shows she's polite, you dashed clothhead," hissed Cuffy in return before he took one of

Alexandra's hands and gallantly raised it to his lips. "How condescending of you to see us, Miss Saxon," he said smoothly, looking at Billy out of the corners of his eyes and daring him to say anything.

"Of course I'm glad to see you all," she contradicted Cuffy happily. "Nutter—bring us some refreshments, won't you, please?" Taking Jeremy's hand, she guided them all over toward one of the trestle tables, past the miniature wigwam where Harold sat stoically staring into the middle distance—completely ignoring the curiously gaping boys.

"Oh, dear," Alexandra smiled as she saw the direction of her young friends' stares. "And I thought you had come to see me. Obviously I am only a means to an end. *Leheléche fli' nítis, Sachema Harold?*" she called. *"Pennó wullíh! Auween knéwa?"*

The Indian reluctantly turned his head in the direction of Alexandra's company, ran his eyes over the young men just then grinning like complete idiots (Billy shyly waving as he stood half behind Cuffy), and then rose slowly to his feet to bow to Alexandra. In a deep rumbling monotone he replied, *"N'leheléche. Geptschátschik, Yengees. N'dellemúske."* Then, without so much as a nod in their direction, he turned on his heel and trod soundlessly away from the boys, heading in the direction of the kitchens.

"What was that all about?" Jeremy asked Alexandra nervously. "We didn't upset him, did we?"

"Uh—er, no, *no*, you didn't upset him," Alexandra stammered back at him, trying to think of some excuse for Harold's rude behavior. In the end, however, the boys badgered her until she was forced to tell them the truth. "I asked Harold if he was well—did 'my favorite friend still draw breath'—and then asked him to look and tell me what he saw. He then told me that he was well—'I exist'—and then, er, and then he told me what he saw. He said, and I *am* truly sorry he said this, 'I see English fools. I am leaving.'" At the sight of their crestfallen faces, she tried to cheer them up, saying that Harold just wasn't very sociable, but Jeremy assured her that it was all right.

"You'll talk him round, Alix, I'm sure," he told her bracingly.

"Better. Dashed marplot if she don't. Plan won't fadge a'tal else, but I'll back her to get the thing done. Mort's as game as a pebble, I say," interrupted Billy incomprehensibly.

Alexandra couldn't help laughing as the two other boys clapped their hands over Billy's mouth. "Now it's I who need an interpreter. Tell me, please, whatever did Billy say—and in what language? Surely that can't be English!"

"It's English all right—at least it's a form of English," Cuffy supplied tersely. "Billy's become enamored of St. Giles Greek, if you wish to call it by that title. It's the language of cant and—Billy! Give Miss Alexandra the book and let her see for herself."

Blushing to the roots of his hair at all this sudden attention, Billy reached inside his jacket, withdrew a badly bent and dog-eared volume, and handed it to Alexandra.

"A Dictionary of Buckish Slang, University Wit, and Pickpocket Eloquence," she read, her eyebrows raised in mock astonishment. "Oh, I say, Billy, this is interesting!" Opening it to the A's, she read aloud the first entry: " 'Abbess, or Lady Abbess; a bawd, the mistress of a brothel.' Jeremy?" she asked, looking up hurriedly. "Are you all right? You seem to be choking on something."

Jeremy could only shake his head in the negative and appeal to his friends with his wildly rolling eyes. Mistaking his inarticulate sounds for physical rather than mental distress, Billy promptly pounded Jeremy on the back, saying, "That's the ticket. You'll be all right and tight."

Keeping her humor hidden with near superhuman effort, Alexandra began to page through the book, looking, she said, for the definition of one of the words Billy had used. "Here it is, *fadge*. 'It won't fadge; it won't do.' Well, that makes proper sense. What else can I find in the F's? Let's see, here's one. 'To flash the hash. To vomit.' Oh, that is good!"

By now Jeremy was almost beside himself. "Get that

book, Cuffy," he managed to gasp. "Lord only knows what all she'll find—*especially* in the F's!"

Cuffy went to do what he was bid, but Alexandra was too fast for him. Before he could grab the book, she had stuffed it down the bodice of her morning gown, saying, "I'll give it back when I'm done with it—heaven only knows I could use the entertainment. Billy," she continued, seeing the boy's downcast expression, "I promise I won't lose it if that's what's worrying you."

Jeremy could see by the sparkle in Alexandra's eyes that she was highly amused by the book, which was in direct opposition to everything he had ever witnessed of the way females reacted to such things. "Just don't tell Nicholas," he begged her.

"He'd have our guts for garters," Billy expanded nervously, earning himself yet another quelling look from his companions.

Nutter arrived then with some refreshments, which, wisely, the boys politely refused. There were then a few moments of silence whilst Alexandra looked up the word *marplot*—discovering that it translated to mean "spoilsport." Returning the book to its hiding place, she asked the boys why she would be a spoilsport if she didn't "talk Harold round" to being more sociable.

"It's just that we were thinking, ma'am," Cuffy began when neither of his friends took up the slack, "and we decided it would be great good fun to catch the highwaymen causing all the trouble hereabouts."

"And while we were thinking," Jeremy broke in, "we figured that having a real, honest-to-goodness Indian in the area would be a big help. They are good at things like that, aren't they . . ." he trailed off, nervously avoiding Alexandra's eyes.

"You mean 'things' like tracking through the woods and such, Jeremy?" Alexandra supplied, a slow smile lighting up her dark eyes. "Oh, yes, I can see how having Harold along on such a venture could be a great benefit to you. But of course you realize that you would need an *interpreter* along, right?" she added hopefully.

The trio exchanged wary glances. "That could prove a bit too dangerous, Alix," Jeremy was forced to point out. "You see, a highwayman can't really be charged unless he is caught in the act, so to speak. Until then he lives high. Why, Dick Turpin—one of our most famous highwaymen— lived quite openly with his father, the innkeeper of the Rose and Crown, in Hempstead. There's a fellow who knew how to live. They all do, at least the successful ones."

Alexandra pointed out that she had already seen the highwaymen who were working the roads around Linton and she doubted they were in Turpin's league. "They seemed more desperate than cunning," she told them. "Harold and I would be in no danger."

Youthful exuberance never being known to be overburdened with prolonged bouts of common sense, the boys soon allowed Alexandra to become one of their group.

The four of them (Harold was still in the kitchens gobbling down spiced meat) then put their heads together, formulating their first moves in the discovery and apprehension of the highwaymen. It was agreed that they must first reconnoiter the area to look for clues. This meant they would undertake to search the hills and valleys nearest the spot where Alexandra and Nicholas had been accosted earlier.

By the time the boys departed, it had been decided that they would all meet the following day at noon in the home woods just west of Linton Hall. Alix waved them on their way, still smiling at Billy's hopeful question as to whether or not Harold would feel compelled to "lift their hair" when he caught up with the highwaymen, and she then went off to curl up with her lunch and the cant dictionary.

Alexandra was happily paging her way through the C's when Nutter shuffled in to announce another visitor. This time her caller was Lord Linton, and he had brought no audience with him.

"Good day to you, my love," he chirped merrily as she came into the Great Hall. "How wonderful you look. Tell me, is that color in your cheeks a lover's blush at seeing me?''

Alexandra stopped dead in her tracks. "The subject for the day is cats," she said, surprising him into attentiveness. "Firstly, there is the cat's paw, as in 'to be made a cat's paw,' so to speak. Someone is made a cat's paw by being made a tool or instrument used to accomplish the purpose of another. *That* is what you are trying to make of me. But, to use the word *cat* in another way, Nicholas, *my love,* allow me to tell you this: you have about as much hope of succeeding as does a cat in hell without claws, which is the same as saying you have entered into this scheme with one who is greatly above your match.''

Nicholas's expression of confusion was comical to behold, as was his dawning comprehension and slowly gathering rage once she brought forth the dictionary and waved it in the air in front of his face.

"Billy Simpson! That paperskulled idiot! How could even he be stupid enough to let the likes of you get hold of that ridiculous book?'' (Clearly, Lord Linton was unhappy.)

Paging quickly through her book to the P's, Alexandra read aloud: " 'Paperskull; a thin-skulled foolish fellow.' Oh, really Nicholas, and here I thought you were above using cant language. Tsk, tsk.''

"A man may use cant—it's expected of him. But women—at least gentlewomen—refuse to allow such slang and bawdiness in their presence. They certainly don't use it themselves!''

"Really? How strange," Alexandra commented, still paging through the book. "It seems like a great piece of nonsense to pretend such things don't exist when there's even been a book published about the subject. See," she went on, looking down at the book. "Here's another one. 'Bawdy,' you said? Well, actually, it's listed under 'Bawdy *House.*' It means—oh no you don't!'' Alexandra warned before expeditiously clutching the book to her bosom just before Nicholas could swoop it out of her hands.

"Give—the—book—to—me," Nicholas gritted out from

between clenched teeth as he advanced on her, his hand outstretched.

Alexandra kept backing away from him, shaking her head in the negative as she reasoned, "If I am to know what not to say, this book can tell me. What better way to learn how to go on?"

"*I'll* teach you," Nicholas pointed out, still advancing on her.

Alexandra raised one eyebrow, said, "No, you won't," and then hastily shoved the book down inside her bodice.

Nicholas smiled, rather evilly, Alexandra thought, and asked, "Was that move meant to stop me blushing in my tracks, madam?" He shook his head in denial of such an idea. "If so, I greatly fear you are to be disappointed. Now, now, love, don't keep backing up that way—you'll be in the fire soon. Just come to Nick, my dear, and let him fetch back Billy's little book. Don't be shy," he crooned as Alexandra covered her bodice with her crossed arms, "Nick isn't going to hurt you. Come on now, open up and let me in."

How this little scene would have ended—with Alexandra wresting the book from her bodice and throwing it at Nicholas's head or with Nicholas conducting his own little search for the tome—will never be known, for at that moment Sir Alexander entered the room calling out a greeting.

"You didn't drag that totty-headed female over here with you, did you, boy?" he asked, casting his eyes about the chamber. "Good. Don't. Nor the offspring either, for that matter. Don't like the stable, neither sire nor dam. Stands to reason I won't like the kiddies. Girl looked to be an insipid bud, and the boy a real clunch—and a regular Miss Molly to boot. Did you spy his high shirt points, Linton? Turn his head too fast an' he'd lop off his bleedin' nose!"

"And good day to you, Sir Alexander," Nicholas returned pleasantly, ignoring the man's character assassination of his house guests. "Do I have your permission to take Miss Saxon out riding?"

Alexandra did not protest this idea, but she surely would have if she had been paying attention. Instead, she was off in a safe corner looking up "Miss Molly," whose definition first puzzled, then angered her. She had of course heard rumors that there were such men—if that's what they were called—but to have her own grandfather use such a vulgar expression in her hearing was the outside of enough.

It then occurred to her that if, as the hateful Nicholas had pointed out, she had been unaware of the meaning of all but a few tame cant expressions, she would have been unaware that her grandfather had used risqué speech in her presence. One could joke about an "Abbess" but there was very little humor in "Miss Molly." Certainly Sir Alexander did not think his granddaughter understood the meaning of "Miss Molly"—it would never occur to him. Cant was, she thought, like a code that men used in order to say anything they wanted to in front of unsuspecting females.

Hiding her chagrin at having Mannering once again proved correct, she, when at last she could be brought back to attention, was almost grateful to get away from Saxon Hall for a space to sort out her thoughts. "I'll get changed into my habit," she told Nicholas hurriedly. "Meet me outside after having my mount brought round."

"Please," said Nicholas.

"What?" asked Alexandra, still clearly distracted.

Nicholas smiled his most infuriating (at least so thought his intended bride) half-smile. "Please," he repeated. "You forgot to say please."

She sighed heavily and spread her palms. "Very well, Linton, if you intend to be so ridiculously disobliging—*please* wait for me outside."

"And—?"

"And *please* have my mount brought round," she ended in exasperation before quitting the room, muttering under her breath.

Nicholas turned to Sir Alexander. "You see, sir? All it takes is a little gentle schooling. I'll have her eating out of my hand within a fortnight."

Alexandra, who was not quite out of earshot, heard every word. "I wouldn't lay odds on it, Lord high-and-mighty Linton," she gritted under her breath. "It matters not who wins the little battles. It is who wins the war. I can afford to gift you with small victories now and then—in the end it is I who shall claim the field!'' As she raced the rest of the way up the spiral staircase, she refused to examine precisely why this thought brought her such small cheer.

After enjoying a mind-clearing gallop across one of Saxon Hall's winter-bare fields, Nicholas reined in his roan and waited for Alexandra to join him. When she drew up beside him—her cheeks flushed partly by the brisk ride, partly by excitement—he dismounted and walked around to assist her to the ground.

Alexandra's smile faded a bit as Nicholas's hands slipped about her waist, and her smile disappeared altogether when, in the course of helping her alight, her body was brought into close contact with his. The moment her feet could feel the ground beneath them, she pulled herself from his grasp, and wrapping her arms about her waist in a protective gesture, she turned her back and walked off toward a small stand of trees.

Nicholas watched her go, wondering if she too had felt it—that magnetic pull that seemed to draw them close and charged the very air they breathed. Her gaze, as he had momentarily held her face level with his own, had locked just as deeply with his as had his with hers, and he could have sworn her sharp intake of breath had not been a sign of revulsion. He ran his gaze up and down her slim back and concluded that she had been more than a little affected by his touch—his close proximity.

In that way at least, his plan would seem to be progressing nicely. Obviously the girl was not dead-set against him, and hopefully, he might just be able to make her believe she was falling in love with him. The only real problem, he told himself as his eyebrows lifted in self-mockery, is how *she* affects *you*, Nicholas, old sport! Surely, he was wielding a two-edged sword—one that could find their battle concluding with deep cuts being scored on *both* sides.

The realization that his heart just might be in danger gave him pause for a second—but not much longer than that. It was not that Mannering was not a deep thinker; he was. But in this case his thoughts and conclusions were so uniformly pleasant that he decided to stop thinking, stand back, and let the Fates take control. He had already decided to marry the girl—and for good, solid reasons at that—so where was the harm in falling in love with his chosen bride?

You could be badly hurt, you fool, he sneered inwardly. Helene's defection didn't make so much as a small dent in your sensibilities, but if a girl like Alexandra Saxon spurns your attentions you may well never recover from the wound! Nicholas frowned as his inner self fought to protect him. But just then Alexandra half turned toward him, the thin November sun outlining her superb figure as she lifted one hand to throw her long, silken black hair back over her shoulder.

"Oh, to hell with my sensibilities!" Nicholas said to the rustling breeze, and tying their horses' reins to a nearby bush, he set off to follow where Alexandra (and his heart) led.

They walked quietly for a while, content to view the beauty of the woods as the afternoon sun filtered through the nearly bare trees and turned the leaves under their feet to gold.

It wasn't until they had stopped for a rest, Alexandra sitting on an old log and lifting her face to the sun, that Nicholas decided to broach the volatile subject of their engagement.

Reaching into his vest pocket, he drew out a small, velvet-covered box and presented it to her. "Here you go, love," he said with maddening insouciance. "Take this."

Alexandra eyed the box much like a mongoose sizes up an angry cobra. "Why? What's in it?"

Nicholas shrugged dismissively. " 'Tis nothing much, just the ancient Mannering betrothal ring—worth little more than, oh, a king's ransom, I imagine. Really, a mere bagatelle." When Alexandra continued to hesitate, he went on, heedless of his seeming insensitivity, "Helene never wore it, if that's what's bothering you. I keep the thing at Linton Hall, you know, and she had broken the engagement before her visit. Go on," he urged, "put it on. We have to lend some credence to this pretend engagement, don't we, if we are to be taken seriously.''

For some reason (a reason she had no desire to pursue), Alexandra's hands shook as she opened the box and looked upon a dazzling sapphire- and diamond-studded gold ring of unbelievable beauty. She stared at it unmovingly for so long that Nicholas sighed, ''Oh, here puss. Let me help you,'' before taking hold of her hand and pushing the ring on her slim finger himself.

''There!'' he exclaimed when the job was done. ''A perfect fit, if I do say so myself. Now how about a betrothal kiss just to seal the thing?''

Alexandra shook herself back to reality. ''If it's a pretend engagement, Lord Linton, you may just *pretend* we have kissed,'' she told him hotly.

''Spoilsport,'' Nicholas teased, leering toward her.

''Marplot,'' she corrected him, ''and the boys have assured me that I am no such thing.''

''Oh yes,'' he remembered, settling down beside her on the log, ''Billy's dictionary of the vulgar tongue again.'' He shrugged fatalistically. ''I can see there is only one way to shut you up.''

Before Alexandra could react, he grabbed her by the shoulders and swept her backward across his lap, leaving her looking up at him in open-mouthed amazement. The smile left his face and he groaned once, as if agonized, before lowering his head to hungrily claim her lips.

Her eyes squeezed closed, then opened to a view of dark branches and blue sky spinning dizzily above her. Hoping to focus her gaze on something more solid, she looked at Nicholas's forehead—that smooth expanse of skin beneath his coal dark hair, marked only by the thin black silk cord of his eyepatch. Looking lower, all that was visible was the patch itself, and since the sight of that rakish bit of silk filled her with an almost uncontrollable urge to reach up and stroke his face, Alexandra closed her eyes once more.

Now she was free to concentrate on the sensations caused by the movement of Nicholas's mouth on hers—somehow familiar, somehow even more exciting than before. To keep herself from falling (or so she told herself) she reached up and encircled his neck with her arms, an action that lifted her toward his rock-hard chest and allowed him even greater access to her body.

His hands roved her back with increasing urgency as her fingers slipped into the hair at his nape and began an investigation of their own. Suddenly Nicholas tore his mouth away, crushing Alexandra's head against his shoulder as he took a number of deep, shaking breaths in order to compose himself. Her close proximity, lying as she was across his lap, did nothing to ease his tension, and he was forced to push her gently away before rising to his feet and taking a few paces away from the log and further temptation.

This left Alexandra free to straighten her riding habit and push some order back into her tangled hair, but it was some time before her breathing returned to a semblance of normalcy. As her passion faded, it was replaced by a deep feeling of shame that took refuge in unjust anger (considering she had been a more than willing participant in the scene just concluded).

His own emotions now once again firmly back under his control, Nicholas turned to face his pretend fiancée. "I apologize, Alix," he said sincerely. "What happened was unforgivable. I don't know how it got so—er—*involved.* I had only meant to tease you, you know, that's all—Jeremy will tell you what an impossible joker I am—but somehow it went beyond a mere joke. Can you forgive me?"

Alexandra was more than happy for Nicholas to take all the blame—it might just keep him from remembering *her* part in the exercise. "Nothing *happened,* my lord—at least nothing of any real importance or lasting damage," she insisted tightly. "Besides—it won't happen again. *Will it?*" she ended, her dark eyes boring into his very soul.

All this show of outraged dignity was too much for Mannering. Saluting her jocularly, he snapped his heels together smartly and crowed, "You may have my word as a gentleman on it, ma'am, it will happen only as often as I can catch you!"

Alexandra jumped to her feet, retorting, "I should have

known, you jack-a-napes. *Oh!''* she exclaimed in exasperation, ''I cannot wait to get back to Billy's dictionary so that I can make a complete list of foul names for you, you—you chuckle-headed, addle-pated, brazen-faced *braggadocia!''*

Nicholas put his hands on his hips and threw back his head to laugh out loud. ''My stars, just think what the chit will say once she gets past the C's!'' he shouted in great good humor, ducking his head only just in time to avoid the clump of dirt Alexandra had sent whizzing in his direction. ''Oh, I say, Alix, sweetheart, *that* wasn't nice!''

But Alix had already hitched up her skirts and taken to her heels, running down the steep hill to their left as if all the hounds of hell were after her. Mannering, naturally, took off after her, only coming to a halt when he saw that Alexandra had taken up a position behind a wide tree trunk and was holding out her hand to silence him.

''What is it?'' he whispered in her ear while casting his eyes alertly about him. ''Is it the highwaymen?''

She shook her head in the negative, and putting a finger to her lips to show him he should remain quiet, she pointed down toward the bottom of the hill where a small stream cut through the trees. ''It's Harold,'' she mouthed under her breath. ''He's taking a sweat.''

Nicholas looked down the slope, but all he could see that was the least out of the ordinary was a small, cigar-shaped cylinder of dirt approximately three feet wide and six feet long that seemed to lie half in and half out of the hill. He imagined the cylinder, if he were to stand next to it, would only come up as high as his chin. There was no sign of Harold, but Nicholas did notice that there seemed to be a bit of smoke or steam rising from the open end of the ''cigar.''

Sliding his arm around Alexandra's shoulders, Nicholas leaned down to whisper in her ear, ''Much as I hate to admit to my ignorance in this matter, my love, could you please be kind enough to explain just what in the blue blazes is going on down there?''

Alexandra looked up at him in exasperation. ''Don't you know *anything,* Nicholas? Harold must not be feeling quite the thing today since he's already had his usual sweat for the week. Poor thing," she sighed slightly. "Grandfather keeps pushing drink on him, you know. Indians can't seem to tolerate spirits too well. Oh, that grandfather of mine—no matter how hard I try, hiding his gin or putting it under lock and key, he always seems to be able to ferret out a new supply. Honestly, the man drinks like a fish!"

"Every man should have a hobby, pet," Nicholas supplied cheerfully, earning himself a none-too-discreet jab in the ribs from Alexandra's elbow.

"Lower your voice, you idiot," she hissed at him, before plunking herself down on the slope so that Harold wouldn't see her when he came out of his sweat oven. Mannering sat down beside her and repeated his request to have her explain Harold's action, and mostly to keep his lordship's mind occupied with thoughts other than their latest bout of lovemaking, she agreed.

She explained that sweat ovens were very much a part of Lenape life, for both men and women. Inside the oven they placed heated stones, making the oven very warm and causing its occupants to sweat. To increase the benefits of this heat, water or medicinal concoctions were poured over the stones, as Harold must just then have been doing, causing steam to rise and envelop the occupant. After a space of time, Harold would throw a blanket about himself and emerge from the oven, his body revitalized and his spirit renewed.

"It's marvelous, the feeling you get when you first feel the cool air on your skin after indulging in a good sweat," Alexandra told him earnestly. "If there is snow on the ground they sometimes roll in it before wrapping up inside a half-dozen blankets—*that* is absolutely wonderful!"

Nicholas sneaked a look at Alexandra out of the corner of his eye. "From the way you talk, I'd say you've indulged in a sweat or two yourself, imp."

"What if I have?" she countered, tilting up her chin. "And wipe that grin off your face—there's nothing funny about it."

"That depends. I cannot imagine Harold is sitting inside that oven decked out in full ceremonial dress. In fact, I'd bet a guinea to a penny piece the man's as near to jay-naked as he can get. Imagining you, my love, in the same charming *déshabillé* state is what brings this leer—never dignify it by calling such a look a grin—to my truly delighted face. Ah-ah,'' he cautioned, easily trapping her clenched right fist as it neared his midsection, ''you forgot Harold's teachings. Never do the expected, remember? Obviously you have had much of theory and precious little of practical application.''

Alexandra directed a long stare at her slim wrist—just now held firmly in Mannering's grasp—and then looked her captor squarely in the face. ''I make no doubt you are enjoying yourself mightily, my lord. One cannot help but wonder how quickly your mood would change if you but knew the power I hold over you.''

Nicholas chuckled. ''That's my savage. Here I am, holding the girl by the arm, defenseless, as it were, at my feet, and *she* threatens *me!* You're a regular Trojan, girl,'' he marveled sarcastically, ''besides being the most tempting morsel a man could imagine.''

Perhaps Alexandra could yet have refrained from blurting out her information, but that was only before Nicholas was so foolhardy as to actually *gloat* over their odd situation. Now she was in a towering rage, and far beyond rational thought or prudence.

Nicholas watched in amused fascination as Alexandra, both her hands now free, inched up her riding habit to disclose a leather pouch tied around her calf. ''You never cease to amaze me, pet,'' was all he said as she untied the pouch and dumped its contents in her lap. ''Truly, I own myself astonished.''

''Stop goggling at me, you ignoramus, and clap your eyes on this instead,'' she told him with no little satisfaction, shoving the parchment into his hands.

With his amusement still showing plainly on his handsome face, Nicholas unrolled the parchment and began to read. As he read, Alexandra watched the amusement slowly drain from his face until at last he looked up at her, his golden eye darkened and narrowed, his expressive eyebrow poised high, like a question mark on his forehead. ''What the devil is the meaning of this?'' he asked, his deep voice ominous.

Alexandra shrugged her shoulders, fighting hard to hide her sudden nervousness. "I think it is pretty clear, Lord Linton.''

"Pray don't be so cryptic,'' he drawled, now looking every inch a lord. "I am breathlessly awaiting your interpretation of this bit of scribbling.''

"All right, Nicholas,'' she rallied. "I'll not tippytoe around the issue. Simply, this paper says that your ancestor, the Second Lord Linton, lost Linton Hall and all its surrounding estate in a game of cards to my ancestor, Bartholomew Saxon, Esquire, in 1703. *You* are living on *my* grandfather's land, my lord,'' she added scrupulously.

"This is nothing but arrant nonsense!'' Nicholas shouted angrily as he jumped to his feet, sending quite a few birds screeching off into the sky from their perches in the trees.

For two pins Alexandra would have agreed with him and thrown the whole thing up, that distressed she was to see Nicholas so upset. "I have the greatest sympathy for you—'' she began placatingly, rising to her feet and resting a hand on Nicholas's arm, before the air was rent with a fierce yell and Harold sprang into their midst, his blackened face running with sweat while the remainder of his body was covered by only a small breechclout and a thick layer of goosebumps.

"N'nitsch undach aal! N'tschittanési!" Harold ejaculated fiercely, eyeing Nicholas menacingly.

"Oh, good grief!'' Nicholas said, clearly exasperated. "It needed only this. What in Hades does he want? Is he eyeing up my hair?''

Alexandra lowered her head into her hands, shaking her head in acute embarrassment. "He wants me to come to him—he says he is strong.''

"He certainly is,'' Nicholas chuckled, his sense of humor allowing him to see the ridiculousness in the situation. "I can certainly see—or should I say, *smell*—the logic in rolling in the snow after a sweat. God, Alix, talk to the fellow—

tell him to stand downwind at least. Tell him I promise not to pounce on you."

Alexandra turned to the protectively hovering Indian and spoke a few phrases, causing Harold to look again at Nicholas, his head tipped inquiringly to one side as if sizing the man up, before he turned on his heel and loped off down the hill.

"He heard the birds, you know. Harold is very wise in such things," Alexandra supplied by way of explaining Harold's appearance. "He's very protective of me. Though I'm sorry if he frightened you."

"Not frightened, pet, merely startled." Nicholas's voice had suddenly taken on an icy quality. Bending to retrieve the parchment, he rose again to say flatly, "I thank you for bringing this to my attention. Naturally, I shall have my solicitors look it over. They're in London, you understand, so it may be some time until we receive their answer. Until that time, I can only beg your discretion in not discussing the matter with anyone. It wouldn't do to have Jeremy unduly upset."

"Of—of course," Alexandra stammered, suddenly very much aware of the chill in the air. "It may all be a hum, you know," she offered, one might think, almost hopefully.

"Having second thoughts about your revenge, infant?" he asked, that maddening eyebrow again flying high.

She had been having second thoughts, she realized, hating Nicholas for having pointed out her weakness. "Put it in a hat, Mannering," she bit out beneath clenched teeth before whirling to stalk angrily back up the hill, Nicholas's mocking laughter following after her all the way.

That laughter rang in her ears for the entirety of her solitary half-mile gallop back to Saxon Hall, and that night she slept with her pillow clamped down tightly over her head, still trying to blot out the sound.

Chapter Six

''I DO BELIEVE this is just about the same spot where the highwaymen attacked Nick—er, Lord Linton and myself,'' Alix told the three boys as they reined in their horses behind her. ''It's as good a starting point as any for our search, don't you think?''

''Then you and m'brother really *did* have a run-in with the highwaymen, Alix. Can't understand why Nick never breathed a word of it to me,'' Jeremy puzzled for about the tenth time since first hearing of the incident a half hour earlier from Alexandra. Then, prudently avoiding her angry glare, he dismounted and began casting his eyes about the area with what he hoped was a look of keen intelligence.

He was soon joined by Cuffy and Billy—all three quickly making themselves busy poking under fallen leaves with their toes and peering into the trees as if looking for signs of the highwaymen.

Meanwhile, Harold loped up beside them on foot having, in the way of the Lenape, shunned all offers of a mount in favor of traveling on his own two feet. A little out of breath, but still game, Harold eyed the boys with open disgust and grunted to Alix, *''Geptschátschik. Yuh' allauwitan!''*

''We *are* hunting, Harold,'' Alix hissed at him under her breath. ''And for pity's sake, stop calling those poor boys fools. Why, even now they are searching alongside the roadway for clues.''

Now Harold fairly burst into exasperated speech as he gestured to the boys to stop in their tracks. Alix quickly positioned herself between the youths and their would-be attacker as she interpreted rapidly, ''Harold says you are

105

wiping away all the signs with your big feet. Sorry, gentlemen, but I do believe he is right—look how trampled-down everything is now. It looks as if an army has passed through here."

All three looked suitably guilty as they carefully backed up until they were once again on the roadway. Then they watched as Harold reconnoitered the area. He passed comments to Alix every so often—comments she dutifully translated for her companions.

"Harold says there were three men on horseback here no more than two, three days ago. That would be several days after their attack on Nicholas and myself."

"Busy little bees, ain't they?" Cuffy commented.

"Hush!" admonished Alix, straining to hear Harold's words as the Indian spoke to her from the trees. "He says there are more footprints under the trees. Come on, let's see them for ourselves."

There followed a lengthy education in the fine art of tracking as done by the Lenni Lenape. Harold explained—as Alix translated—that three white men had stood about in this area, probably waiting for passersby they could rob. That they were white men was proven by the fact that the feet trod the ground toe "out," rather than toe "in" as Indian feet would.

"That ain't so brilliant," Billy sniffed. "Of course they was white—who'd he expect, a passel of ravin' Chinamen?"

Alix ignored this jibe and continued, "Harold also says the men were careless, leaving a clear trail leading back into the woods. Come on, he's motioning for us to follow him."

Everyone raced to their horses, mounted, and hastened to catch up with Harold, who had loped off into the woods ahead of them. They followed along easily for nearly a quarter hour—the woods being neither dense nor crowded with undergrowth—before Harold motioned for them to dismount and tie their horses.

Then the Indian went down on all fours and sniffed at the earth before rising once more and setting off in a southeasterly direction.

"He smells 'em!" Billy whispered excitedly.

"*Smells* them," Cuffy sneered disdainfully. "He's an Indian, you looby, not a bloody hound."

"*Shh!*" Alix cautioned, seeing Harold raise one hand for silence. "And Billy's right, Harold does use his nose to sniff them out—but it's the earth he's smelling, not the men. See," she motioned, pointing to the ground. "The men obviously dismounted here and began walking their animals. Harold says footprints from several directions converge here. Luckily, the ground is soft and Harold can sniff at one of these deep footprints and tell how long ago it was made. Now stay here a moment and let me find out what Harold wants us to do."

So saying, Alix bent low and raced soundlessly toward Harold on her moccasined feet, holding the skirt of her riding habit up above her ankles. When she returned, the boys had just finished tying their horses to nearby branches and were fairly dancing about in the excitement of the chase.

"What did he say? What did he say?" Jeremy questioned eagerly. "Are we closing in on them?"

"Brought my ruffles," Billy volunteered, dangling an evil-looking pair of handcuffs in front of Alix's astonished eyes.

Cuffy shook his head slowly in disgust. "The fella's really revolting, you know that? Ruffles, indeed."

"Yeah," interposed Jeremy. "It's like it says in his book: he has about as much wit as three fellows—two fools and a madman!"

Alix positioned her hands on her hips and set one moccasin-clad toe a-tapping. "If you are quite done insulting poor Billy here, may we please get on with it?" After Cuffy executed a flawless leg in her direction, followed by two lesser, more humble bows from his fellows, Alix informed them of Harold's plans.

He would, in true Indian fashion, go on alone, following the tracks the highwaymen had so conveniently left behind. Then, once he had ascertained the thieves' location, he would backtrack to a place he felt safe and signal for the rest of his trackers to join him.

"What's the signal?" Jeremy asked, now well and truly caught up in the adventure of the thing. "Will he shoot a flaming arrow into the air?"

Trying to keep a straight face, Alix told him it would be nothing quite so dramatic. "He will make the call of the wild turkey."

"Well, if that isn't above everything silly," Cuffy drawled sarcastically. "*Any* fool knows turkeys don't call in the wintertime; he'll set the highwaymen to scampering sure as check."

"Cuffy's right. Probably how they lost the wars in America. Stands to reason, don't it, if turkey calls were the best they could come up with," Jeremy added, more than a little crestfallen.

Alix refused to enter into an argument with the boys but merely shot them a quelling look before plunking herself down on a nearby fallen log to await further developments.

About a half hour later the call came as Harold's wild turkey imitation set all the smaller birds in the area into flight. Bodies bent nearly in half, the four scurried off in the direction of Harold's voice. Soon all five of them were hunkering down behind a small stand of trees, their eyes riveted on the scene Harold pointed out to them.

In a small clearing just ahead of them stood a ramshackle cottage that had definitely seen better days. Half of its thatched roof was missing, rags were stuffed into gaping holes where windows had rotted away, and the only visible door to the hovel hung drunkenly from its single remaining hinge.

But it was not the cottage that caused their eyes to widen and their mouths to gape; rather, it was the sound of voices coming from its interior that had their complete attention.

"It's them—it's the high toby men!" Billy rasped, nearly exploding with his knowledge. "Let me at 'em!" he blustered, brandishing his ruffles.

Both Cuffy and Jeremy were hard pressed to hold back the enthusiastic Billy, struggling silently as they each held tightly to one of his ankles, but the noise made by the heavy iron manacles clanging together as Billy swung his arms wildly about was more than enough to alert the thieves.

All in a moment, it happened. A mean, dirt-streaked face appeared in the doorway, rapidly discerned the cause of the commotion, and hastily withdrew his head to warn his fellows that "some coves have rumbled our lay!" Before Harold could do more than throw his body over Alix's in an attempt to shield her, three shots rang out, two of them snapping through the branches near the boys and the third cutting a deep furrow in Harold's bearskin blanket.

While their would-be capturers nervously embraced the damp earth beneath their prone bodies, the thieves burst from the cottage already on horseback—as their less than refined tastes did not see any reason not to share their living quarters with their mounts—and hightailed it off into the woods.

"Well, that's that," commented Cuffy, spitting out a mouthful of moss and rolling over onto his back to contemplate the sky.

"Tipped us the double," Billy agreed—admitting that the highwaymen had gotten cleanly away—before both his friends began pelting him with leaves and clumps of moss, letting him know just whose fault it was the thieves got away.

It was left to Harold to restore some order to the group, which he did by neatly knocking the boys' heads together and growling menacingly as he held out a portion of his abused bearskin robe, his finger pushed up through the bullet hole it had sustained.

"We're in the basket now," Jeremy said, shaking his head sorrowfully. "Alix would have taken that bullet if it weren't for Harold here."

At that, Alix, who had been vainly trying to regain her wind after Harold had knocked it clean out of her with his crushing embrace, raised herself to her knees and stared at the bearskin in some fascination.

"N'tschútti—my dear, beloved friend—thank you," she told the Indian, placing a hand on his arm.

Harold seemed to grow another foot taller as he rose,

straightened his shoulders, and threw his head back majestically. *"N'nitsch undach aal!"* he pronounced regally—come hither, my child!

Alix got to her feet, brushed off her habit, and quietly followed behind Harold as he strode off through the trees—no longer an interesting oddity or a figure of fun, but every inch the great warrior, to be looked upon with awe and respect.

The three boys, greatly subdued, followed meekly some paces to the rear on the ride back to Saxon Hall—the four horses walking behind the loping Lenape who led the way.

It wasn't until Alix was safely inside the inner bailey that Harold allowed himself to swoon—collapsing gracefully on the ground at her feet.

Lord Linton was furious! It had been bad enough to hear that the nutting expedition the boys had told him was the outing they had planned for Alix had in reality been merely a ruse to cover a childish attempt to trap the highwaymen, but to discover that they had actually been chuckle-headed enough to put Alix in danger was too much to be borne.

Jeremy's admission that they had "made a muff of it" was just the understatement of fact to set Nicholas off into a raging fury. Capping his anger was the admission that Harold, in the act of protecting Alix, had taken a ball in the shoulder and was even now lying unconscious at Saxon Hall.

Leaving the three boys behind at Linton Hall to nervously await his return and the punishment that would surely follow, Nicholas set forth toward Saxon Hall on his fastest horse.

That he was not as welcome as the flowers in May was soon apparent, as Alix greeted him abstractedly before ducking inside Harold's wigwam to tend to her patient. This left Sir Alexander as the only other occupant of the Great Hall, and that distinguished gentleman made no bones about whom he felt to be at fault for putting his only granddaughter in peril of her life.

"That hare-brained bunch of hooligans is under your guardianship, Linton, and I hold you personally responsible for this near-disaster,'' Sir Alexander told Nicholas none too quietly as he jabbed at the Earl's chest with one pudgy finger. "Bedlam-bait, the three of 'em, that's what they are. You have my word on this, Linton—if they ever dare to show their faces around Saxon Hall again, I'll have their livers carved out and set up on poles for the crows. Sink me, if I don't just do that!"

"Such a piddling punishment, Sir Alexander? Pray, don't be lenient out of any consideration for me," Nicholas soothed the enraged man. "For my part, I was considering setting the scoundrels themselves up on poles for the crows."

At that the old man laughed, slapping Nicholas on the back thumpingly, and called to Nutter to bring two goblets of gin. "Should have known you had nothing to do with it—seeing as how you're to be my grandson-in-law and all," Sir Alexander told the Earl, his humor much restored, and the two seated themselves at one of the long tables and discussed Harold's condition.

"The ball passed clean through one of those oversized lumps of muscle at the top of the savage's arm," Sir Alexander informed Nicholas. "Alexandra's already cleaned out the wound, piffling little thing that it is, although the heathen did lose a lot of blood, I guess. That's why he fainted, y'know. Alexandra didn't even know he was wounded—says he used that animal fur to sop up the claret, and no one the wiser until the bloody idiot passed out at their feet. Got to admire the man, I guess," he added grudgingly. "He did, after all, save m'granddaughter's life, yet I can't help but know if he hadn't been a part of the scheme none of this would have happened at all."

"On the contrary," Nicholas told him, his golden eye twinkling, "I believe Alix would have gone haring off with my brother and his harum-scarum friends irregardless of whether or not she had Harold's sanction. Much as I had dismissed our Indian friend as an eccentric fool, I now believe your son Charles's faith in Harold to have been well placed. Obviously the fellow dotes on Alix."

Sir Alexander made no answer to this but just grumbled

something about going to the kitchens for more Hollands. Nicholas, happy to have the subject shift away from his being responsible for today's near-disaster, got up from his seat and walked over to stick his head inside the wigwam.

"Hello in there," he called softly, causing Alix to turn her head in the direction of the opening.

"Shh!" she hissed angrily before turning again to continue wiping Harold's brow with a cool wet cloth. This action had caused the black paint on Harold's forehead to come away, leaving him in, as it were, only half-mourning, but Nicholas decided to keep this observation to himself as he could see Alix was in no mood for levity concerning her Indian friend.

Alix continued to minister to Harold for some few minutes more before backing out of the wigwam and facing Nicholas, a belligerent look on her face. "I suppose you are come to ring a peal over my head? Well, I can tell you that you have wasted a trip. Between m'grandfather's ravings and my own guilt over involving Harold in the scheme, I am truly chastened."

"Funny," Nicholas returned with a grin, taking in Alix's flashing eyes, "you don't *look* chastened."

Alix loudly plunked down the bowl of water she had carried with her out of the wigwam. "Of course I don't," she countered, her cheeks flushed with heat. "That's because I'm mad—darn mad! How dare those—those lowlifes take potshots at Harold like that?"

"Why, I do believe those lowlifes might have called it self-defense," Mannering replied with some humor. "After all, you were out to capture them, weren't you? Or perhaps I am mistaken in my notions and you all only wished to make their acquaintance so that you could join them in their exploits, um? Upon second thought, the latter seems just like something my brother and his idiot friends would try."

Now Alix's face contorted in fury as she advanced menacingly in Linton's direction. "Don't be any thicker than you can help, Nicholas. I didn't mean the highwaymen had no *reason* to shoot at us. It's just that—well, they had no *right* to do so. Do you see what I mean?"

Nicholas put his arm around Alix's shoulder in sympathy. "Poor infant, your concept of right and wrong is so touchingly innocent. Of course you were in the right and the nasty robbers were most clearly in the wrong. But being right doesn't necessarily ensure victory. Sometimes the bad fellows do triumph—but it is usually a short-lived victory."

"Exactly so," Alix said firmly, disengaging herself from Linton's embrace. "Our turn is coming—mark my words!"

All traces of humor disappeared from the Earl's handsome face and he looked quite fearsome wearing the scowl of anger that replaced it. "God give me patience," he ejaculated. "The chit means to continue with this madness—don't you, girl?"

"Oh, come now, Nicholas. You didn't really think I would let Harold remain unavenged, did you?"

"I forbid it," Nicholas told her feelingly.

"You have nothing to say in the matter, Nicholas," she replied with maddening calm. "You may, of course, do as you see fit concerning the boys, but as for Harold and myself—why, Nicholas, do you seriously believe you can exert your control over *us?*"

"If I have to tie you both up and chain you to your beds," he gritted back, his golden eye narrowing to a mere slit as he leaned down into her face.

"Let me go my own road, Linton," Alix warned, tilting her chin.

Suddenly Mannering's expression changed and he placed one finger under Alix's chin. "Ah, love—would that I could," he breathed huskily before indulging himself in the unknowing invitation of her softly parted lips. As had been the case with them since the very beginning, this close physical contact set off a mutual flare of passion that burst even more immediately into flame owing to their already highly charged emotions.

The kiss may have had its roots in anger but it swiftly grew into one of mutual desire—with their two bodies fused together in an embrace so close-knit that it seemed as if they would melt together and become one. There, in the middle of the Great Hall—with Sir Alexander apt to come upon the scene at any time and Harold lying injured not ten feet away from them—they stood locked together, oblivious to all but their sudden hunger for each other.

It was Alix who returned to her senses first—some niggling thought deep in her brain telling her that if her grandfather did happen upon the scene it would only be to comment that Nicholas was "handling" her just as a fiancé should. Well, Alexandra Saxon would not be *handled*—at least not once she loosed herself from Nicholas's physical grasp. Breathless but determined, Alix pushed hard at Linton's shoulders until she was released and gasped, "Is that your answer to everything, Nick—passion?"

Linton raised one eyebrow and grinned. "I doubt if the method would work during times of war, but yes, I'd say my idea is worthy of some merit. It shut you up, for one thing, and as a way to settle arguments, you've got to admit it has pistols at ten paces beat all to flinders."

Alix was nothing if not honest. "I agree that these—er—interludes you seem to favor do have their benefits. They do not, however, take the place of honest argument and sane, sensible solutions equitable to both parties." Drawing herself up to her full height, she concluded, "In plain words, Linton—you may kiss me till I turn blue, but that will not alter my determination one tiny jot. I want those highwaymen and I mean to have them. You may be able to conquer my body but you shall never gain control of my mind. Did you really think I would be controlled so simply?"

"You don't mince matters, you Americans, do you?" Linton admitted with a shrug. "Very well, my love, since you see so neatly through my strategy—although I admit to a fluttering in my breast as I think of how you so freely admit I do have some control over your body—I will bow to your independence of mind and spirit. It was shabby of me to treat you so cavalierly. Obviously you are a woman of great strength of mind. But," he seemed to ponder the question, "do you trust those three young buffoons to be a workable portion of your plans?"

Alix laughed and shook her head. "I wouldn't *trust* those

three to find their way home from the village. No, it is up to Harold and myself to capture the baddies, I fear.''

"And a pretty botch you have made of it so far," Nicholas informed her without rancor. "As it will be some days before Harold is up and about, may I suggest you leave off your thief catching for a while—only if this is agreeable to you, of course—before allowing me, poor one-eyed specimen that I am, to join you in your quest?''

Alix appeared to consider the idea for some moments before slowly nodding her head in agreement just as her grandfather staggered back into the Hall, much the worse for having had free access to his Hollands for the first time in over two weeks.

"What ho!" he shouted as he weaved his way toward the pair. "Is the savage all right then? Hate to see him tucked up to bed with a shovel just when I've found a new partner at cards. Don't talk so much as Nutter—don't play half so well neither. Bloody waste to lose him now, if y'ask me.''

"Grandfather! You're drunk!" Alix accused the old man.

"O'course I am, you conniving female," he countered belligerently. "What the devil else is there to do around here anymore? Can't feed my belly without you yapping at me to stop tossin' m'chicken legs on the floor. Can't wager with the vassals without you comin' down on me like some fire-belching Baptist. Can't even play at cards now that your black-faced Indian went and got his fool self shot. O'course I'm drunk—nothing else left to do.''

Nicholas looked at Alix and saw how tear-bright her eyes were as she valiantly held on to her self-control. She'd had, all in all, a very trying day. Deciding to ease the tension a little he told the old man, "If it's excitement you're after, Sir Alexander, Alix and I were just discussing our plans for trapping the highwaymen. I'm confident your addition to our party would be greatly appreciated—wouldn't it, my love?''

Sir Alexander leaned forward to study Linton through narrowed eyes. "Sink me if the lad ain't serious!" he exclaimed, nearly toppling over backward as he tried to straighten his enormous body. "You really mean to take m'granddaughter along to track down thieves? You must be bloody lushy!'' He tilted his head and peered slyly at the Earl. ''You found where she hid my private stores, Linton, is that it? You've been tipplin' at my Heart's Ease, haven't you? Out with it, man!''

Nicholas spread his empty arms wide, proclaiming his innocence. ''I am quite sober as you can see, sir. It's not drink that has me asking your assistance—it's just that I can see no other way of keeping your granddaughter from having a hole blown through her when she goes haring out after the highwaymen. She is quite determined to capture them, you know.''

The old man took a deep breath and let it out slowly. ''Just like her grandmother. Once set a trap for a poacher, y'know. Caught him too, she did, and then had him horsewhipped. Nasty piece of work your grandmother, when she got her dander up.'' Turning from Alix, he addressed his next words to Mannering. ''You'll not tame this one any easier than I tamed her grandmother, boy. Come to think of it, never did quite break her to bridle—more the other way around.''

''Then you see the wisdom of riding with Alix rather than simply forbidding her to act, knowing full well she'll disobey the moment our backs are turned?''

''Would you both please stop talking about me as if I were not here?'' Alix interposed angrily. ''And stop acting as if I were some incorrigible hoyden or, worse yet, some scatterbrained ninny who would needlessly endanger herself just to be obstinate.''

''If the shoe fits—'' Nicholas drawled, bowing in her direction.

Before Alix could make a suitably cutting retort, her grandfather belatedly answered Nicholas's last question in the affirmative—declaring in a loud, clear voice that he would be honored to be a part of the party that would rid the community of the dastardly highwaymen—before his face took on a slightly greenish hue and he lurched from the room, one pudgy hand clamped tightly over his mouth.

''Now see what you've done,'' Alix cried at Mannering

indignantly. "You've just exchanged three fairly harmless youths for one overage knight errant. It'll be no small miracle if he doesn't ask me for a favor to wear on his sleeve as he rides out to do battle encased in full armor with Nutter riding beside him as page. Oh, Linton, you have really gone beyond the excusable now. I warn you—if anything happens to my grandfather, I shall never forgive you!"

With that, Alix quit the room—her skirts whipping about her ankles as she slammed up the stone stairs in a fine fury—leaving Nicholas quite alone in the Great Hall.

But not quite entirely alone. Just then the flap over the opening to the wigwam was drawn back and a half-black face appeared in the doorway. Harold looked the tall, well-dressed man up and down as if measuring him before slowly shaking his head and commenting sadly, *"Yengees—geptschátschik,"* and withdrawing back into the wigwam.

"I don't know what you said, friend," Nicholas told the absent Harold as he picked up his hat and prepared to take his leave, "but it's a guinea to a pennypiece you're absolutely correct."

Chapter Seven

THREE succeeding days of November weather so wet, damp, and dreary even Sir Alexander could not find it in himself to protest at Alix's disparaging remarks about his "damp island" were to pass slowly before Saxon Hall was again blessed with a visitor from the outside world.

This time Alexandra could not hide her surprise as Nutter ushered in not Jeremy and the boys, not Nicholas—dragging with him an audience of Mrs. Anselm and daughter as he playacted at being a loving fiancé—but the last person Alix would have expected to set foot in the Great Hall—Rupert Anselm.

"Beastly weather we've been having, don't you know," he trilled merrily as he minced into the room on high, red-heeled slippers. He bowed over Alix's reluctantly held out hand before turning to Sir Alexander—who was just then sprawling at his ease on one of the huge thronelike chairs, his left leg draped over one carved wooden arm. Rupert swept Sir Alexander an elegant bow before looking pointedly at the open fire in the center of the room and, lifting his scented handkerchief to his rouged lips, coughing discreetly a time or two. "A bit—er—*smoky* in here, eh?"

"Too smoky by half," muttered Sir Alexander, taking in Rupert's elegant, silk-covered figure. "What d'ye want here, you man-milliner? Mama sent you, I wager. But to what end—that's what I want to know. Sink me, if I don't."

Rupert's thin face took on a look of injured sensibilities. "Why, sir, you wound me deeply. I have come, of course, with my mother's wish to inquire after Miss Saxon's servant speeding me on my way. But I assure you, sir, the idea for this visit was entirely mine.''

''In a pig's eye,'' Sir Alexander muttered into his soiled ruff before pushing his velvet cap down over his eyes and withdrawing from the conversation.

Profoundly grateful to be so quickly ignored by the astute old man, Rupert returned his attention to Alexandra, telling her how he had risen this morning to see the sun once again adorning the sky and his first thought had been to take the lovely Miss Saxon out for a ride in his high-perch phaeton.

''A high-perch phaeton?'' Alix asked, not recognizing the term. ''Sounds like something birds sit on, doesn't it?'' she joked, earning herself a low chuckle from her grandfather's direction.

But Rupert was undaunted. ''No, no, Miss Saxon,'' he told her, forcing himself to laugh a little at her sally, ''a high-perch phaeton is merely the most daring, most smack-up-to-the-mark conveyance made today. *Mine* has yellow wheels trimmed in black,'' he added rather proudly.

''Ah,'' Alix pursued, enjoying Anselm's discomfort hugely. ''Yellow and black wheels. Surely then I was in error. It's not a vehicle for *birds*—it's for the other half of that old axiom—it was made for the *bees*. All right, Mr. Anselm. If only for the chance to ride in this elegant-sounding equipage, I accept your kind offer of a ride, thank you.''

''I was sure you would,'' Rupert smiled, bowing yet again.

''Damned presumptuous ass,'' Sir Alexander snorted sotto voce as the two took their leave, and then he promptly took advantage of Alix's absence by picking up a deck of cards and heading in the direction of the recuperating Harold's wigwam.

Once outside in the clear, cold air, Alexandra dutifully admired Rupert's new toy—privately thinking she was risking life and limb by merely standing near the delicately framed structure. But after being lifted up to sit beside Anselm on the lofty perch, she began to see the attraction of the phaeton and almost believed she could pass a few hours in

Rupert's company riding through the countryside without becoming bored to distraction.

And bored she was not. Rupert, it soon became obvious, was no good judge of horseflesh. His snowy white pair was showy, highly tempered, and totally in control of their driver—who was definitely out of his league in anything but a pony cart.

Fortunately, after a brisk, half-wild ride down the hillside outside the castle, Rupert's showy cattle were content to plod along at their own pace, only mildly taxing Anselm's whipmanship, and Alix could begin to enjoy a bit of fresh air after three days of nursing Harold. Not that the Indian was a bad patient—he was really quite stoically brave about the entire matter—but conditions inside the wigwam were not conducive to comfort over any prolonged period of time.

Now she reveled in the breeze as it blew her long black hair about her, and she even smiled once or twice at the inanities Rupert spouted as to the beauty of her smile and the flawless perfection of her skin. His small store of flattery finally exhausted, and believing his duty to his mama fulfilled, he let a bit of his true self show through as he commented on the sad lack of activity to be found in the country during the winter months. "I find it insupportably flat, don't you?" he asked her.

Alix thought back over her various adventures since first setting foot in Linton and suppressed a smile. "No, Mr. Anselm, I can't say that I do," she replied tongue in cheek.

"Ah, yes," he went on condescendingly. "I do hear that young girls in the country amuse themselves by weaving fantasies about heroes like Byron and the like. Even some fellows of my acquaintance fairly wax poetic over living the simple life in the country—almost weeping over the innocent romantic times spent lolling about on hillsides with a blade of grass stuck in their mouths. I cannot understand it myself. I enjoy the hustle and bustle of town life—the thrill of having an entire city at my fingertips."

Not having spent time in any city but Philadelphia, and having enjoyed her homeplace and its amenities immensely, Alix was interested in hearing all about London. She pushed

Rupert—only the slightest of nudges was needed, actually—into telling her a little bit about the great metropolis.

If she had thought to hear about the many historic landmarks, architectural monuments, or artistic treasures of the city, she was soon to be disabused of this notion. Instead, Rupert launched himself into a recitation of his own activities in the city—an endless round of parties, balls, and gaming halls that had Alexandra openly yawning within the space of fifteen minutes. She almost hoped the horses would bolt—anything to shut Rupert's boring mouth.

Seeing he was fast losing his audience, Anselm decided to tell Alix of one of his most recent excursions—a trip to Bedlam with a group of his cronies.

"Bedlam?" Alix asked, interested. "What is that—a museum?"

Rupert exploded with laughter, momentarily startling his horses into a brief canter. "A museum—oh, that is rich! No, no, Miss Saxon, Bedlam is no museum. It is a hospital—Bethlehem Hospital to be exact—devoted to the care of the hopelessly insane."

"You *visit* there?" Alix asked, incredulous.

Rupert nodded his head in agreement. "They let you in for a few pennies every Sunday afternoon. It's jolly good fun, really. We take a few bottles along with us, of course, and scented hankies for our noses, but it is totally natural to meet your friends in the promenade past the public cells—rather like attending the sideshow at the Bartholomew Fair, you know. Of course you must watch out for pickpockets."

"Are you trying to tell me it is socially acceptable to pay money to gawk at poor unfortunates?" Alexandra pressed him.

Oblivious to her disgust, he happily expounded on some of the fine sights to be seen at Bedlam. He told her about the leopard man, a very cunning fellow indeed, along with a group of longtime inmates who charge a penny to perform small dramas for the visitors. "Of course it doesn't pay to get too close to any of them—they are liable to toss their chamberpots at you if you do," he ended warningly.

"I don't blame them a bit," Alix countered, the heat of

battle in her eyes. "Now stop this ridiculous vehicle at once and let me off."

"Wha-what?" Anselm blustered, taking in the militant set of Alexandra's chin. "Why, we are at least two miles from Saxon Hall. You can't be serious." His small, colorless eyes met and held her dark ones for a moment before his gaze faltered and he looked away. Not even his mama ever appeared so intimidating. He hauled on the reins and the phaeton came to a halt in the middle of the roadway. "Please, Miss Saxon," he began to beg, remembering his mama's order to do the pretty with this outrageous chit or pay the consequences, "you cannot possibly walk all the way back to Saxon Hall in this cold weather."

Anselm's entreaty seemed to give Alix pause for a moment as she tilted her head in thought. Then a small smile appeared on her face as she mentally recalled Anselm's high-heeled slippers. "You're absolutely right, Mr. Anselm. No frail *woman* could possibly traverse the two miles to Saxon Hall on foot. On the other hand, the three or so miles to Linton Hall should seem as no more than a stroll through the park to a *man,* should they not?"

Anselm, who hadn't exactly been brimming over with joy at the thought of escorting Miss Saxon in the first place, was beginning to regret he had ever been born. "Now, Miss Saxon," he cajoled nervously, "you certainly can't be saying that you wish me to abandon you out here in the wilderness alone simply because you dislike my taste in entertainment?"

"But, Mr. Anselm," Alix responded with a dazzling smile, "that is exactly what I am saying. Do but think upon it a moment, Mr. Anselm. Which is worse—walking back to Linton Hall to face your mama, or returning to Linton Hall in your lovely new phaeton alone, to face Nicholas Mannering and, shortly thereafter, Sir Alexander Saxon. Gracious," she trilled archly, "I do believe even Harold may have to force himself from his sickbed to take umbrage with a man who would leave a woman afoot alone in the countryside with highwaymen about."

Alix could almost see the gears turning in Rupert's head

as he mentally listed the pros and cons of his situation. The highwaymen and his mama warred with the certain wrath of Linton, Saxon, and that fierce-looking savage—the last truly, he thought, an ugly customer—and quickly he made his decision.

Handing the reins to Alix he muttered wretchedly, "Good day to you, ma'am. Please be careful of my horseflesh. They have tender mouths."

"They have mouths like shoe leather, thanks to your cow-handed driving, Mr. Anselm," she replied pithily, "but I will take extreme care not to damage your fine yellow wheels. Good day to you, sir." And so saying, she whipped up the horses and, turning them smartly, set off in the direction of Saxon Hall, leaving Rupert Anselm alone in the roadway to contemplate his fate.

"I still don't see why we have to go haring off to Linton Hall, Alexandra," her grandfather whined, holding on to one of the carriage straps for dear life as the ancient, badly sprung Saxon Hall traveling coach sought and found every rut and hole on the roadway from the castle to the Mannering estate.

"We are going, Grandfather," Alix replied wearily, "because we returned their invitation to dinner in the affirmative—at least you did. I, if you recall, was all for chucking the blamed thing in the fire. It was you who said you'd enjoy spending an evening watching Matilda Anselm trying to look down her nose at us while that same appendage was so sadly out of joint."

Sir Alexander chuckled, his enormous belly moving up and down as he shook with merriment. "By Jupiter, how could I forget! Can't remember the last time I had such a good laugh. Even those hey-go-mad boys were near to splitting their sides when they came by to pick up that fool popinjay's bumblebee contraption—told me Anselm near belly-crawled into Linton Hall jabberin' that the nasty highwaymen were going to get him; his bloomin' red sissy-shoes stuffed into his pockets. Oh, Matilda must have well and truly torn a strip off his hide. Yes, indeed, missy. When those boys told me we was invited to share their mutton Saturday night, I fair leaped at the chance to see that snooty dragon Matilda stewing in her own juice. Does an old man good to have a bit of a giggle once in a while, you know," he ended, throwing Alexandra a broad wink.

Alexandra relaxed at her grandfather's return of good humor and made a small half-bow in his direction. "I live only to please you, sir. Indeed, had I known how much enjoyment you would derive out of my insulting the Anselms, I assure you I would have done my utmost to have arranged with the highwaymen beforehand to have them meet up with poor Rupert upon the roadway and strip him of his fine clothes as well as his wallet."

"I don't doubt that you would have, either," Sir Alexander roared back at her. "Ramshackle past reclaim, that's what y'are, lass. Charles let you run wild, I can see that now."

"Chas was more than a little preoccupied with his good works," Alix ruminated cheerfully enough, "but he always saw to it that I was well taken care of. He gave me Harold, didn't he?"

"Hummph, that he did—and more of an albatross around your neck I cannot imagine. No proper English miss drags a black-faced savage with her everywhere she goes. Ain't proper; by Jupiter, it ain't. Besides, if a female's to have a second language, it's supposed to be a few *la-de-da* words in that Froggie tongue, not some heathen gibberish that sounds like you've got something stuck in your craw and you're tryin' to get it out."

Alexandra thought it might be prudent to change the subject before her grandfather got himself worked into a real temper, which wouldn't auger well for the dinner party—or herself, for that matter. She carefully redirected the conversation to the evening ahead, telling Sir Alexander that she was looking forward to seeing her three co-conspirators—just to see if they would still be eating their dinner standing at the mantel as Jeremy had told her they had been.

"Ha! That would serve them right—if Mannering indeed had taken the birch rod to their behinds," Sir Alexander chuckled. Much to the delight of his interested granddaughter, he then went on to reminisce about some of his own grasstime exploits—a recitation that neatly filled the time until they reached their destination at Linton Hall.

They found Mannering and his houseguests all assembled in the large saloon—waiting impatiently for the Saxons and the hoped-for diversion their visit should provide from the rather strained relations that had been evident around Linton Hall the last few days.

Jeremy, for one, could barely contain himself. His feelings of guilt over Harold's injury—encouraged as they were by Nick's lecture as to the folly of involving others in mad schemes—had kept him nervous and off his food for three whole days. Billy seemed to be likewise affected—taking to mumbling cant phrases under his breath and going off for hours to sit alone in the third branch of the old beech tree that overlooked the south lawn.

Only Cuffy appeared unchanged. He remained his usual urbane self, filling his days with seemingly aimless wanderings through the house and applying himself with the greatest civility to drawing out the shy, mother-dominated Miss Anselm. Most remarkable was that he kept his acerbic tongue completely off the hapless Rupert—perhaps seeing him as too easy a target and therefore not worthy of his sarcasm.

If the servants were grateful for the temporary lull in social activity caused by the weather, their gratitude was offset by the heavy burdens Mrs. Anselm placed on them. It seemed that the woman had taken it into her head to completely rearrange the furnishings at Linton Hall—calling them too austere and masculine to be borne by a person of her sensibilities.

While stopping short of actually ripping down draperies and ordering new furniture (although she spoke quite openly of the merits of creating an Egyptian room in the current solar and using elephant feet as table bases in the morning room), she had the servants racing to and from the attics morn 'til night hunting out knickknacks and falderals that she placed on any bare surface to "give the place some personality."

Now that the rain had stopped, she told Poole she planned to do some thinking regarding the grounds surrounding Linton Hall—an idea Poole heartily endorsed, believing it would at least keep the meddling woman out from underfoot in his butler's pantry.

While Rupert sulked, Helene simpered, Mrs. Anselm schemed, and the boys shuffled about aimlessly, Linton himself was busy in his library-office, searching out old documents and tracing his family back to the infamous Linton ancestor whose signature appeared on Alexandra's condemning parchment scroll.

He had already made a copy of the scroll and sent it off to his solicitors in London, but he found he could not let the matter rest there and had begun his own private investigation into the validity of the thing. So far his search had uncovered no similar parchment in his own family archives, but that did not mean one did not exist.

Deep in his own pursuits, he did not notice or refused to lend credence to Mrs. Anselm's meddling in the domestic affairs of Linton Hall. Poole and his servants put this down to their master's being caught up in the throes of True Love and excused him.

They were more than a little perplexed, however, that the Anselms were still in residence and making no preparations for leaving, even now that the weather had cleared. Surely that encroaching old woman could not really believe their master would break his engagement to Miss Saxon and take up with Helene Anselm again. It wouldn't be proper, for one thing, and besides, the master had compromised the poor girl, hadn't he?

And that's just what Sir Alexander was telling that same encroaching old woman within five minutes of taking up his glass of gin and depositing himself inelegantly beside her, dangerously straining the construction of the small loveseat they now shared. "Don't want this bruited about, Matilda," he said baldly, "but Linton *did* compromise m'granddaughter, you know. So if you're hanging about here

126

thinkin' he'll come up to scratch with your die-away daughter over there, you're sadly mistaken. Don't wish to hurt you, Matilda, but there it is. Best pack your bags and move on to greener pastures. The chit ain't exactly in her first youth anymore, is she?''

Mrs. Anselm raised one pudgy hand to her small diamond necklace and leaned toward Sir Alexander. "You mean to tell me the gel's pregnant, Alex?" she whispered, her expression more lascivious than aghast.

Sir Alexander jumped back on his seat as if he had been suddenly poked in the posterior with a loose cushion spring. "Matilda!" he ejaculated, feigning shock. "You have a filthy mind, you know that?"

Watching this interchange from across the room, Nicholas thought it might be safer to remove Alexandra from the saloon for a little while and let the two old adversaries spar without the subjects of their duel as witnesses. Before Alix could protest, he slipped a hand neatly under her arm and guided her into the hallway. "Since we still have some time before Poole calls us in to dinner, I thought you might like a small tour of your future home—only to impress my house guests, I assure you." At Alexandra's nod of consent (the conversation between her grandfather and Mrs. Anselm had not gone undetected by her, and much as she would like to think she was above such feelings, she was still experiencing some embarrassment over what she had heard and did not quite trust her own voice), Nicholas led her toward the center staircase leading up to the second floor and the family apartments.

"I believe there are several interesting rooms on this floor—filled with paintings and other works of art my ancestors have collected over the years—but there is one type of room I am convinced you will find most intriguing. We have several such rooms, you understand, but I shall only direct you to one of them."

"If you're talking about the Linton family bedchambers, I assure you I have no great desire to step foot in any of them ever again," Alexandra told him, finding her voice once

127

more. "But recall, Nicholas, it was a Linton bedchamber that got me into this muddle in the first place."

The Earl allowed himself a small smile of reminiscence before telling her, "Although I admit the thought of luring you into my personal bedchamber on the ruse of giving you a tour of my household does hold a certain charm, the room I had in mind is a water closet."

"What!" Alexandra fairly shouted, stopping dead in her tracks.

"You heard me," he replied silkily. "Let me see now. It was around about 1775 when that dear man Mr. Alexander Cummings developed the first water closet, although Linton Hall waited for Joseph Brahmah to improve on Mr. Cummings's idea and our household sports the Brahmah closet, actually."

Alexandra put her hands on her hips and faced Linton. "What would make you think I would be interested in seeing a stupid water closet?" Her belligerent stance openly dared him to answer her.

Linton shrugged his shoulders in feigned innocence. "Nostalgia?" he offered. "After all, living at Saxon Hall all this time, you may have developed an attachment of sorts for articles you have not seen lately."

"Funny, Nicholas," Alix told him tightly. "Very funny. Now wipe that asinine smile off your face before I push you headfirst down the stairs."

A look of dejection came over Nicholas's face before he seemed to brighten with inspiration. "Perhaps you would rather have a tour of the grounds before it gets too dark," he ventured eagerly. "There's a lovely Ruin m'grandmother had built in the east garden."

"She did what?" Alix was forced by curiosity to inquire, while all the while nursing a deep foreboding that once again Nicholas was enjoying himself at her expense.

"I said m'grandmother had a Ruin built—a Gothic Ruin. They were all the rage a while back, you know."

Alexandra looked perplexed. "Why would anyone want to build a Ruin? I don't understand."

Linton shook his head and agreed with her. "Truth to tell,

I can't understand the reasoning behind it myself. Why, I've heard it said some people even *live* in ruins—imagine that!''

Alix opened her mouth, realized that whatever she said would lead her only more deeply down the path Mannering had so neatly set her upon, and closed it again. Live in a ruin, indeed! How insufferable he was to keep pointing out the shortcomings of Saxon Hall. Well, if he thought such strategy would lead her to see marriage to him as some sort of salvation, he had another thought or two coming! Turning on her heel, she tramped back downstairs to the saloon, her head held high. How dare he think she was so soft as to allow creature comforts to override her resolve!

Just as she was about to enter the saloon another thought struck her and she whirled about to face her tormentor, nearly causing him to cannon into her, so abrupt was her aboutface. ''Besides,'' she said, taking him totally unawares, ''if the scroll proves legal I won't need to leg-shackle myself to you just to gain your sumptuous Brahmah closets—they'll be mine by right. You'd best be good to me, Linton. Stay on my right side and I may allow you to take up residence at Saxon Hall until you can find a decent job someplace to earn your keep. I regret to say I do not know the name of the person who invented the garderobe, but as you would only spend your time cursing the poor soul as you endure those cold winter mornings, I cannot say I am sorry.''

Linton bowed deeply in front of Alix. *''Touché,* my love,'' he told her handsomely. ''But I suggest we wait until your conquest is official before we let the others in on our little secret, if you don't mind. Jeremy, remember—I'd hate to upset the boy without reason.''

This mild rebuff bringing a rush of color to invade Alexandra's cheeks, observors of the little scene came to their own conclusions as to what was passing between the engaged couple—causing delighted smiles to come to the faces of some of them and deep scowls to register on others.

Poole entered then, summoning them all to a dinner that Mrs. Anselm had planned personally. The dinner table was arranged in the strictly formal manner—with Linton at the head, Mrs. Anselm and Sir Alexander on either side of him, and all the younger members of the party seated below the salt. Helene, naturally, had been placed by her mother at the foot of the table, where she sat looking totally out of place in her assigned role of hostess.

"How's old puff-guts taking it?" Billy whispered out of the corner of his mouth to Alix, who was seated beside the young man. "Is he still cutting up stiff over our ruckus?"

Struggling to keep the smile off her face, Alexandra assured the nervous Billy, "Square-toes has become most mellow on the subject of the thief chasing—ever since Nicholas promised to include him on the next expedition, that is."

At Alix's statement Jeremy choked on his wine and had to be roughly thumped on the back by Cuffy, who articulated for his gasping, coughing friend. "Square-toes, Alix? Never say you're still deep in Billy's book of cant? Must be," he went on, answering his own question, "else how would you know puff-guts meant a fat man—your grandfather, of course. That would mean you've gotten to the P's—and the S's as well. Still, much as I abhor Billy's use of cant—it can become so wearing at times—I do believe my favorite description for a fat man is to say he's got a 'glorious corporation.'"

By now Jeremy had regained his powers of speech. "Hang the slang and cant, Cuffy. Wasn't that what made me choke on my wine. Didn't y'hear Alix say her grandfather was to become one of an expedition out to catch the highwaymen—an expedition, if my ears are to be believed, to be headed up by none other than my brother himself!"

"You ain't tippin' us no gammon, Alix?" Billy asked, eyeing her askance.

Alix assured them all that she was telling the truth—adding that, although she regretted to tell them this, they were not included in the search party. This did not depress them half as much as she had feared, and their exchanged glances and almost audible sighs of relief gave her the uneasy feeling that they had already begun planning an expedition of their own.

Once or twice during the interminable meal made up of course after course (more, Jeremy quipped, like a Carlton House fête than a simple country dinner), Rupert tried to ingratiate himself back into Alexandra's good graces—obviously on orders from his mother. But these attempts were so neatly blocked by Alix that he soon gave up the fight, and since the three boys had long ago established that they wished nothing to do with the fellow, he was left very much to himself most of the time.

Helene was likewise a very quiet member of the dinner party. It was not that anyone bore her any ill feeling; it was just that after their initial tries at conversation had been answered only by negative shakes of her pretty head, no one felt sufficiently interested in her to try again.

At the other end of the table it was an entirely different matter. Nicholas was kept busy mediating between Mrs. Anselm and "old puff-guts," hoping to keep the two of them from coming to blows over the *Ragôut à la Françoise*. It seemed that they could not find a single area of agreement, be it politics, society at large, or even, so thought Nicholas, the proper size for peas.

As the meal at last came to a close, Poole and his helpers placed small colored glass bowls full of water before each person at the table. While the rest of the party daintily dipped their fingers in the scented water before wiping their hands dry on their napkins, Sir Alexander—in the manner of his forefathers—lifted the bowl to his mouth, sucked up a great quantity of the fluid, gargled noisily, and then returned the fluid to the bowl.

After repeating this procedure several times—the whole while being goggled at by Mrs. Anselm as if he had run entirely mad—he dipped his napkin in the bowl and proceeded to thoroughly wash his hands and face, ending his ablutions by drying himself with a corner of the fine linen tablecloth.

All this proved to be too much for the three boys, who had been watching the entire performance with avid interest. After exchanging winks among themselves, they—on the pretext of trying to make their guest feel at home—imitated Sir Alexander's actions down to the last gargle and wipe.

131

The ladies then retired from the table—Alexandra reluctantly, as she dreaded sitting alone in the saloon with the female Anselms, and the two Anselms hurriedly, both holding their hankies delicately to their mouths. They left behind a disgusted Rupert, three giggling young scamps, one old man (whose face shone rosy red with cleanliness) totally at sea, and one absolutely delighted Lord Linton, who had not been so amused in a very long time.

After drinking their port, the men rejoined the ladies and Alexandra sought out the boys like a lost soul in search of her saviors. "Thank goodness you have come to rescue me," she told them as they sat together in one corner of the saloon, in Nicholas's mind, as close as inkleweavers.

"What's amiss, Alix?" Jeremy questioned facetiously. "Never say Mrs. Anselm's been grilling you?"

"Grilling me?" Alix countered in disgust. "That dratted woman's just lucky I don't give her a good drubbing. Do you know she has yet to open her mouth without insulting me one way or the other?"

"Somehow I don't see the old gorgon getting the best of you, Alix," Nicholas drawled smoothly, coming up from behind her and nearly scaring her out of her wits. Still standing behind her, he motioned for the boys to shift themselves off, which they did. They soon became deeply involved in matching one feather against another with Sir Alexander as they laid bets on the fuzz descending from Mrs. Anselm's moulting boa wrap with the intensity of seasoned gamesters, the first feather to hit the floor being declared the winner.

Seating himself beside Alix on the wide windowseat, Nicholas pressed her to tell him what had gone on while he remained at table with his male guests. "She started on me the moment we came in here," Alix told him heatedly. "I sat down on the sofa over there, and she eyed me like I was some wet cat someone inadvertently let in and told me, talking down her nose, you know, 'girls don't cross their legs.' "

Not being able to bring himself to believe that Alix had let this insult pass, Nicholas pressed her to tell him how she responded to this obvious dig.

"I just looked her straight in the eye and said, 'this girl does,' " Alix confided, a bit of a grin hovering about the corners of her generous mouth.

Mrs. Anselm had then become more subtle with her digs, pretending to start a conversation with Helene about the latest fashions and then neatly slipping in, looking at Alexandra's gown, "Didn't you have a frock like that once, dear? About five years ago, I believe?" But Alix didn't bother repeating that little bit of feminine poison to Nicholas, whom she was sure wouldn't understand just how very much the woman's remark had hurt her. Crossed legs were one thing, but a reference, no matter how veiled, to her straitened economic circumstances was just the pinprick to draw blood.

Instead, she told him how Mrs. Anselm had tried to ferret out Alexandra's lineage. "She asked me who my mother was, and I told her she was simply the daughter of a Philadelphia shopkeeper. 'Oh,' the old cat purred at me, 'then you're—' She let her words die away while she looked me up and down and I told her, 'I'm as common as gooseberries, ma'am.' "

"But you're the granddaughter of a baron, Alix; surely you reminded her of that," Nicholas offered.

"As a matter of fact, I didn't have to remind her," she went on, beginning to smile in earnest. *"She* told me—even said I could now be proud of my name." Even now, several minutes after the incident, Alexandra sat up very straight in her seat as she ended, "I told her, 'fool that I am, madam, I had never thought to be ashamed of it *before* I knew a drop or two of blue blood flowed through my veins.' "

"Good for you!" Linton complimented her sincerely. "You did just right, love. Don't let the Anselms of this world make you believe everyone judges you by your ancestors. And pity us if everyone should! Lord, look at mine— one of the bloody idiots may even have gambled away my inheritance, or so says your piece of parchment."

Nicholas hadn't noticed that Helene had come up beside him (being ordered by her mama to go over to the window embrasure and "break those two up"), and she looked back and forth between the two of them before saying in her breathless way, "Nicholas, I could not help but overhear you. Are you in some sort of trouble?"

Just then the Earl had an inspiration. If Mrs. Anselm got wind of the possibility that her daughter had made a lucky escape by breaking her engagement with a penniless man—a man who did not even own the roof under which that same woman was now housed—she would gather up her offspring and depart. So thinking, he quickly sketched in the details of Alexandra's find, carefully swearing Helene to secrecy concerning Jeremy, but deliberately not forbidding her to tell her mother.

Helene sat quietly for some moments, her childlike face screwed up in concentration before a hand flew to her mouth and she gasped, "Nicholas! Does this mean you could lose *all?*"

Alix leaned over and whispered in Linton's ear, "Devilish acute, ain't she?" and Nicholas only preserved his countenance with difficulty while he whispered back, "Minx!"

This byplay passing completely over Helene's head, the girl was left to her own thoughts for a few more moments, and she used this time to show that, if her intelligence wasn't of the highest, she at least possessed that most basic of instincts—the talent for using information for her own best interests.

"Nicholas, Alexandra," she began, looking from one of them to the other, "since you have confided in me, I feel it only fair, in my turn, to confide in you." Seeing she had their undivided attention, she leaned more closely to them and whispered passionately, "I'm in love!"

Alexandra was the first to recover. Folding her hands in her lap, she sat back and said, "Now why do I get the feeling it is not friend Nicholas here who has set your little heart a-tapping?"

"Oh, Alexandra—may I call you Alix?—I just knew you'd understand," Helene replied, blushing hotly under her auburn hair. "Of course it isn't Nicholas—it never was." Looking toward Mannering, she shrugged her shoulders nervously and apologized, "I'm sorry, Nicholas, but it was Mama's idea to encourage you. Not that I don't think you are a fine gentleman. I don't mind the patch either—that too was Mama's idea. You see, I had heard you had died at Waterloo, and I believed Fate had allowed me a second chance with my Reginald. That's why I fainted when you appeared at the door that day.''

"Reginald?'' Nicholas interjected calmly. "I take it Reginald was on the scene before you and I ever met?''

Now Helene spoke rapidly, all her shyness forgotten at the mention of her beloved's name. "Oh yes, Nicholas. I have known Reginald for ever so long. His papa's estate is just next door to ours in Kent, you know, and we have played together since we were in leading strings.'' Then her smile faded. "But Reginald's father lost everything due to rash investments and then promptly hung himself up by his cravat in the herb garden. Reginald is now near penniless, and Mama says I must forget him.'' Her large, round eyes filled with tears as she ended, tragically, "But I can't forget Reginald. He is the love of my life!''

"Oh, brother,'' Nicholas heard Alix mutter under her breath, and he jabbed her pointedly in the ribs.

But Alix wasn't as coldhearted as she appeared. She was truly touched by Helene's story, even if she was at the same time convinced that matching Helene with her Reginald would be ensuring another generation of weak-chinned Englishmen the likes of which her own countrymen made the butt of countless jokes and cartoons. Even before Nicholas's jab in the ribs she had decided to help the poor girl— although how this was to be done she had no idea. But help her she would—for many reasons. It would thrill Helene, yes. But it would also serve to remove Mrs. Anselm from Linton Hall so that she and Nicholas could put an end to this charade of an engagement and settle the matter of the parchment once and for all with no outside disturbances. And it would well and truly put a spoke in that same insulting Mrs. Anselm's wheel—which could only be looked on as an added bonus.

Indeed, the idea of helping Helene and her Reginald held nothing but appeal for Alexandra. So why did the thought of ending her engagement to Nicholas seem to cast a shadow

over the remainder of the evening? Refusing to think anymore about it, Alix drew Helene off into a corner, where
they talked at some length about the absent Reginald and
Alexandra stored away her newfound knowledge for later
use.

Chapter Eight

TO SAY that things were beginning to get somewhat complicated would be much like saying that Nutter, who still had not realized Harold was an Indian, was "just a tad" nearsighted.

First, take the problems besetting Nicholas Mannering, a gentleman who, through no fault of his own, suddenly found himself neck-deep in dilemmas. It had been bad enough when he was only trying to keep a tight rein on Jeremy and his two ramshackle friends while attempting to run his estate and recover from his war wound.

But to add—in descending order—a reluctant fiancée, an outraged grandfather, an old love, that old love's managing mama and twit of a brother—not to mention some assorted highwaymen and one large Indian—was perhaps pushing credulity too far.

On the other hand, his reluctant fiancée's life was no bed of roses either. Alexandra Saxon was simultaneously trying to juggle the needs of a cantankerous, tippling, gaming grandsire; a wounded, overprotective, overaged Lenape warrior; an odiously overbearing—not to mention *persistent*—fiancé; three hey-go-mad young adventurers bent on capturing three already proven violent highwaymen; and a trio of tiresome Anselms, two of whom inspired disgust and one who somehow engendered Alix's compassion.

Not that Nicholas's dilemmas could be said to vary perceptibly from Alix's, but at least, on top of all his other problems, *he* did not have to contend with Saxon Hall's ancient plumbing!

But the major issue—the complication that could safely be

said to dwarf all the others—was that damning piece of parchment that hung over *both* of them like the Sword of Damocles. For, much as they had not yet trusted each other with the confidence, Alix and Nicholas were more than a little in love with each other, and the matter of the parchment had to be settled before they would feel free to confess that love.

Each unaware of the other's motives, Alix and Nicholas independently decided that the only way out of their separate dilemmas would be to resolve all the other, lesser complications so that they could concentrate on the one thing that really mattered.

So thinking, Alix was more than amenable to Nicholas's suggestion that the next fine day should find her, Nicholas, Sir Alexander, and the recovered Harold out in the countryside in search of the highwaymen.

Ah yes, as the days moved swiftly on into December, the cauldron surely began to boil.

"This is a serious business," Nicholas said tersely. He stopped to cast incredulous eyes over his little group of listeners. "A *dangerous* business," he emphasized, then shook his head sadly. "I cannot believe you are approaching this thing with the degree of gravity it deserves."

It was easy to see why Nicholas was concerned. Wellington may have ranted and raved a bit over his officers' entertaining the thought of going into battle with unfurled umbrellas over their heads, but Mannering could not begin to imagine the Iron Duke's reaction to the motley crew of warriors now standing before him.

Harold, it suddenly came to the Earl's mind, actually seemed the most normal looking of the group. At least he only looked as he always did—black face and all.

Nicholas then cast his eyes up and down Sir Alexander's ample form—complete to a shade in the battledress of his worthy ancestors—and suppressed a shudder. The only piece of equipment that seemed to serve any real purpose was the neat brace of dueling pistols tucked into the man's wide leather girdle. As Jeremy had said, the man, for all his girth, could shoot the pips out of a playing card at twenty paces. However, the three-foot-long broadsword, as well as the evil-looking mace—strictly a Middle Ages weapon used mostly for cracking open an enemy's skull—seemed somehow superfluous. The fact that the man also sported a face smeared with bright, greasy, beet-red paint (also the Lenape color for war) and had three red-smeared wampum belts strung around his neck did little to enhance the man aesthetically, although Nicholas declined to bring this to his attention. With any luck, Sir Alexander, like the Prince Regent, would not be able to mount his horse without the aid of a winch, and would, in the end, be left behind anyway.

But it was Alix's appearance that most unsettled the leader of the little group. For some reason unknown to the Earl, Alexandra had at long last decided to wear the buckskin dress Harold had given her. Not that she didn't look quite fetching, he admitted to himself, fidgeting a bit as his eyes took in the expanse of Alix's smooth skin where it was exposed from knee to shapely ankle, but the thought of any eyes but his own seeing her in such a state of—his proprietary feelings were growing by the moment—*déshabillé*, caused him to absolutely *itch* to throw a blanket over her and carry her off—to where? Well, he thought with an evil half-smile, his bedroom might be as good a place as any.

Before his mind became so muddled as to seriously entertain the thought that Jeremy and his erstwhile friends might make a better hunting party (a truly ludicrous idea), Nicholas told the group to mount their horses so they could be on their way.

Their initial objective was to return to the cabin in the woods where the thieves had first been spotted, and then go on from there. However, when it came time to dismount and continue on foot, Sir Alexander balked, telling anyone who would listen that knights did not go tramping through the damp undergrowth like common folk.

"He probably thinks he'll rust," Nicholas commented in an aside to the now giggling Alix, before saying more loudly, "Exactly, sir. It is always good to have a rear guard." Again under his breath he whispered to Alix, "Although some of us have a bit more 'rear' than others." As Nicholas watched Alix's face turn slightly red in her efforts to keep from bursting into laughter, he told himself ruefully, "If you can't beat 'em, Mannering, you may as well join 'em."

They walked along in single file following Harold's lead, since he already knew the way, until they reached the spot where Harold had been wounded, whereupon they halted for a moment while the Indian mumbled a few well-chosen Lenape curses Alix did not bother to translate for the Earl's edification.

Then it was on to the cottage, Nicholas now in the forefront, creeping stealthily toward one of the gaping windows to ascertain whether or not the place was still inhabited. He was sure the thieves had deserted the place long since, but perhaps Harold could pick up a few clues by examining the area. Once assured there was no one inside, Mannering motioned for Alix and Harold to follow and stepped through the door ahead of them.

"What a mess!" Alix exclaimed once she had joined him. "Though," she continued, one finger pressed to her chin, "it's nothing that couldn't be fixed with a little bit of work."

Now it was Nicholas's turn to chuckle. "Leave it to my little housekeeper. Given enough pails of water and sufficient dustcloths, I do believe you could set this entire island to rights."

Alix merely glared at him and moved toward the slanting wooden table, suppressing the impulse to right the overturned mug she saw lying there. "Harold," she said, looking at the Indian, "why are you just standing about? Don't you want to look for—"

"Wulli ta pépannik!" the Indian hissed, motioning to Alix to drop to the floor. Quickly Alix did as he ordered, hissing to Nicholas, "Harold says they are coming. Get down!"

Within the space of a heartbeat the three were on their knees on the filthy floor (the same floor where the thieves had stabled their horses), and Nicholas was scrambling on hands and knees to the window to peer out into the woods.

Harold, he soon saw, had been correct. The thieves were indeed coming toward the cottage, leading their mounts behind them. They were not as yet close enough to make them out, but Nicholas primed his pistols, ready to take two of them out quickly before throwing himself bodily at the last one.

They were almost in his sights now, and he took a steadying breath before he took aim. His finger was just beginning to squeeze the trigger when all at once Harold threw a body block on him, tumbling the both of them to the grimy floor. "What in bloody hell—" Mannering shouted, struggling to regain his feet.

"La kella geptschátschik, geptschat!" Harold spat, clutching one pistol to his chest and out of Mannering's reach.

"What?"

Alix, who had been more than a little frightened, released her breath in a rush and said, "To translate, Lord Linton, Harold said, 'It is the fools, *fool!*' "

Sure enough, just then Jeremy stuck his head in the cottage door, gulped, "Crikey, the jig is up!" and quickly pulled his head out again.

Now it was Alix's turn to physically hold Nicholas back from committing mayhem on his sibling. "Now, now, Nicholas, don't fly into a pet. They are only boys, you know."

"Boys, is it? Well let me tell you this, missy. If I have my way about it, they'll never make it to full manhood!" he bellowed back in exasperation as hasty hoofbeats faded off into the distance.

The great thief-catching expedition, fizzling as it did so soon in the day, then came to a complete halt as the skies opened, sending down heavy sheets of rain that soon dampened their already sagging spirits. The small party hastily rejoined its "rear guard," then returned to Saxon Hall, where Sir Alexander and Harold sat down in their wet clothes to drink a bumper or two to their adventures, while Alix went off to her chamber to change out of her wet, foul-smelling buckskins, and Nicholas, his temper still not of the best, rode hell-bent for Linton Hall, growling his brother's name once or twice and, in general, muttering a lot.

"I imagine you're wondering why I have sent for you this morning."

Alix, looking quite regal seated as she was in Sir Alexander's huge, thronelike chair, looked over the nervously shuffling trio standing before her and surpressed a smile. If ever she had seen a crestfallen, chastened group, Jeremy, Cuffy, and Billy were it.

Young Master Cuthbert was the first to locate his voice. "I wager it is to ring a peal over our heads for that little fracas in the woods yesterday," Cuffy piped up bravely. "If it isn't, you're the only person this side of the channel not to have *something* nasty to say on the subject."

"If you are referring to Lord Linton in particular," Alix responded more soberly, "I don't believe anything he could say would be too harsh. After all, coming within Ame's Ace of shooting one's own brother is bound to be an unsettling experience."

Cuffy, mentally reliving the scene the day before with the eloquently irate Nicholas Mannering, and still chafing under the effects of that same tongue-lashing, nevertheless objected. "Well, I for one think he was out-of-reason cross. After all, there was no real harm done."

"Sure was in one of his crotchets," Billy added quietly. "Glimflashy, he was, saying we was all dicked in the nob or else we should be bummed, laced up in darbies, and tossed in the bilboes. Oh, gloomy hour—what a brangle."

"Anyone care to tell me what Billy here just said?" Alix asked, her humor greatly restored by the young boy's tangled speech and woebegone expression.

Jeremy, who had been nervously running a hand through his red hair in expectation of yet another sermon, gladly interpreted. "Nick was very angry; so angry his glims, or eyes—although in Nick's case that means one eye, which is more than enough, let me tell you—seemed to flash. He swore we were either crazy—dicked in the nob—or else we should be arrested, put in fetters, and carried off to gaol. All in all, Alix, Billy says it is a terrible mess.'' Jeremy's head hung as he ended, ''He's right too. We just wanted to help and all we've done is cause more trouble. Poor Nick—he's certainly had his hands full lately, hasn't he?''

Sensing that Jeremy's words had given him an opening, Cuffy quickly put in, ''And that's it exactly, ma'am. Nick did his possible, all that could be asked of him in such a tangled situation, but we sensed that it was all getting to be a little too much for him. What with us tripping over Anselms morn 'til night, and you telling him you were going to catch the highwaymen, poor Nick just had too much on his plate. We just decided to lend him a little bit of a hand, so to speak. That's why we were in the woods—to catch the highwaymen for him and ease his mind a bit.''

''I see,'' Alix replied straight-faced, hoping she looked suitably impressed. ''I imagine you believe you all deserve medals for what you attempted to do—or a commendation at the very least! Such a devoted, concerned brother. Such altruistic sacrifice from that brother's two bosom chums.'' She shook her head in wonder. ''My goodness, I do believe I might cry.''

''Burn it, ma'am, if you ain't a card!'' Cuffy exclaimed, dropping his sophisticated pose. ''You see through us like we were all panes of glass, don't you? We was just out cutting a rig, as usual, right, boys?'' he admitted, turning to his friends. ''I told you she was a right 'un, though, didn't I?''

Billy sighed in relief, seconding Cuffy's endorsement of Alix as being really ''tip-top,'' but Jeremy still couldn't seem to shake off his fit of the sullens. ''Nick's in bed with the devil's own headache, you know, and it's all our fault. It's his war wound, Alix; sometimes it pains him something awful.''

As Jeremy again pushed his hand through his hair, locks that Cuffy had taken great pains to arrange in a flattering Brutus for the boy just an hour earlier, Master Simpson felt he had to put Nicholas's headache into its proper perspective. ''Ease up on yourself, friend. That was no war-wound headache. I have it directly from his valet that your brother was well over the oar last night when Bates found him in his study. He's just got a banger of a hangover this morning, that's all. Though I guess he *might* have got cupshot thinking over how he almost parted your hair with a bullet." Cuffy sighed in exasperation. "Which is how it looks now. Really, Jeremy, how do you ever expect to go to London as a top-of-the-trees fellow if you insist on raking through your hair like some backwater chawbacon?"

Although watching the three boys tangle was almost as good as a play, Alix thought it was time she brought their little meeting to order. This she did by clapping her hands together briskly and then, when that failed to capture their attention, by inserting the little finger of each hand into the corners of her mouth and letting out with an ear-splitting whistle that successfully put a period to any further discussion of Mannering's headache, proper grooming, or any other subject—save one.

Once Billy had elicited her promise to teach him how to whistle like that—"you're as good as any coachie on the Mail!"—she had their undivided attention. She then presented her plan for their consideration.

"I say, Alix," Jeremy jibed, once she had finished, "have you given up Billy's book of cant and begun on Mrs. Radcliffe? Sounds like something out of some gothic novel."

"A Penny-dreadful," Billy added, giving his own interpretation of the idea's source.

"No, no," Cuffy objected. "Straight from the Minerva Press, I'm sure. M'sister reads that stuff all the time. Hides herself under the bedcovers at night devouring the drivel like sugarplums. Still," he said, tipping his head to one side and placing a finger to his cheek, "it's so outlandish it might just work."

Once their leader had given the plan his approval, the other two boys began to see some merit in the idea.

Relieved that she had gotten so neatly over her first hurdle—convincing the boys to go along with her plan—Alix filled them in on the details of her scheme, which she dubbed "Save Helene from a Fate Worse than Death," (which was what Alix considered living under Mrs. Anselm's domination to be).

The boys would, according to Alix's plan, make some excuse or other to Nicholas—perhaps saying they were off for a few days to visit another chum who had been sent down early from school—and instead post themselves off to Reginald's estate, which was just a stone's toss from Dover. Once Helene's swain was corralled, they would hie him back to Saxon Hall, where he would be reunited with Helene.

"It'll have to be cap over the windmill, you know," Cuffy put in reasonably. "Mrs. Anselm will never allow the match."

Jeremy, the last of his melancholy banished under the excitement of this new chance for a lark, hopped up from his seat and did a fine impersonation of Helene's simpering mama. "Oh, the shame, the *ab-so-lute mortification!* My own daughter—to bring such *ruin on us all.*" Clutching his chest, he trilled, "I have nurtured a snake at my bosom," before he dissolved into laughter, taking two modest bows before resuming his seat.

"Cuffy," Alix said, trying to bring the interview to a speedy conclusion before her grandfather, whom she had not yet apprised of her plan, heard the commotion and decided to investigate, "I am sure you will know just how the travel arrangements are to best be contrived. I'm putting you in charge of the expedition—and in charge of explaining the seriousness of the situation to friend Reginald. He must understand that Helene is totally beyond salvation if he should fail her now. From what Helene has told me, they are deeply in love."

"Then they both have my *deepest* sympathies," Cuffy shot back impishly before turning serious. "Helene isn't a bad sort, even if her mind is filled with feathers. Brother's a conceited fribble though, and the mother's a mean cat I'd truly enjoy seeing thwarted."

"I knew I could back you to get the thing done," Alix

said bracingly, while wisely not agreeing aloud with Cuffy's sentiments even though she shared them totally.

Cuffy blushed, a habit he could have sworn he had outgrown, and preened, "Oh, I say, Alix—I mean ma'am—that's mighty decent of you!"

"And if Nick objects once we tell him *all*—which will, of course, be *after* the fact—you may lay the idea for the whole thing in my dish," she added, more than a little caught up in the excitement herself. "As you boys were astute enough to see for yourselves, Nick is so beleaguered with problems that it is left to us, as his—er—*friends*" (and here Alix, who could count on the fingers of one hand the times in her life when *she* had blushed, suddenly felt her cheeks growing warm) "to do our utmost to untangle at least this little bit of the coil he has innocently found himself caught up in. Don't you agree?"

It was left to Jeremy to ask the most important question. "You know," he pointed out reluctantly, "Cuffy's right when he says it will have to be a cap over the windmill match. That means a trip to Gretna Green. That's in Scotland," he added for Alix's benefit, "and I can't see Mrs. Anselm not giving chase and catching them before they get there."

Alix knew Jeremy was right. Mrs. Anselm had her own cap firmly set on Helene's marrying Nicholas, and a little thing like a threatened elopement would serve to put only a temporary crimp in her plans. Helene's happiness meant next to nothing to that horrid, scheming woman, who was on the lookout for a nice, deep gravy boat to swim in the rest of her life, and Helene's marriage to Lord Linton would serve her purposes to a cow's thumb. Once she knew Helene and her Reginald were on their way to Gretna, Mrs. Anselm would move heaven and earth to hie them back to Linton Hall. "We will have to throw a rub in her way then, won't we, boys?" she winked at the trio, their smiles telling her that they trusted her to find a way to solve this last problem.

Sir Alexander entered the Great Hall, and feeling magnanimous—thanks to a goblet or five of gin provided by that turncoat Harold (who was just then snoozing off a snootful under a table in Nutter's buttery)—invited the boys to share a potluck lunch with them.

"We've got brawn today, boys, a real treat," he told them.

"What's brawn?" Cuffy hissed in an undertone to Alix.

"It's the meat of a pig's head, cooked up in a sharp sauce that will set your eyeballs to sweating," she whispered back, adding, "I've made myself some soup, which I shall eat in the privacy of my chamber. I don't have enough for all of us, but Grandfather has plenty of brawn, I assure you. I do believe there's also some white curd and beef cooked in almonds Nutter was working over this morning, as well as some pig stuffed with spiced forcemeat."

Master Cuthbert, looking suspiciously green about the gills, made an eloquent, if hasty, excuse to Sir Alexander and, pushing Jeremy and the confused Billy before him, quickly made to quit the premises.

"You'll keep our—er—conversation confidential, boys, won't you?" Alix called after them.

"Mum's the word, missus," Billy yelled over his shoulder as Jeremy, suddenly remembering Nick's vivid description of the lone meal he had ever eaten at Saxon Hall, tugged at his friend's arm. "I can keep my chaffer closed when I want to!" Billy shouted as he was pulled out the door.

Once the boys had departed, Sir Alexander asked Alix, "Just what in Jupiter has those loonies in such a twitter?"—which earned him a quick kiss on the forehead and no explanation whatsoever as Alix skipped off upstairs, humming under her breath.

Nicholas had been out riding for some time, lost in thought, before he at last dragged his mind away from his problems to realize that he was in the same clearing where—when was it? a week ago? a lifetime ago?—he had given Alix his family betrothal ring. Remembering the heated kisses they had exchanged, kisses he knew would burn in his memory forever, he dismounted, tied his horse to a nearby tree, and walked in the direction of Harold's peculiar sweat house.

Once seated on a fallen log at the top of the hill, he noticed that once again a thin stream of steam was rising from the structure. "Harold must be employing his Indian sweat box to rid himself of yet another blue-ruin-induced headache," he ruminated aloud, shaking his head. "Poor Alix. Instead of reforming her grandfather, she has lost her stalwart Harold to demon gin."

He watched the steam awhile, lazily tracing its path toward the sky, and gave his mind over to remembering the curious excitement his brother and his two friends had shown at luncheon. Something was afoot again—as usual, considering the trio's larcenous proclivities—but he was at a loss to understand what they were about this time. Perhaps he should have withheld his consent to have them go off visiting this school chum of theirs they seemed so bent on burdening with their presence. But the mere thought of having them out from underfoot for several days was so heady that he eventually gave in to their outrageous pleadings. (They had been packed and gone within the hour.)

Mannering could understand their wanting to be shed of Linton Hall, his own bad temper, and the depressing presence of the Anselms—Lord knew Nicholas himself would have appreciated a bit of time away—but something, some slight suspicion, persisted in niggling at his brain. That niggling told him the boys would not so easily abandon their search for the highwaymen unless something better—even more exhilarating—had come along to set their mischief-making instincts a-tingling.

He drew a thin cheroot from his pocket, lit it, and leaned back to lose himself in the enjoyment of a good cigar. What was he so worried about, anyway? Having the boys a few counties away would certainly make his chances of catching the highwaymen that much easier. At least he wouldn't have to worry that he might run the chance of blowing a hole in one of the youths while aiming at the highwaymen.

He also, he grimaced ruefully, then might be able to banish from his memory the thought of the boys catching any more glimpses of Alix in that indecent buckskin dress. Not that Jeremy or Billy had really taken too much notice of the expanse of shapely leg Alix had shown when she'd run outside the cottage, but he did not at all like the gleam that had appeared in Cuffy's eyes. That boy was too observant by half, and even now Nicholas's hands clenched into fists as he recalled Cuffy looking back at the cottage as he rode away. The scamp had shouted delightedly, "Oh, I say, ma'am. Good *show!*" before giving Alix a smart salute and proceeding to make good his getaway. If he wouldn't have felt so much a fool for doing so, Linton would have taken Cuffy to task over the incident, but he knew he had been wiser to leave the subject alone. Cuffy would probably just have said something else even more provocative, and Nicholas would have been left to either rant with impotent rage or call the youth out—the latter thought being almost too ridiculous to contemplate.

"Ah, well," he told himself, "at least they are already on their way. I do believe going home today shall be that much easier. Between Jeremy's mother-hen hovering, Billy's inane cant, and Cuffy's knowing looks, I might soon have been driven to Heart's Ease m'self. Now if I could just see my way clear to blasting the Anselms to kingdom come without running afoul of the local constable, I might be able to find life reasonably tolerable."

Just as he was about to rise to his feet and make his way back to his mount, he caught a bit of activity at the entrance to the sweat house and decided to stay and watch Harold at his ablutions. If the Indian seemed much restored by the procedure, he might just give the sweat house a try himself.

However, it was not the tall warrior that Nicholas saw emerging from behind the flung-back flap, but a near-to-naked girl. Wearing naught but a small tan breechclout, Alix rose to her full height outside the sweat house and, her back to the hill and her dumbstruck audience of one, lifted her hands to free her hair from its prison beneath a towel wrapped turbanlike around her head.

The sun slanting through the trees lent a glow to her perspiration-slicked body, and as Nicholas's gaze took in the straight perfection of her legs below the breechclout and the concave sculpting of her smooth back above it, he felt a sheen of perspiration dampening his own skin. Every movement of Alix's lifted arms took the form of sweet torture for the man who sat tensely on the hillside, and his sigh of disappointment was almost audible as her long black hair, once freed from its prison, cascaded down the length of her back, covering her past her waist like a dense cloak.

Nicholas knew that, as a gentleman, he should just then be rapidly making himself scarce. But he also knew that—where Alix was concerned at least—he was no gentleman. He did stand up—more to ease his sudden discomfort and at the same time gain for himself a better view of his betrothed—but he made no move to leave the area. Holding his breath lest she somehow hear his painful, labored breathing, he watched as Alix daintily picked her way through the stones to the edge of the water.

She did not dip a tentative toe into the cold stream, but walked into the water without hesitation, not stopping until she was covered to her middle. Then she stopped, spread her arms wide, and quickly submerged herself three times, lifting her head to the sun each time she emerged from beneath the surface.

"I've died and gone to heaven," Nicholas murmured to himself. Then, "Oh, God, she's coming out!" He felt the need to hold on to something solid as Alix turned and began making her way back toward the bank. "Her dratted hair is in the way," he hissed under his breath. "Come on, Alix, sweetings, push your hair out of the way."

As if in compliance with his impassioned plea, Alix raised her hands to gather her hair above her head. "Ah," Mannering sighed, lost in the rapture of the moment, "there's a love!"

Her rounded hips pushing sinuously against the slight current, Alix continued to make her way slowly toward the shore and the blanket that waited for her there. Nicholas was suddenly beyond all rational thought. He began struggling with his neckcloth—unfortunately tied in the intricate knots of the Mathematical—convinced that Alix wouldn't mind if he joined her. As he shrugged hastily out of his jacket, he cursed the coat's tight tailoring, the need for clothing at all, and for the first time in a long time, the fact that he had but one eye with which to see the beauty before him.

Then the sun seemed to go behind a dark cloud, casting Nicholas in shadow. But it wasn't a cloud that hid the sun, he soon discovered; it was the towering bulk of one highly indignant Lenape Indian. Abandoning his current project—he had just then been vainly trying to tug off one of his Hessians while hopping about on one foot like an indignant stork—Nicholas stood up straight and tried for a look of dignity as he stood before Harold, his neckcloth undone, and one shirttail hanging out over his riding breeches.

Harold was making low, growling sounds that, although he could not understand them, Nicholas was sure were not meant to be an exchange of simple pleasantries between gentlemen. "Don't get your spleen in an uproar, Harold, my friend," Mannering said placatingly. "Honestly, I meant no harm." Seeing the dark scowl on Harold's equally dark face, Nicholas was brought back to complete reality, belatedly facing the fact that the sight of Alix's exquisite body had sent him—an educated, urbane man of the world—posthaste into the very depths of depravity.

"I'm truly sorry, Harold," he apologized again, still wondering—in some dark corner of his mind—whether he was sorry for his *actions* or merely for the untimely *interruption*. But Harold was still talking, his throat working as he spat out his guttural condemnation of Linton, for even an affianced bride was not to be so abused by her betrothed.

As Nicholas retied his neckcloth and pushed his arms into the sleeves of his hacking jacket—taking his good, sweet time about it while more than once casting his eyes in Alix's direction—Harold became impatient at the Earl's dawdling and poked at him with one large hand. "All right, all right," Nicholas responded testily, for truly he was upset, "stop cackling like a hen with one chick. I'm leaving."

Sounds of the commotion at the top of the hill finally traveled down to Alix as she was reaching down to pick up her blanket and she raised her head to see what Harold—for who else could it be but her protector, who had stationed himself on the hillside while she took her sweat—was so upset about.

Her shock-widened eyes locked on Nicholas just as he was turning to take one last glimpse of her. She did not, as he fully expected, shriek, faint, or even fumble wildly in an effort to cover herself with either spread hands or the blanket. Another woman perhaps, but not Alix—not his sweet savage. Instead, she raised herself to her full height and stared him right in the eye—never flinching as he smiled, bowed deeply from the waist, and then threw her a kiss.

Enough was enough and too much was just too much. Harold spat an angry oath, placed his body between Mannering's and Alix's and pointedly put his hand on the hilt of his knife. "No need for violence, Harold, old boy. I'm leaving," Nicholas said, beating a hasty retreat up the hillside.

Once a good twenty feet separated the two men, Nicholas turned one last time to see Alix still standing as she had been, a statue carved in living flesh, and more beautiful than any ancient Greek treasure. Suddenly a knife blade sank into the trunk of the tree just slightly to the left of Nicholas's head. Clearly this was his final warning—Harold could easily have killed him. But even the Indian did not want to so permanently dispatch (in Harold's mind) Alix's last hope at escaping spinsterhood. "Spoilsport," Nicholas told the Indian, raising one hand to finger the glittering blade, and then he saluted the angry warrior and departed without another backward glance.

Once back at Linton Hall, even the pudgy Poole's whining complaints about Mrs. Anselm's plans to refit the drawing room in red velvet could not erase the smile from his lordship's face or remove the spring in his step. And once left alone in his study, he reached for a calendar and happily began marking off the days until January—and his wedding day.

Chapter Nine

IT HAD been five days since Alix had last seen Nicholas—
five days during which she relived the incident at the
stream over and over again in her mind; alternately angered,
embarrassed, or amazed at her reaction to lifting her eyes
and seeing Mannering grinning down the hill at her.

The Earl had been wise to stay away from Saxon Hall for
at least the two days it took Alix to get over the urge to
skewer him on sight with her grandfather's sword. For the
sake of her blushes, it was also considerate of him to absent
himself a further two days, during which time Alix debated
whether she could ever face him again.

But now, on the fifth day, Mannering was doing himself a
great disservice. For she had, after much long thought,
come to the conclusion that, although she knew the emotion
to be most unladylike, she had felt a definite wave of pleasure at Nicholas's obvious appreciation of her feminine
form.

Not that she wouldn't thoroughly upbraid him for his
audacity—indeed, Harold was still grumbling over the
man's insolence—but she was woman enough to know that
Nicholas had very much approved of what he had seen.
Mannering might be arrogant, overbearing, infuriating, and
obstinate, but he was also the most exciting, interesting,
amusing, and *attractive* man she had ever met. If he presented himself at Saxon Hall while she was in this mood of
tense excitement that had kept her pulses racing with the
remnants of last night's rather unladylike dreams of the
man, she might just have leaped into his arms like some
love-crazy hoyden.

But, alas, the Earl did not appear. He was, for once, trying to be the Compleat Gentleman—giving the lady time to recover her poise before he placed himself in her—or the knife-wielding Harold's—vicinity again.

Alix's hopes were raised when Nutter came to fetch her from her efforts to make some order out of her grandfather's cluttered chamber—the place gave new meaning to the term *Gordian knot*—saying she had visitors waiting in the Great Hall. After racing to her own chamber to make hasty repairs on her appearance, and pausing a moment more to press her hand to her breast to steady her erratic breathing, she made a graceful descent to the lower floor—only to find the Unholy Trio taking up residence just outside Harold's wigwam, and a fourth, nervously shivering figure standing somewhat in the shadows near the closest exit.

Cuffy was the first to spy her out. "What ho, ma'am? Here we are, returned from our mission all right and tight. Jolly good fun it was too—though I did at first feel a bit like dear Mother Windsor."

Knowing that Mother Windsor was an infamous procuress in London's King's Place—and also knowing that Alix would demand to know who the lady was—Jeremy quickly jumped in to divert her attention away from his large-mouthed cohort. "Your plan went off with nary a hitch, Alix," he said quickly, then turned in the direction of the cowering shadow. "Come, come now, Reggie, old man. Front and center it is. You must make your bow to your hostess for the next few days."

Slowly, and oh so cautiously—his eyes never leaving the open flap on the wigwam (where Harold's head had appeared briefly some moments before)—the man called Reginald tippytoed his way toward Alix. As he made his painful progress across the room, Billy sidled up to Alix and whispered rather loudly in her ear, "A regular Captain Queernabs, ain't he?"

Alix's sporadic perusal of Billy's cant dictionary allowed her to know that he meant friend Reginald to be a shabby dresser, and her first clear sight of the man only reinforced Billy's comment.

"Welcome to Saxon Hall, Mr. Goodfellow," Alix smiled warmly, extending her hand to the unprepossessing creature standing before her. "We are all *so* very glad you could come."

Reginald mumbled something inaudible and made a jerky bow before returning once more to his dark corner.

"Told ya," Billy pronounced. "Captain Queernabs. Don't flash tatler nor fawney. Coaxes his vampers too, I wager, smack down in his beater cases. And his coat's sleepy."

Cuffy admonished his indiscreet friend. "So he doesn't wear a watch or ring—so what? And as to him pulling down his darned stockings to hide them in his shoes, why, Billy, I've seen you do the same numerous times at school. Leave off the fellow, will you?"

"Yes," Jeremy warned, joining the small group standing in the center of the chamber. "He might bolt else, and then where would we be?"

But Billy had one more insult left in his quiver. "He's beetle-browed," he muttered stubbornly.

Jeremy took a good look at Reginald's rather bushy eyebrows. "Stubble it, Billy," he ordered, trying hard not to laugh. "Those thick brows are his one redeeming feature!"

While Jeremy and Billy cast daggers at each other—clearly the lightning-fast jaunt back and forth across the country had set their nerves on edge—Alix asked Cuffy what his cousin meant by saying Reginald's coat was "sleepy."

"It means old Reggie's coat hasn't had a 'nap' in a long time," Cuffy supplied, his eyes twinkling, and Alix had to hide her face until she could once again gain control of herself.

"Really," she admonished, turning back to Cuffy, "Billy's cant can prove extremely wearing at times, but then again, there are *times* . . ."

"I know what you mean," Cuffy agreed. "Then again there are times when it seems so very appropriate, doesn't it?"

Their badinage at last dwindling, Alix reminded the boys

that only half of their plan had been accomplished. There was still the elopement to consider—and at least one consultation with the eloping bride.

"What if Helene balks at marrying over the anvil?" Jeremy questioned, some of the enormity of what they had done coming home to him. "Then we'd have three Anselms *and* friend Reggie here cluttering up the place!"

"That is not to be thought of!" Alix insisted, passionately. "Our plan will work—it *has* to work!"

The unsuppressible Billy stepped into the breech, saying, "We just lug them off to the gospel shop, have the Autem bawler spout a few whiners over 'em, and—ta da!—they're shut up right and tight in parson's pound. Less, o'course, the old lady tumbles our lay," he added reluctantly. "Then we'll all be put to bed with a mattock and tucked up with a spade. That means"—he performed his own translation of this last; perhaps his anxiety was getting the best of him—"Mrs. A. will *kill* us if she catches even a sniff of what we're about."

Alix, with more bravado than conviction, assured Billy and the rest of them that Mrs. Anselm would never get wind of the elopement. After all, who would tell her? Helene certainly wouldn't jeopardize her one chance at happiness, and Reginald would stay safely secreted at Saxon Hall until the very night of the elopement. Nothing, she assured them, could possibly go wrong.

"One slip and we're for the bubblebath and it'll be the briars for you," Billy warned one last time, obviously quite concerned for their safety.

"I'd rather be in the bubblebath than the briars, Billy," Alix confessed, smiling. "Besides, why must I be stuck with thorns while you all loll about in a pleasant tub?"

"Probably because Nick will know it was you who masterminded this little plan and go after you with blood in his eye," Jeremy told her grimly. Then another thought hit him. "What about your grandfather? What does he say about it?"

Cuffy gave a theatrical sigh. "Ah, yes, Sir Middle Ages. What does he say, ma'am, or have you thought you could hide Reggie here in the dungeon with none the wiser? Your grandfather, I fear, pardon me ma'am, does have the disposition of a curst warthog—not that he's not a famous sport sometimes too, when he's in the mood to be amusing.''

Alix told them that she had finally apprised Sir Alexander of her plan, and as she had expected, the old man had been thrilled with the idea of putting a crimp in Matilda Anselm's matrimonial plans.

Before the boys left—scant moments after Nutter came to announce luncheon—Reginald had been installed in a chamber upstairs and Alix was making plans for a mandatory trip to Linton Hall where she could inform Helene of her beloved's presence in the neighborhood. She warned the boys not to say a word to the girl—as she wished to prepare her for what would doubtless be a bit of a shock.

"You really like Helene, Alix," Jeremy said. "That's awfully sporting of you, seeing as how she's dashed in the way."

"Don't be silly, Jeremy," Alix denied pleasantly. "I don't care a button for such a dead bore of a girl. I'm merely clearing the field for a battle of my own."

"You don't like her at all?" Cuffy asked, clearly puzzled. "Then why go to all this trouble to help her?"

"Oh, I guess I do like her a bit, although she is, you must admit, a particularly spineless chit," Alix expanded a bit. "Like m'grandfather, the idea of besting Mrs. Anselm has gone a long way toward making this a pleasant project. But as I also said, I have my own battles to fight. Above all things, I desire anyone not involved in my war out of the way before I take to the field."

"Nicholas," Jeremy nodded, sure he was correct in his assessment when Alix suddenly looked a bit flustered and unsure of herself. "Do us all a favor, Alix, will you," he begged with an exaggerated shiver, "and warn us when this battle is to take place. I don't know whether I wish to be a hundred miles from here or if I'd rather sell tickets to the spectacle. But I do know I will want to be a good distance away from the line of fire. You and m'brother battling— why, it makes Waterloo sound like a picnic in the park!"

The boys left then and Alix returned to her endless house-cleaning. It wasn't that she truly enjoyed working with a mop and a pail; it was just her love of order that kept her working—that, and a strong desire to keep herself too busy to think about things best left alone. But this afternoon she found even the chore of cleaning the chicken bones out from beneath Sir Alexander's bed was not sufficient diversion.

Nicholas was on her mind—again. Her brave words to the boys about this eagerly awaited battle she had been contemplating for so long had fallen hollow on her ears. She had known for some time now—even if she had not before admitted it to herself—that she had no desire to see Nicholas stripped of his lands and fortune.

Now, she worried even more about Mannering's stubborn *pride*. Taking aim at his lands and fortune was bad enough, but a direct hit in his pride—which was what proving the parchment legitimate would be—would also be the death knell to any relationship between the two of them.

And suddenly Alix wanted that relationship more than anything else in the world.

Alix's quick scrutiny took in the people occupying the room, and she gave an almost audible sigh of relief when she saw that Nicholas was not one of their number. She had dreaded seeing him again, but the need to talk with Helene had overborne her sensibilities, and here she was—Sir Alexander bringing up a reluctant rear—once again a dinner guest at Linton Hall.

"Ah, you have arrived at last, Miss Saxon," Mrs. Anselm observed unnecessarily, spying her out. "Come, come now, dear," the lady went on cuttingly, "one must not stand about gawking when one is being entertained in a gentleman's home. No, no! One must at least take on a semblance of knowing what one's about—like greeting one's hostess, for one thing. Come here, girl, and let me look at you."

As Alix, choking down the urge to give the smirking Mrs. Anselm a poke in her hatchet nose, came closer, she limited herself to only a verbal poke, saying sweetly, *"One* must first discover a hostess in residence, mustn't *one*, Mrs. Anselm? As you too are a guest in this house, perhaps you would be so kind as to point her out? Although," she added, seemingly as an afterthought, "I did not know that in England it is customary to greet a hostess whose only presence in the residence is in a likeness captured on canvas." Alix's eyes slid to the portrait of the late Countess of Linton hanging over the fireplace before once again settling on the flushed face of Mrs. Anselm.

"Helene!" Mrs. Anselm whined, touching a hand to her brow. "I feel quite faint. Fetch me my lavender drops at once."

By now Sir Alexander was already in possession of his first drink of the evening—but not his first of the day, not by a long chalk. "Oh, stubble it, Matilda," he said most unkindly. "You're as strong as a brace of donkeys. Why don't you just admit it—you've been bested by my granddaughter here. She has more than just the look of her grandmother, y'know; she's got her same sure way around a set down. Best keep your tongue in check, old girl, 'cause even if you do fill out that settee you're perched on, you aren't up to m'granddaughter's weight!"

While it was to be expected that such a statement should reduce Cuffy, Jeremy, and Billy to near insensibility—so manfully were they trying to suppress their giggles—it was with some surprise that Alix observed Rupert smiling broadly into his lace cuffs, obviously quite amused at his mama's discomfiture. So that's how the land lies, Alix thought, storing away the knowledge for possible future use.

Just then the host of the little party made his own entrance, and Alix, her back turned to him, stiffened noticeably as she heard his voice raised in apology for his tardiness.

She turned slowly at his individual greeting, sure she would dissolve completely once subjected to his sure-to-be-insolent eyeing of her person. Her eyes searched his handsome face with a look so fraught with uncertainty that Nicholas, in his turn, was hard-pressed not to gather her into his arms and croon to her that he would never do anything to harm a single hair on her head.

Time seemed to stand suspended as the two exchanged these silent looks, time during which the rest of the room and its occupants faded away, leaving them alone on their own private island. Slowly, as she realized Nicholas was not going to give her away, Alix's brow cleared and she was able to give him a small smile of thanks. But when Mannering then nodded his acknowledgment, the spell was broken, and Alix found herself becoming quite angry with the man. How dare he condescend to *allow* herself his protection when it is *he* who should be hauled out of here and drawn and quartered for his horrid conduct!

Nicholas saw the different expressions fleeting across Alix's face and knew all the way down to his toes (just now curling inside his shoes) that it was the devil to pay now for sure. Once Alix had him alone he would get the sharp side of her tongue—not that he didn't deserve it.

Acknowledging to himself that it was only a matter of time before the ax would fall, but also cognizant that Alix would not deliver the blow until they had no risk of an interested audience, Nicholas accepted the drink Jeremy was holding out to him and took up a stance at the fireplace, eager to have this before dinner ritual of drinks and polite conversation over with as soon as possible.

Helene, noticing that it might be up to someone of a gentler disposition to inject a little politeness into the tense atmosphere, took up a position near Alix and began to ask her about Harold, for lack of any other subject coming swiftly to mind. "I understand from Jeremy that your Indian paints his face black as a show of mourning for your father. Isn't that rather odd?"

Before Alix could comment, Mrs. Anselm—with more brass than brains—opened her mouth once more. "*Civilized* gentlemen limit themselves to black gloves, or perhaps a black armband, you know."

"Yes, Mama, that's right," Helene agreed, adding, "and even the ladies wore black ribbons on their dresses when brave Admiral Nelson was killed."

The insertion of Nelson's name into the conversation kept Alix from swiftly pointing out that a truly "civilized" person did not go around talking about another behind that person's back, and she only observed mildly, "I was amazed to read in my guide book of all the various monuments you people have put up for Nelson. Do you know, we Americans have not a single monument honoring our own great President, George Washington, in our own country, save one done by some Frenchman that stands in the Virginia state capital. I cannot decide if we honor our heroes too little or you honor yours too much."

Alix had made a tactical error, for her grandfather was not about to sit back and listen to anyone, even his granddaughter, belittle his country. "By Jupiter, girl, how dare you mention our Nelson and that upstart Washington in the same breath?"

Now Mrs. Anselm pricked up her ears, eager to get some of her own back. "Now, Sir Alexander, don't be too hard on the girl, I pray you," she trilled with patently false concern. "After all, as the girl says, she is not *truly* English. What can an American know of such things as honor and reverence—they who turned their backs on us and dragged us through two dreadful wars?"

"Both of which those upstart Americans won," Rupert put in quietly, once again proving that even such a mincing puppy dog as himself possessed some wit.

Mrs. Anselm, sighing the deep sigh of the truly afflicted parent, pushed herself against the back of the settee and waved her handkerchief about her face, filling the air with the cloying mint of patchouli. "Rupert," she purred with underlying iron in her voice, "you will kindly refrain from such nastiness in my presence. Really, I do believe a sojourn in Germany with your Uncle Maximillian might be in order for you."

At this open threat to banish him to his uncle's ancient *schloss,* Rupert knew himself bested and retired from the conflict. Alix decided there and then that, while Rupert might applaud from the sidelines whenever his mama was bested, he would refrain from ever openly standing against her. No, Rupert could not be counted upon to help his sister, that was as plain as the beauty patch on his face.

Nicholas watched this give-and-take with a heavy heart. He had been slowly chipping away at Mrs. Anselm's resolve to have Helene become his bride, and last night he had at last come to believe the woman had realized she was building mare's nests with her hopes after her latest, most daring scheme of all had fallen through.

He had gone to his darkened chamber after a late night spent hovering over the estate books and had been in the process of stripping down to the buff—which was his normal routine, as he slept in the nude—when a slight whimpering from the direction of his bed caught his attention.

Hastily jumping back into his clothes, he lit his bedside lamp and discovered the frightened eyes of Helene Anselm peeping out at him from under the bedcovers. In an instant he knew that Mrs. Anselm (and a servant or two she had collared to witness the compromised pair in bed) was hovering about just outside his chamber door until she was sure he was abed. But Helene, bless her, did not possess either the starch or the inclination for such intrigue and had alerted him with her noisy sobs. Putting a finger to his lips, Mannering had held out his hand to the trembling girl, drawing her to her feet before sneaking her out to the side hallway through his dressing room. Once he had shooed her back to her own room, he took a quick trip down the backstairs before returning to his chamber, stripping, and climbing into bed. "Oho!" he then had cried loudly, "What are you about, *lying in my bed?*" When Mrs. Anselm, followed by one reluctant-looking underfootman, had burst into the room, the Earl was standing in the middle of his room, naked as the day he was born, holding up one gray and black striped kitten he had purloined from the kitchen.

Even now Nicholas could not suppress a smile as he remembered the look on Mrs. Anselm's face as she turned and ran from his chamber like all the hounds of hell were after her. He had truly believed that the lady had now shot her bolt—there were no other ploys for her to try—and she would pack up and be on her way. But now, now that Alix had so carelessly let herself be drawn into showing herself in a bad light, Mrs. Anselm was smiling with a burst of new hope. She'll dig in now for the duration, he told himself grimly, finishing his drink in one angry swallow. Trust Alix to put the cat among the pigeons.

While Nicholas had been ruminating on the events of the previous night, Alix had been happily talking with the three boys, all of whom seemed to have a great interest in how things were done in America as opposed to their own English traditions.

At that moment she was—propelled by some imp of mischief that had taken up residence in her brain—describing the outlawed but still practiced mode of courting called bundling. "Oh yes, boys," Nicholas overheard her saying with a remarkable lack of guile, "it was quite the custom to have the courting couple lying, fully dressed I must tell you, in the same bed, with only a bolster keeping them apart. It can get quite cold in America, you see, and it was done to preserve heat in the cold weather. I understand that, even though it has been against the law to practice bundling since 1785, it is still widely in use in at least the western parts of my home, the Commonwealth of Pennsylvania."

"Well, I must say, Alix," Cuffy put in irrepressibly, "it sounds like a whacking great custom to me. Pity the government had to go and get their backs up about such a perfectly splendid idea." At Nicholas's frown the boy added belatedly, "To conserve heat, sir. It was a good idea to save heat—that's what I meant!"

Fortunately, Poole chose that moment to call them all to dinner, not that Alix's mood had eased enough for her to see the sense in keeping her mouth shut and letting others toss the conversational ball back to within the bounds of polite dinner table talk. Oh no, she was not about to do any such thing.

They were not at table five minutes when she turned to Jeremy—she and the rest of the younger generation were, thanks to Mrs. Anselm, again seated below the salt, while only Helene was somehow put at Nicholas's right hand—

and began telling him about the time Philadelphia had played host to royalty.

"From 1796 until his departure in 1799 France's Louis Philippe resided in our city, his lodgings in a solitary room above a tavern. He called himself the King of the French and boasted that he would one day rule France—he was a Bourbon-Orléans, you know.

"Well," Alix went on, sure of the interest of her audience, "while he was peacocking about in society he took it into his head to ask for the hand of the well-to-do daughter of our senator, William Bingham. The senator forbade the match, however, pointing out that if Louis were indeed to be King of France, he was too good for his daughter, and if he were *not*, then the senator's daughter was quite above Louis's touch! It was perhaps fortunate for Louis that the senator was so astute, for I have read that in 1809 Louis was married to a daughter of the King of the Two Sicilies and is now living on the Orléans estates in France."

Nicholas heard everything Alix had been saying and, knowing her grandfather had little love for the French (actually, the man had little love for anybody), tried to bring her tale to a hasty conclusion. "I hear even now the republicans wish to make him a citizen king over Charles X—not that any French government lasts for more than a sennight," he said with an air of finality on the subject.

But Alix was not to be thwarted. "Ah, yes, that word brings back memories of my childhood—*citizen,* that is. We Americans were very sympathetic with the French and their revolution—having had one of our own against oppression not that long ago—and even took to calling each other *citizen* when we met on the streets. I remember, although I was quite young at the time, being taken by my father to watch a reenactment of the beheading of Louis XVI at The Sign of the Black Bear theater and tavern."

"Bah!" Sir Alexander exploded. "It figures that rogues would stand together. Damned Colonials and damned Froggies—two of a kind. Mannering, I need a cup of the creature to wash out my mouth. Where in blazes do you keep your gin? Last thing I need is this namby-pamby

Froggie wine you're serving!'' As Poole ran to fetch a decanter, Sir Alexander muttered under his breath, ''Probably knows all the words to that cursed Frenchie song and all the rest of that damn bilge. My own flesh and blood—who would believe it!''

''You mean the 'Marseillaise,' Sir Alexander?'' Mrs. Anselm egged the man on sweetly, drawing out the full flavor of his anger against his granddaughter.

''I don't mean 'God Save the King,' you daft female!'' the man was goaded into responding before Poole arrived with the decanter and Sir Alexander slumped over his glass, intent on getting himself well and truly drunk.

The remainder of the meal passed well enough, with Mrs. Anselm pushing Helene at Nicholas's head and Alix determinedly flirting with the three boys. Sir Alexander again served to amuse his tablemates (some of them) by once more nearly diving into his fingerbowl as he cleaned himself up after his meal. Then, shunning all entreaties to the contrary, he stayed at table sipping gin long after everyone else had retired to the drawing room.

The company then seemed to divide itself into separate parties consisting of all females and all males as the gentlemen discussed politics and the ladies listened to Mrs. Anselm talk. She went on at great length too, telling Alix of her ambitious plans for the gardens at Linton Hall. ''I envision a copper umbrella in the west garden, a large affair with a circular iron seat underneath to sit upon if one desires some shade. And of course there shall be an aviary built in the flower garden.''

''I dislike the idea of caging birds, no matter how pretty their prison,'' Alix said disgustedly, above all things wishing the lady would take the hint and shut up. Really, however was she to have a coze with Helene if her mama continued sticking to their sides like a barnacle!

Mrs. Anselm, her plan being to show how firmly she was entrenched at Linton Hall, went on doggedly, ''And what do you think about building a garden wall on the east prospect—covering it with moss and lichen to make it homey looking?" she pressed Alix.

"To be truthful, ma'am, I think very little about it either way, as my interests don't lie in that quarter."

"That's true enough, Mama," Helene said conversationally, not understanding this byplay a jot. "Alix is much more interested in housekeeping—or so I once overheard Nicholas tease her when he asked if she had run out of dustcloths yet."

"Really?" Mrs. Anselm exclaimed, eyeing Alix distastefully down the length of her long nose. "How very—er—*domestic* of you, dear. *I* have always left that sort of thing to the servants, you know."

Alix bundled her hands into tight fists, torn between a desire to fling something in Mrs. Anselm's snickering face and an even stronger urge to kick Nicholas—the loudmouthed looby—in the shins. In the end, she said nothing and Mrs. Anselm was left to savor her victory, for just then Cuffy wandered over, eager to try out an idea of his on the ladies.

"I've been thinking, you know," he began before Jeremy, who had followed along as a matter of course, piped up irrepressibly, "There's a first!"

Turning quelling eyes on his friend, Cuffy cleared his throat and began again. "As I was saying before I was so *rudely* interrupted," he pursued doggedly, "I was thinking, since we seem to be a sort of house party here anyway, and the holidays are coming on—what do you say to putting on a pantomime or some such thing?"

His idea was met by shouts of "Good show!" from the younger members of the party and a groan of despair from Nicholas—who now gave up the last lingering traces of hope that he would be able to shove the Anselms out before January. The way his luck was running, the countryside would then be hit with the worst blizzard in a decade and the whole bunch of them would be sponging off him until the spring thaw!

Quickly, Nicholas voiced his objections to the idea, saying rather firmly that Mrs. Anselm had told him only that morning at breakfast (after he had confronted her about her activities of the night before) that she and her children would be removing to their own residence within a week.

"That's time and enough to do something," Cuffy objected, unaware or uncaring of any underlying tensions. "It wouldn't have to be anything elaborate—just a single evening with a few skits and some dancing."

"What exactly did you have in mind?" Alix asked the youth, her agile mind turning over a plan of her own. "Will there be costumes involved—or *masks?*"

It was Jeremy who realized what Alix was thinking. It would be so easy to slip Reginald into Linton Hall in the midst of a party, especially if there were masks involved. Who would notice the eminently unnoticeable Reggie when he entered alongside the county gentry—or when he slipped out again, Helene by his side? It was perfect—so perfect he was sorry he had not thought of it himself. Immediately he began voicing his strong desire to have Linton Hall thrown open for such a party and even began casting the others in the roles they should play in the pantomime.

"Nick, you must be Lord Dashaway, of course," he bubbled merrily, "and Cuffy is perfect for Lord Flirt Away."

Cuffy, not one to be left out of anything—and especially not one to be left out of something he had instigated—piped up, "Billy will make a perfect Spantu Long Tong Song, don't you know, and Rupert could be Lord Dumble Dum Deary to the life!"

"What about me?" Jeremy asked with some trepidation.

"Lord Lollypop," Billy supplied promptly, earning himself a roar of laughter all round.

"And the ladies?" Nicholas asked, resigning himself to his fate.

"Helene would perhaps like to be Lady Languish," Jeremy suggested, "but I don't know about Alix and Mrs. Anselm."

"How about Mrs. Strut for Mrs. Anselm?" Nick suggested, knowing his sarcasm would flow neatly over that woman's empty head. "And as for Alix," he went on with the air of a man who would as lief be hanged for a pig as a shoat, "Alix is Fanny Fandango to the life!"

"Oh, I say, Nick, that's famous!" Jeremy agreed enthusiastically. "I know we have some old scripts about somewhere. What say we put our heads together? Cuffy, Billy—you too, Rupert—come with me to the library. I'm sure we'll unearth something useful."

"Oh, but I had hoped we could dance for a bit this evening," Helene complained, right after receiving a sound nudge in the ribs from her mama. "Mama plays quite nicely, you know, and has volunteered to provide the music for us."

Reluctantly Jeremy, remembering his manners, agreed to the scheme and they adjourned to the music room, where Mrs. Anselm took her place at the piano and began beating out a tune. Nicholas, of course, partnered Helene as she was his house guest, and Jeremy led Alix into the lively country dance while Billy, Cuffy, and Rupert propped up the walls with their shoulders.

As an idea for pushing her daughter into Linton's arms, it was not a resounding success. Even Mrs. Anselm could see how shadowy Helene's milk-and-water looks appeared next to the flash and verve of Alix's vibrant coloring and features. While they were still with their original partners, Mrs. Anselm struck up a waltz, determined to take advantage of every opportunity that presented itself.

"I don't know how to waltz," Jeremy apologized, his steps coming to a halt after he had trod on Alix's toes three times in as many moments. "Sorry."

Seeing another way to slay two birds with one stone, so to speak, the redoubtable (and hopelessly obtuse) Mrs. Anselm trilled, "Oh, my Rupert is at home to a peg on the dance floor. He shall partner you, dear."

"I should be delighted!" Rupert said, taking his cue.

Suddenly Nicholas had had enough of the whole thing. The dancing was just one more bad idea heaped on top of a huge pile of bad ideas, and the thought of Rupert's lily-white hands touching his Alix was just too much.

"Delighted my Aunt Alice!" the Earl nearly shouted, so overborne was he. "Do, and I shall likely toss you down the stairs!"

"Nick!" his brother was startled into exclaiming. "I know she's your betrothed but you're coming on a bit strong, ain't you? You can't fly into a pet just because she dances with someone else."

"In a love fit," Billy pointed out with more honesty than tact.

It was left to Cuffy, of all people, to step into the breech, as no one else seemed to be doing anything more constructive than standing about staring at each other, and he did so with his typical blend of sophistication and youthful candor. "No need for anyone to fall into a twitter," he said calmly, placing himself between Nicholas and the person who seemed most likely to plant the Earl a facer, his fiancée. "May I suggest that Helene and Alix, who I know have been yearning for a few minutes of female talk, retire to the drawing room while Mrs. Anselm and I tidy up in here? Billy, you and Rupert and Jeremy go spy out that script in the library. And Nick—" He turned to face his host, who was just then standing with a look of suppressed fury on his handsome face. "I do believe someone should check on Sir Alexander. It is entirely possible, considering his mood when we left the table, that the poor old fellow has drunk his way into a slight decline."

As the party seemed universally receptive to having someone telling them just how they should go on—for indeed the atmosphere in the music room was become uncomfortably *warm* and they all would like nothing more than to escape it—everyone readily fell in with Cuffy's plan and quickly scattered to their assigned areas.

After a few minutes spent helping Mrs. Anselm reassemble her music sheets and convincing the woman she looked rather pulled and should perhaps decide on an early night (with his usual lack of subtlety, Cuffy's comments on Mrs. Anselm's appearance had the woman racing to her mirror to inspect herself for indications that the end was near), the aspiring diplomat joined his friends in the library, where they discussed the pantomime and, after Rupert's departure from the room, Alix's obvious, to them at least, plans for the elopement to take place that same night.

In the meantime, Alix and Helene shared a settee in the drawing room while the former apprised the latter of much the same thing—holding Helene's trembling hand and administering a sniff of burnt feathers when the silly chit decided to swoon dead away at the thought of seeing her beloved Reginald once more.

It seemed, to Alix anyway, to have taken an unconscionable amount of time to explain the elopement plan to Helene (once the girl had roused from her swoon), and even now, sitting alone in the drawing room after the fainthearted girl had been safely delivered into the hands of her maid, Alix had more than a few misgivings as to whether or not the chit possessed the backbone to so defy her mama.

Alix rose from her seat and walked to the glass doors overlooking the garden. "How did I ever get caught up in this coil?" she asked herself aloud, before sighing deeply and stepping onto the flagstones outside, hoping the chilly night air would help to clear her mind.

"Come out here to make your own plans for redesigning the grounds, have you, *hmm?* I warn you—I'll brook no miniature Indian village on the south lawns."

"Nicholas! You startled me." Alix peered into the darkness beyond the light cast from the chandelier in the drawing room and the Earl emerged from the shadows, a cheroot stuck in the corner of his mouth.

"Sorry, darling," he apologized insincerely, tossing away the unlit cigar. "I have just spent a very trying half hour helping Poole and two footmen disengage your grandfather from his death grip around my gin decanter. He's sleeping it off in the study right now, and with any luck we'll be able to heft him into your carriage for the ride home within the hour."

Alix hung her head. "I am sorry my behavior at table prompted poor Grandfather to dive into your gin supply. I was mean-spirited enough to try to disconcert that odious Mrs. Anselm and forgot your warnings about Sir Alexander's antipathy toward foreigners."

Nicholas smiled warmly, his white teeth flashing in the

moonlit night, and suggested that perhaps a certain discomfiture with being faced with his presence for the first time since the "incident" at the stream may also have muddled her thought processes a bit.

"Oh!" Alix sneered scornfully. "I should have known better than to think you wouldn't comment on that. It seems I have made two errors tonight—trying to get some of my own back on Mrs. Anselm and inadvertently setting up Grandfather's hackles, and trusting you to act the gentleman when doing so would have set a precedent you could never live up to if you lived a thousand years!"

"Now, now, my savage," Nicholas interposed hastily before Alix could turn on her heel and run away, "you are being most unfair. An English gentleman, I'll have you know, considers his reputation as a gentleman to be his most valuable possession. I'll not let you destroy my good name so easily. To be considered a real English gentleman, you see, means that such a man must not lie, go back on his word, or flinch from the consequences of his actions. Nowhere does this code advise being such a gudgeon as to leave so earthshaking an event as the one shared by us at the stream unmentioned—to do so would soon build a wall between us that might be impossible to tear down. I hereby present the subject, prepared—nay, eager—for the consequences."

"Piffle!" Alix answered indignantly.

"That's one way of putting it, I guess," Mannering acknowledged with a shrug, "but at least having the subject out in the open now, we can perhaps discuss it and clear the air."

"I'd rather close the subject, thank you anyway, by the simple expediency of *never speaking to you again!*" So saying, she turned sharply as if to leave him, but she had taken no more than two steps before Nicholas took hold of her arm and whirled her back to face him.

"I said we'll talk about it, dammit!" he growled with some force. "I can't sleep, I can't eat—all I can do is think about it—I *have* to talk about it!"

"Force those thoughts from your mind then, my lord,"

Alix responded icily. "Find yourself an engrossing hobby, and employ a soothing draught at bedtime."

Nicholas bit off a pithy laugh. "Ha! Only a heavy red brick applied sharply to the side of my head could ever put me out too deep for dreams—very *disturbing* dreams. No, I feel my only hope for sanity is to exorcise the demons from my brain by living out my fantasy."

Suddenly Alix found herself clamped tightly in Nicholas's arms as his lips came down to claim hers in a kiss born of desperation. Neither of them content with namby-pamby shows of affection, the two vitally alive, tinglingly aware forms at once melted together in an explosion of passion that left them both trembling when it was over. Standing closely together, still locked in each other's arms, Alix murmured shakily against his shoulder, "I do believe you've compromised me yet again, my lord."

Nicholas placed nibbling kisses up and down the smooth column of her throat, pausing only long enough to whisper into her ear, "Compromise no longer has anything to do with it, puss. I love you, you know."

Alix stiffened in his arms, then relaxed against him. "Truly, Nick?" she asked, her voice wavering just a little bit.

"Truly," he promised, his tongue making tiny circles behind her ear and devastating inroads on her heightened emotions.

"I—I have found myself growing quite—er—*fond* of you too," she confessed, her right hand sliding upward and making tentative contact with the dark hairs that curled slightly at his nape.

"Fond of me, are you?" he teased. "Pray, continue. You edify me extremely."

Alix should have known he wouldn't let her off so easily. For some reason, one she could not explain even to herself, she found her inhibitions swept away like cobwebs whenever he held her in his arms. But to voice her feelings— actually put them into words—made her vulnerable to whole worlds of insecurities she had found alien only a short time ago (about the length of time she had known Mannering, as a matter of fact).

But now the time had come for truth, and he wasn't about to let her go without a full confession of her feelings for him. Sighing deeply, she then squared her shoulders and moved to look him full in the face. "I love you, Nicholas," she stated firmly, earning herself a renewed assault on her senses as the Earl then began, by means of an immediate demonstration, her education of the heights to which two people who love each other can travel.

It wasn't the cold that at last drew them back to reality, nor was it a show of reticence by an innocent young woman perhaps a bit frightened by this serious excursion into delight. No, it was Lord Linton himself who broke things off between them before his passion, burning exceedingly high at that moment, overtook him completely and he carried Alix off to his chamber willy-nilly. Reluctantly pushing Alix away from him, he straightened her gaping bodice and led her back into the still-empty drawing room, indicating she sit down while he took a moment to pour himself a half-beaker of strong brandy. "We have to talk, sweetings," he told her with a heaviness in his voice that set her nerves a-tingling.

He came over to the settee and, rather than sitting beside her, dropped to one knee on the floor at her feet. "Alix," he said, finding his voice only after the air in the room had become decidedly tense, "you must know how much it means to me to have my love for you returned—you *have* to know that. It will make it easier, never easy, for me to now tell you that I don't think I can marry you."

Alix didn't understand. "Is it Helene?" she asked, searching his face for the answer while, inside, something beautiful that was just then beginning to flower, withered and died.

"A pox on Helene—and her mother too!" the Earl denied hotly. "If only it were that easy. No, it is not Helene. It's the parchment."

"What has that silly scrap of paper to say to anything?"

Alix argued, already knowing her worst fears were being realized.

Nicholas rose and began pacing the carpet in front of the settee. "You were right in saying I was no gentleman, Alix, for I already knew our marriage was not to be before what just happened—or should I say, very nearly happened—in the garden. Only a cad could take advantage of your sweetness like that, but I had to have one last moment of happiness in your arms, tell you I loved you, before releasing you from our engagement."

He turned to look down at her. "You see, Alix, I received a letter from my lawyer in yesterday's post—just as I was about to indulge my impulse to ride over to Saxon Hall and confess my love for you, as a matter of fact. I wasn't just teasing you when I said I haven't been sleeping since I saw you at the stream. I've been like a man demented—aching to hold you in my arms."

Alix had begun to stiffen in her seat. "Go on."

He shrugged. "The contents of the letter stopped me in my tracks, but, weak-kneed jellyfish that I am, I could not hold myself back when I came upon you tonight outside. It shouldn't have happened, Alix, but I cannot apologize for what will doubtless become, in my memory, the happiest moment of my life. But the fact remains—we cannot wed. The parchment is entirely legal."

Springing to her feet, Alix cried hotly, "So what? What does it matter if Linton Hall is actually a Saxon possession? It will revert back to you as soon as we're married anyway, won't it? I fail to see what all this fuss is about—unless you are just looking for an easy way to have your cake and eat it too?" she ended, her voice hardening.

"You're not thinking rationally, Alix," he corrected. "If you are thinking I want your charms without banns, you must remember that I would still be losing Linton Hall."

She hung her head. "You're right, of course. I wasn't thinking—just reacting." She looked up again, pinning him with her eyes. "But I still don't see why the authenticity of the parchment, if, and I do mean *if,* your lawyer is correct, bans a marriage between a Mannering and a Saxon?"

"You will have to excuse this pale imitation of an English gentleman, but I fear my folly knows no bounds. I find I can marry you for love, but I cannot marry you for material gain."

"But all you English lords and ladies do just that," Alix protested with a dismissing sweep of her hand. "Why are you so different?"

"Have you never, then, heard of 'honor,' Alix?" he sighed, his golden eye searching her now tear-stained face for understanding.

Alix returned his look for long, anguished moments before she turned away, saying with a definite air of defeat, "As usual, your arguments are unanswerable, Nicholas." Alix was down, that was certain, but she was a long way from out. Shortly she rallied, whirling to say, "How sure is this lawyer of yours? Surely you will not simply take his word for it without another opinion?" She spread her arms wide. "Barristers, solicitors, counselors—there must be thousands of them. Surely we should seek other advice before accepting any judgment as final. Think, Nicholas, damn your honorable hide, *think!*"

Mannering stood back and applauded softly. "Well done, Alexandra! We could have used you at Waterloo. You're right, of course. As Cervantes said, 'Faint heart ne'er won fair lady.' I *shall* consult someone else, I promise."

"Right!" Alix pronounced, with more bravado than conviction. "No need to be downpin until we're certain." Privately, in her heart of hearts, she was nowhere near as confident as she made out to her betrothed, but it wouldn't do to let him know. Then there was the idea fast taking hold of her brain—finding a way of so compromising his lordship that, parchment and honor be hanged, he would have no *choice* but to wed her. No, it wouldn't do to let him know that either. Suffice it that they take this thing one step at a time. Who could say? Perhaps another lawyer would declare the parchment invalid. If not—well, she would think about that later.

For now she was content to convince Mannering that, seeing as how they were still at least officially affianced, they could indulge in just a teeny bit more kissing and such before rousing Sir Alexander. But her efforts to draw him into her embrace were thwarted by his firmly disengaging her arms from about his neck. "No, my torment," he denied her whispered entreaties with a slow shake of his head, "we cannot. It isn't right."

Alix suddenly became angry—quite angry. "Enact me no tragedies, Nicholas," she warned, obviously incensed. "This honor you speak about so earnestly is becoming more than a little bit of a bore. You demonstrated no such sensibilities when you all but seduced me under the azalea bushes not so many minutes ago. I find this honor of yours to be convenient for you while it is tedious for me. Either you love me or you don't. Honor—bah! Sometimes, Mannering, I think you're no more than a pompous English *ass!*"

For some reason Alix's outburst, combined as it was with a becoming flush to her cheeks and a truly remarkable heaving up and down of her scantily covered breasts, served to restore a good bit of Linton's customary good humor. Feigning a look of supreme hurt at her injustice, he remarked casually, "It seems a marked friction has developed between us, madam."

"I'll give you a marked friction all right—square between the eyes!" she shouted. "I'm going home. Call Poole to help you heave the old man into the coach."

When Nicholas made no move to do as she had bid, but merely stood in the center of the room grinning like the village idiot, Alix marched huffily over to the corner of the room and gave the bellpull hanging there three mighty tugs.

Now, considering the fact that bell ropes had found no place in Charles Saxon's modest Philadelphia home, and considering the fact that bell ropes had not even been invented before 1760 and such modern conveniences would never have been allowed in Saxon Hall anyway, it was perhaps forgivable for Alix to have walked all the way to the corner of the room to tug on this particular rope rather than to pass close beside the so-obtuse Nicholas to reach the pull she had seen him use on other occasions.

Yes, it was forgivable. But it was also very, very funny—or at least so Nicholas thought when he at first began to warn her, then just as quickly decided to do no such thing, but just to stand back and watch what happened.

Alix's strong tugs on the rope set off a loud clanging somewhere at the top of the house, a tremendous, raucous, clanging of Linton Hall's *fire bell. "Oh, make it stop!"* Alix shouted above the din, clapping her hands over her ears.

Within moments the drawing room was near to overflowing with people: servants carrying blankets and hatchets; Cuffy and Jeremy shouting for someone to "bring buckets! bring water!"; Helene—still in her gown, for she had decided to dream about her Reginald for a while before retiring —giving delicate little screams and looking about for someone to save her from a fiery death; and Rupert, clutching to his chest three or four jackets from Weston that he prized almost as much as he did the little black engagement book he now held clenched between his teeth.

"Nick! Are you all right?" Jeremy shouted above the noise. "Where's the fire? Water!" he yelled toward the group of frightened servants. "Won't somebody bring me water!"

Just then Mrs. Anselm raced into the drawing room, her hair done up in papers and a near pint of night cream on her face. Clutching her pink, ruffled peignoir closed across her ample bosom, she too shouted, "Yes, Yes! Water! Somebody fetch some water! *Hurry, before we are all burned!"* Then she turned once more toward the hallway, obviously about to flee the inferno, only to run smack into Billy, who—being a dutiful soul and not one to panic in such a situation—was running full tilt into the drawing room carrying, quite naturally, the bucket of water everyone had been bellowing about.

They collided with the force of two cannonballs meeting in midair and then bounced backward, landing rump down on the hallway floor, the bucket still firmly in Billy's grip, but the water now all relocated on the person of Mrs. Anselm.

As everyone in the drawing room stood stock still,

stunned into silence, Sir Alexander careened drunkenly into the picture, looked down at Mrs. Anselm's soaking wet, sputtering form, and remarked with drunken incredulity, "By Jupiter, either I'm more cupshot than I think or that's Matilda Anselm sitting there on the floor looking for all the world like one of m'hounds when he comes in out of the rain. Come on now, speak to me—or bark or something— anything to tell me I'm not seeing things."

"Oh shut up, you old fool!" the lady shrieked hysterically at Sir Alexander as he bent over to peer down at her with his bloodshot eyes. "Get away from me! Rupert! Get over here and help me up. What are you waiting for, you stupid child? Hurry, before this drunken sot falls on me!"

Somehow order was restored and the drawing room was again returned to some semblance of sanity—the servants banished, the guests assured there was no fire, and Mrs. Anselm (now wrapped in a blanket, a few bits of sodden paper and night cream clinging to her cheeks and the tip of her nose) reclining against the long couch, her ministering children at her side.

"It was just a drill, people," Nicholas was apologizing for the umpteenth time, manfully shielding Alix from embarrassment.

"And *I* say it's a mighty queer time for a fire drill," Mrs. Anselm accused him, wagging a finger in his direction and then sputtering as a piece of one of her night papers got caught on her tongue.

"What's the sense of having a fire drill in the daytime when everyone's alert?" he countered. "I was checking on my household's ability to handle such a danger at night— when everyone is relaxed, off their guard."

"We were that, all right," Jeremy inserted, unable to look anyone in the face for fear he'd destroy the uneasy peace by bursting into loud peals of laughter—for Mrs. Anselm surely did look a fair treat. "Could have at least told the ladies, though, Nick. Warned them, you might say."

"Yes," Mrs. Anselm attacked from her couch. "It was very vexatious at the least to have frightened us so. Besides," she added, yet another plan forming in her devious mind, "between the effects of the shock you have dealt Helene and me, and the putrid cold I am sure to develop after being doused with icy water, I do believe I shall be in no fit state to travel within the next fortnight. We will have no choice but to infringe upon your hospitality until then—or longer if I am not quite recovered. It is really too bad of you," she ended rather more gently, seeing as how events had once again somehow worked in her favor, "and I had *so* wanted to spend Christmas at home."

"Christmas! Why that's nearly a month away," Cuffy pointed out, dreading the thought of the Anselms still being underfoot for the holidays. Then he remembered the pantomime set for the following Saturday night and the elopement that was to follow it and relaxed. "Yes, well," he began, "you may yet be home in time for Father Christmas, if everything—"

"Cuffy!" Billy cut him off. "Dub yer mummer!" Cuffy, quickly brought to the realization that he had nearly put his foot in his mouth, quickly shut up, and within a few minutes the party dispersed, Mrs. Anselm going off to a hot tub and the rest of the group declaring they were for bed as it had proved a long, exhausting night.

"Thank you, Nicholas," Alix whispered to the Earl as he handed her into the Saxon coach. "I really made a muff of things with my stupid temper, didn't I?"

Nicholas smiled and kissed her hand. "Personally, I think the incident topped off the evening rather nicely. But really, my darling," he added on a more serious note, "I do not blame you for being angry with me. I was a perfect cad to take advantage of you when I already knew what I know. Can't you see? That's why I could not compound my villainy by allowing myself the pleasure of any more of our lovemaking."

"I applaud your reasons while I abhor their results," she confessed honestly. "I may be a shameless hussy, but I *do* love you, Nicholas Mannering. Women care little for honor when their hearts are involved."

"Look at me like that much longer and I may just tell my honor to take a swift hike to hell," he told her, giving her nose a tweak. "Get thee gone, woman, before all my best intentions go up in flames and Billy has to douse *me* with his trusty pail of water!"

"Nicholas," Alix called out the window to the man watching after the coach as it moved off down the driveway, *"N'ktahoalell!"*

Although he had never before heard this particular Lenape phrase, Nicholas replied under his breath, "And I love you, Alix," before he turned his back on the coach and reentered Linton Hall—his birthplace, he told himself sorrowfully—but no longer his birth*right*.

Chapter Ten

WHY DID everything have to be so complicated? This wasn't the way love was supposed to go, Alix thought as she attacked one of the trestle table tops with a soapy rag. "We that are true lovers run into strange capers," Shakespeare said, she told herself ruefully. That being the case, she and Nicholas must be the truest lovers since Adam and Eve—and the most harassed.

Like Eve, Alix knew it was she who had bolixed up the works, dangling that wretched piece of parchment in front of his face. She had never really *meant* to ever make use of the dratted thing even if it was legally binding—she had just been trying to show him (and her grandfather) that she would not be carted off to the altar willy-nilly on *their* say-so.

Admit it, she admonished herself, slapping the rag back into the bucket with such force the water splashed all over her gown, you only did it to get some of your own back—to show Nicholas you were not without options of your own. You sure did do it too, she grimaced, wiping soapy water from her cheek. Now you have to figure a way to *un*do it!

And so, for the next three days, Alix figured and figured. Because she always seemed to think better when she was occupied with physical labor, she also cleaned and cleaned—driving Nutter and Sir Alexander to the brink of strong hysterics. Deciding something had to be done to get his granddaughter's mind off whitewashing his bedchamber and onto something else, Sir Alexander sent off a message to Linton Hall begging the Earl to set a definite date for their next assault on the highwaymen.

Mannering, eager for some respite from the tensions of waiting for the solicitor he had contacted the morning after the fire-bell fiasco to reply to his inquiry; aware that the boys were too involved in their ridiculous plans for the pantomime to take notice of what he was doing and interfere; and desperate for any excuse to see Alix again, set the date for that Wednesday night and included in his note detailed plans for setting a trap that would capture the highwaymen.

They all met just outside the high walls of Saxon Hall soon after dusk—Alix not wishing Nicholas inside the castle, where he might just discover Reginald in residence and throw a damper over all her plans by pointing out the flaws in the scheme (of which she knew there were a great many) by refusing to let his brother take part in what many people would call the "ruining" of Helene Anselm.

Sir Alexander, snug inside his traveling carriage, which was loaded to the roof with a small mountain of luggage to make it look as if he were in the midst of a long journey (and more prone to be carrying jewels and a quantity of cash), acknowledged Nicholas with a wave as the latter rode up on horseback.

"All rigged out in your best Sir Galahad armor again, I see. And who is that with you?" Mannering asked, peering inside the coach to see another, smaller form quavering in the far corner.

"Nutter, of course," Sir Alexander answered ingenuously. "You didn't think I'd travel without my page, did you? Ain't fitting, by Jupiter."

Looking upward to the driver's box, the Earl commented, "Then what is Harold's designation, hmm? Swordbearer? He looks armed to the teeth sitting up there beside your coachman."

"Harold's got some ideas of his own for this night's work, your lordship," Alix said, moving her mount up beside Nicholas's horse. "He plans to lay some traps in the woods to capture the bridle culls." She spoke rapidly, hoping the heartbeats she heard dinning in her ears were not audible. Oh, he looked so fine sitting there on his stallion and all dressed in black like some dangerous sea pirate—right down to his black silk eyepatch. How she longed to throw herself into his arms, begging he ride off with her into the night and, as the novels said so intriguingly, "have his way" with her.

For his part, Nicholas had stiffened perceptibly at the sound of Alix's voice, and only when he felt himself once more in control did he turn in the saddle to look at her. Once again she was dressed in the buckskin dress Harold had made for her. She sat her mount astride—astride and bareback—her legs uncovered from the knee down to her deerskin moccasins. As was her custom, her long black hair fell loosely down her back, but tonight it was held away from her face by means of a thin strip of leather tied around her forehead—a long white feather tucked into it at the rear.

Never, he told himself, audibly sucking in his breath, had she looked so exotically beautiful. It was all he could do not to sweep her into his arms and then spur his horse into an immediate gallop—taking them far away from highwaymen, house guests, and incriminating parchments where they could lie together under the stars and make the wild, passionate love he could only dream about during the long, lonely nights in his empty bed.

The two were silent for some moments, long seconds that passed ever so slowly as they peered hungrily at each other, before Mannering at last remembered where they were and, his quick tongue coming to his rescue, said only, "Devilishly fetching headgear, Alix. Although I guess a bonnet would look rather silly anyway, wouldn't it, all things considered? Shall we be off then?"

But Alix had lost all powers of conversation after that exchange of looks, and opening her mouth to reply and finding no words coming out, she only nodded and pushed her knees into her mount's flanks, urging him forward to follow behind the lumbering coach.

They rode in silence for about five minutes, lagging some ways behind the coach as to be out of sight of its bright carriage lamps, before Nicholas could no longer endure the tense silence and burst into speech.

"Have you any idea why we are riding on the left-hand

side of this road, Alix?'' he asked conversationally. ''I mean, we could jog along on the right just as easily, couldn't we? It wouldn't do at all to sashay straight down the middle of a roadway, but why pick the left side and not the right?''

Alix knew what Nicholas was doing and she appreciated his effort to put their relationship back on its former bantering footing. ''Since this is a world full of right-handed people, and since the right-hand side is considered to be the one most honored, I can only guess that—being English and therefore prone to the most arbitrary of notions—the people in charge of these things decreed it so just to confuse everyone.'' She turned slightly in order to look at him more closely and ended facetiously, ''Now that I have so willingly responded to the bait—not without getting in a dig or two at you English in the process—you may show off your superior intelligence by telling me the real reason.''

Mannering took on an air of injured innocence. ''How you malign my motives, sweetings. I was only hoping to pass the time with an interesting bit of trivium—as surely the reason for riding on the left, though obscured through the ages, is based soundly on logic.'' Raising his right arm as if he held a sword, he demonstrated by means of a few flourishes: ''We ride on the left in order to keep our right arm—for as you say, this is a right-handed world—free to hack at approaching horsemen who could be bent on attack. If we rode on the right side of the road, it would prove deuced awkward if it came to defending ourselves, you see.''

''One can only marvel at the problems besetting the left-handed,'' Alix replied with a chuckle. ''Just think—being placed at such a disadvantage could find him lopping off his own nose whilst trying to ward off an attacker.'' Alix laughed aloud at the image this thought conjured up before ending, ''Beset with such a problem, I imagine there's a real dearth of left-handed highwaymen about, wouldn't you say?''

Nicholas thought about this a second and then suggested that once they caught the highwaymen tonight they interview them on the subject. ''Only think of the many left-handed fellows our English sense of order has saved from a life of crime.''

Just then they noticed the coach slowing a bit. ''What's your grandfather about? I don't want him to stop here; we're still not deep enough into the countryside.''

''Harold is climbing down,'' Alix informed him. ''Lenape make it a rule to walk everywhere, shunning any transportation other than that provided by their own two feet, but because of his recent injury, I have been allowed to persuade him to ride at least a part of the way. Now he will disappear into the woods, to follow parallel to the coach but out of sight. Once we arrive at our destination, Harold will scout out the area and prepare some surprises for our expected company.''

''But we have nearly three miles to go,'' Mannering protested. ''The old boy will be winded long before and left in our dust.''

Alix shook her head in disgust. ''Ah, Nicholas, you have much to learn. Lenape, even those like Harold who have had many summers, can cover great distances on foot, traveling day and night without stops for rest.'' At the Earl's hoot of disbelief Alix merely shrugged. ''Any time you wish to pit your endurance against Harold's, you have only to ask—but please don't be overly upset if I lay *my* blunt on Harold!''

Nicholas watched as Harold, having leapt to the ground with remarkable agility, bent into a slight crouch and, his bow, quiver, and a length of rope slung over his back and a long spear held in his right hand, trotted off into the woods alongside the roadway. ''He moves well enough,'' was all Mannering would say. ''I shall reserve my judgment until the night is over.''

It was completely dark when they had at last reached the area where the highwaymen had been known to strike. Now it was time to implement the first part of Nicholas's plan.

The driver hauled the traveling coach to a full stop, aiming it slightly toward the shoulder of the roadway, and hopped down to tend to his horses.

Opening the off-door, Nutter edged his ancient bones out

through the opening, lowering the coach steps as he went. Sir Alexander then emerged, bellowing in a loud voice, "Why have we stopped? I've urgent business in Cambridge, damn your eyes, and if these jewels are not delivered before noon tomorrow I'll nail your hide to the stable door, coachie, by Jupiter I will!"

From their vantage point some ways back and near the trees, Nicholas whispered, dismounting, "Overacting a tad, don't y'think? Perhaps he's a frustrated thespian."

Alix stifled a giggle and only crouched deeper into the weeds to await further developments while Mannering tied their horses to a nearby branch.

Sir Alexander and the coachman then enacted a long, loud scene wherein the coachman pointed out that the off-leader had cast a shoe, and his passenger bellowed that he didn't give a tinker's curse about anything other than the fact that "the jewels" be delivered safe to Cambridge, while Nicholas and Alix were kept busy scanning the trees for any sign of the highwaymen.

Mannering judged himself to be a man of good instincts and clear (if limited) eyesight, so he was more infuriated than startled when Harold suddenly appeared at his side with Nicholas never being aware that the Indian was even in the area. Harold and Alix exchanged a few short, guttural phrases—Harold pointing to several different spots in the distance as he spoke—before the Indian lapsed into silence and dropped to balance himself easily on the balls of his feet, his hands wrapped loosely around his knees.

Nicholas looked at Harold in a dispassionate way, turned his head to observe the pseudo-Indian maiden crouched on his left-hand side, and then slowly shook his head. "Wellington would never believe it," he muttered, almost to himself.

Then Harold's stomach growled, loudly setting up its protest at being left without food for too long. "What the blue blazes was that!" Nicholas hissed, swearing to himself that the noisy grumbling had been enough to send the sleeping birds winging from the branches above them.

"It was Harold's stomach," Alix told him unnecessarily.

"Indians always go out hunting on an empty stomach. A full belly makes an Indian careless and lazy."

"It also makes him damned hard to hide, if that racket keeps up. Throw him a bone to gnaw on or something, will you?"

Alix had no chance to answer as Harold growled something (something rather nasty concerning the character of Mannering's antecedents, actually) and soundlessly took to his feet and melted away into the trees.

"The man's spooky, that's what he is," Nicholas found himself saying. Then he turned his gaze once more to the roadway, allowing himself to be slightly amused at the sight of Sir Alexander berating his coachman—his mail-covered torso and flailing arms making him look for all the world like a turtle turned on its back.

And then, all of a sudden, it wasn't so amusing anymore. For just then three riders emerged from the darkness farther down the roadway and began advancing purposefully on the disabled coach squatting across the road.

"Here we go!" Nicholas rasped, rising to his feet in one swift motion. "You stay here!"

The largest of the trio of horsemen—easily discernible as their leader—reined in abreast of the coach and quickly took in the scene with a sweep of his narrowed eyes. "Well, look-ee 'ere, mates," he said, extending a hand in Sir Alexander's direction. "It's a bleedin' knight I've clapped m'peepers on, damned if 'e ain't. Hey, square-toes, huntin' dragons are ye?"

While his companions laughed heartily at this sport, their leader's grin faded and he reached inside his full-skirted coat, drawing out an ugly-looking pistol and pointing it squarely in Sir Alexander's florid face.

Nutter was the first to raise his hands in surrender, followed quickly by the coachman. "That's the ticket, coves, hoist them fambles and keep yer blubbers mum. You too, puff-guts, else yer'll take yer next ride on six men's shoulders."

The entire time the leader had been talking, Nicholas had been stealthily creeping up on the group, looking for the best way to catch them off-guard. When he suddenly halted to plan his next move, Alix cannoned into his back, forcing him to grab her sharply by the shoulders else they tumble to the ground and give themselves away.

"I thought I told you to stay back," he hissed, totally out of patience with her. "I swear, woman, you have no more sense than a newborn babe—as do I for that matter, allowing you to come along at all. Whatever do you think you're doing?"

"Oh, don't be so provoking, Nicholas," Alix retorted in a fierce whisper. "Did you really expect me to stay back there twiddling my thumbs while you all risk life and limb?"

Nicholas sighed in exasperation. "Ask a stupid question—" he mused aloud before dropping a quick kiss on the end of her nose and giving her drooping white feather a gentle tug. Then he turned his face back toward the direction of the coach and found that there was no end to the folly he was to endure this night, for just then Harold could be seen entering the roadway, crouched low to the ground and carrying something in his hand.

By now the three highwaymen had dismounted and were busily engaged in emptying Sir Alexander's pockets and searching beneath the coach seats for hidden pouches of riches. Harold, moving with the stealth of a tracking lion, approached the three horses and began sprinkling a dark powder in a large circle around their feet. Then, as quickly as he had appeared, he disappeared back into the darkness.

Once he realized that nobody was paying the slightest attention to the Indian, Nicholas sat back on his heels and watched the little play with amused fascination. The man moved like a ghost, that was for sure, Nicholas thought, but he'd be damned if he could understand, even if they could not *see* him, why the highwaymen did not *smell* Harold's presence. Perhaps, he told himself with a shrug, bear-grease-smeared Indians and grubby highwaymen smelled much of a piece.

Everyone's attention was suddenly drawn to the highwayman situated half in and half out of the coach as that man suddenly let out a shout and emerged holding up a heavy pouch. " 'Ere's 'is boung!'' he announced at the top of his lungs.

The leader smiled his satisfaction, exposing a mouth sadly depleted of teeth, and admonished his fellow thief: "Keep yer breath to cool yer porridge, Jenkins, or yer'll 'ave all the world and 'is wife down on us. All's bob, let's buy a brush an' lope. Clap yer bleeders to yer gallopers, mates!''

"They mean to ride off,'' Nicholas whispered to Alix unnecessarily—for she remembered enough of Billy's book of cant to know what the highwayman was talking about.

"I know that, you dolt,'' she replied with an air of impatience. "The first thief said he had found Grandfather's purse of 'jewels' and the leader told him to be quiet or someone would hear him. Then he said everything is fine and they should leave—using their spurs on their horses as they are in a hurry. So what?'' As Nicholas meant to rise, his pistols at the ready, Alix pulled him back down by his coattails and grumbled, "Honestly, Nicholas, for a bright man you are sometimes excessively dense. There's no need for histrionics—those men aren't going anywhere.''

And as Mannering struggled to release his coat from her grasp, still looking at the highwaymen, he found that Alix was correct. They weren't going anywhere—at least not on horseback, they weren't—for the horses wouldn't budge, no matter how hard they were spurred.

"I don't believe it,'' he said, awestruck. "I see it—but I don't believe it. What did Harold do to those horses?''

"He merely sprinkled some dried blood—blood of some animal or another—and some secret powder mixture around the horses. They're too frightened to move,'' she told him with an unholy grin lighting her features. "Now watch. The highwaymen will have no choice but to dismount and try to get away on foot.''

Of course, that is precisely what the highwaymen attempted to do—cursing and swiping at their recalcitrant horses as they managed to keep Sir Alexander and the rest safely within range of their pistols. With no other option left open to them, they then turned to make their way into the trees, planning to get themselves far away before some passerby came along and caught them.

They had taken no more than three steps when an arrow came whistling through the air to land point down in the dirt at the leader's feet—this first arrow followed quickly by two more that figuratively pinned the remaining highwaymen where they stood.

"Wot the bleedin' 'ell?" the leader exclaimed, whirling where he stood, half expecting attack from the rear. While all three thieves cowered in expectation of more arrows to follow, there came a blood-curdling yell from deep in the darkness—the Lenape alarm-whoop—calculated to strike terror into the hearts of anyone within earshot.

Although Nicholas had heard such a whoop before, listening to it now, coming as it did from the throat of a real Lenape warrior rather than a beautiful young woman, sent ripples of goosebumps shooting up his arms.

The thieves were petrified with fright, so paralyzed that it became mere child's play for Sir Alexander to reach inside the coach, pull out Harold's heavy war club (loaned for just such a purpose), and bring it down neatly on the side of one of the thieves' heads.

Now there were just two.

"I own myself astonished at the brilliance of this plan," Nicholas admitted to Alix as they now stood most openly in the roadway, the better to watch the fun. "In fact, lovely one, I am feeling quite superfluous—unless I was only allowed to come along to serve as an appreciative audience to this masterful strategy."

"Don't be silly," Alix retorted matter-of-factly. "It was your idea to set up a decoy, Nicholas. It's just that Harold and I decided it would be less dangerous to handle the actual capture this way rather than to go about shooting holes in everyone." As Alix spoke, they were walking rapidly toward the coach, Nicholas refusing to pocket his pistols even though the second highwayman was now on his knees, his hands clapped over his ears, begging anyone who would listen to make the awful noise go away, and the leader of the group was busily trying to drag his now hysterically rearing horse down the roadway.

When the leader saw Nicholas approaching—his frightened eyes not quite taking in Alix's bizarre appearance at his side—he dropped his mount's reins and bolted for the cover of the trees that lay on the opposite side of the road from whence the ear-splitting whoops were coming.

Sir Alexander, feeling very much in his prime, brandished Harold's war club, successfully keeping the kneeling highwayman in check, while Nicholas broke into a trot, following the escaping thief.

"Nicholas, don't!" Alix shouted after him. "There's no need—honestly!"

"The hell there isn't!" Nicholas muttered under his breath, breaking into a run. "Bloody old men and a wet-behind-the-ears girl—making me feel about as useless as a wart on the end of Prinney's nose, by God!"

Once in the woods, Nicholas stopped to get his bearings. He could still hear Alix calling to him to turn around and come back, but he ignored her pleas, choosing instead to listen for sounds of the thief moving in the underbrush. As the man was concentrating all his efforts on flight, not stealth, it wasn't hard for Mannering to hear him—the hapless highwayman was charging through the trees with all the finesse of a wounded elephant.

The thief ran as if the hounds of hell were after him, looking back over his shoulder as he went, although the outcome of his flight would have been no different if he had been watching where he was going. One moment he was beginning to think he could outdistance his pursuer, and the next he was hanging upside down by one leg, his thrashing arms reaching helplessly toward the ground beneath his head.

When Nicholas arrived on the scene, the highwayman, thinking the devil himself had come to fetch him, began blubbering something unintelligible and making the sign against the evil eye while his furious leg kickings set him spinning about like a child's toy top.

It was just too much. Mannering stood looking at the hapless captive for a few moments, realizing that his sole function in the man's capture would be to cut him down from Harold's deer snare and haul the fellow back to the coach, and loosed a pungent oath. Then, leaving the highwayman to dangle until Harold deigned to collect him, he turned to make his way back to the roadway.

Perhaps he was too busy nursing his wounded ego to take much notice of where he was stepping, or perhaps he just didn't give a damn—but whatever the reason for his inattention, Nicholas had taken no more than ten steps before there came a small, snapping sound, followed closely by the sight of a thin sapling whipping past his head, followed even more closely by the rapid inversion of his person.

When Alix found him, he was looking quite urbane—one leg crossed over the other and his arms folded negligently across his chest. The fact that he was upside down did not seem to faze him in the least.

"Nicholas!" Alix was startled into exclaiming. "You're in the deer snare!"

Mannering turned his head from side to side, then looked up and down, seeing stars hovering above his feet and a patch of moss below his head, and replied in a tightly polite voice, "So I am, sweetings. It's so good of you to bring it to my attention—I'd never have noticed otherwise." Then his voice hardened and he unleashed his frustration in a loud shout. *"Get me down from here!"*

Not knowing whether to be solicitous and commiserate with the poor fellow, or whether to use her well-developed sense of preservation and run for it—leaving Harold to face Linton's wrath once he was cut down—in the end, Alix did the very thing calculated to bring Nicholas's fury down around her ears.

She laughed.

She plopped herself down on the ground and she howled. "Oh, Nick," she chortled, pointing a finger in his direction as she held her other hand to her smiling mouth, "you look *so funny!*"

Nicholas's voice was like chipped ice. "How that gratifies me. I live only to amuse you."

Then, her sense of the ridiculous riding high, Alix

creeped toward Nicholas on all fours, and bracing his shoulders with her hands so that he would not swing away, she planted a kiss on his upside-down lips.

"A plaguey queer time to be billing and cooing, if you ask me," pointed out Sir Alexander, as he lumbered into the small clearing and saw Nicholas and his granddaughter locked in a rather bizarre embrace. "Linton! What the deuce are you about—hanging around in trees like a bloody bat? Good thing Harold and I were able to subdue the highwaymen, for all the good you've been. Thought you was with Wellington. Wonder we ain't all talking Frenchie, if all his men were like you."

"Grandfather, that is too bad of you," Alix scolded, smiling only a little bit at his teasing. "Poor Nicholas couldn't have known about Harold's snares."

Mention of the Indian distracted Sir Alexander, and he embarked on a lengthy recitation of all that had gone on that evening—his and Harold's parts in the adventure taking on the glimmerings of what soon could become an epic poem—before informing his audience (one could almost say "captive" audience) that Harold would be along shortly to tie up the last highwayman and cut Nicholas down from his ignominious position.

"Jolly decent of him," Mannering muttered. "But if you're entertaining the notion of commissioning some artist to capture the events of this evening on canvas for the sake of posterity, I'd as lief you left me out of it. I have no great desire to have my descendents referring to me as 'The Inverted Earl.' "

Sir Alexander bridled. "And why should you think you'd have any part in such a thing anyway? All you've done is get yourself trussed up like a chicken whilst Harold and I did all the real work. Besides," he added, pointing out just another of the Earl's misconceptions, "it's not a painting I'm thinking about but a tapestry. Look good in the Great Hall, don't you know."

"Oh good grief," groaned Nicholas, pushing at the ground with one hand and setting his body into a slow turn—away from Alix's laughing eyes.

* * *

Twenty minutes later the worst was over. The three high-waymen (none of them left-handed—Alix had asked) were neatly tied up like birthday presents and stashed in the boot of the coach, their legs hanging out the back like streamers, and the coachie, with Sir Alexander sitting alongside him as guard, lumbered off in search of the local constable.

That left only Harold, Alix and Nicholas, and five horses—three of which refused to budge an inch when the Earl tried to turn them about. Mannering tugged; the horses resisted. Mannering pulled; the horses reared, then dug in their heels. Mannering cursed; the horses merely blinked at him.

"Well that's the last straw!" Nicholas exploded, venting his pent up fury any way he could. "Tell me, Alix," he purred, turning toward the pseudo-Indian maid, "now that Harold has succeeded in turning these nags into immovable statues, does his vast store of Lenape magic extend to including a way to get them moving again? Or on second thought—do you think we should just have them bronzed and made into bookends?"

Alix spoke a few words to Harold, who then extracted another small leather pouch from beneath his bear skin and began pouring its contents on top of the dried animal blood he had sprinkled about earlier. "That's milk," Alix said unnecessarily. "It will cover the smell of the blood and the horses will move again. It's really very simple, actually."

"Simple," Nicholas repeated dully. "That certainly is one word for it."

Harold returned the now-empty pouch to its hiding place and picked up the horses' reins, easily leading them into a large circle that ended up heading them toward Saxon Hall. Then, stopping beside Nicholas, he held out his right hand in a sort of salute and intoned gravely, *"Itah, Issimus."*

"What did he say?" Mannering asked. "Has he found yet another way to call me a fool?"

"You should be honored, Nicholas," Alix told him. "Harold said, 'Good be to you,' and then he called you

194

'Issimus,' which means brother. Harold has only ever called one other person that—my father. Now that Chas is dead—''

Alix's words broke off abruptly as she clapped a hand to her careless mouth. Surely now Harold would start in to wail as he had done every time someone mentioned Chas's death. But Harold did not begin the eerie keening that was his way of mourning his great friend. The Indian only bowed his great black-faced head and intoned softly, *"Bíschi, n'tschu gámink. N'palléha."* Then he faded into the night, the three horses following along docilely behind him.

Alix stood very still, watching Harold as he began the measured loping gait that he would sustain throughout the long trip back to Saxon Hall, as Nicholas watched Alix's stiffly held back and her proudly held chin that was etched so clearly in the moonlight. Then, as he watched, her slim shoulders began to shake, and he reached for her, turning her toward him so he could see her tear-streaked face.

"He—he said," Alix began, visibly controlling her features, "Harold said, 'It is indeed so, my friend is across the river. I am sor-sorry.' Oh, Nick, it's so sad. I'm sorry t-too. So very, very sorry.'' Then her face crumpled and she began to cry—really cry—for the first time since Chas's death.

Nicholas gathered her into his arms in the middle of the dark roadway and let her weep. What a paradox Alix is, he thought—part child, part savage, and more than any female he had ever known, all woman. Left alone in Philadelphia with only an eccentric half-breed Lenape—a living anachronism actually—for a companion, she had set off for a strange land and an uncertain welcome from her only living relative, who turned out to be yet another living anachronism.

But she had not allowed herself to be defeated—not even when her life became even more muddled with the addition of an unwanted fiancé. No, she had not buckled under, had not given in. She had kept her fighting spirit intact. She would have won out against him too, he realized shamefully, if her heart hadn't gotten in the way. Poor Alix. Harold's quiet acceptance of Chas's death seems to have been the last straw. She must feel so dreadfully alone now—with her father gone and me, with my stiff-backed pride, denying her offer of love.

He tightened his arms about her shoulders. "Hush, darling," he crooned into the curve of her neck. "I'm here. I'll never leave you, Alix, I swear it."

Her sobs slowly died away into a quiet sort of sorrow, but she did not release her fierce hold, her arms wrapped around his back. "I love you, Nicholas," she whispered into his shoulder.

"I love you too, darling—more than life itself."

Alix took a deep, shuddering breath and looked up into his face. Dredging up all her courage, she pushed out a smile that brought a dimple to her left cheek and asked, "Does that mean you'll marry me, my lord?"

He pushed her a little bit away, holding her by the shoulders, and peered down into her face—so dear to him, so heartbreaking in its mixture of hopefulness and anxiety. How could he deny her?

She was waiting for his answer. He could feel her body trembling under his hands. It wasn't fair to keep her on pins and needles—not now, after she had bared her very soul to him. Love warred with honor—and love won.

He looked deeply into her eyes and a slow smile turned up one corner of his mouth. "Yes, my dearest savage," he said gently, "I will marry you."

When they were at long last mounted and headed toward Saxon Hall, holding hands as they rode along in the path of the moonlight, the silence that followed their loving was loud with their unspoken thoughts—thoughts that, they both knew, could reach out at any time and destroy their newfound happiness.

Chapter Eleven

MATILDA Anselm did not admit defeat gracefully—as her late, harassed husband would have been the first to say (as long as he first made quite certain his wife was not within earshot). She had planned long and hard, determined her Helene would wed the Earl of Linton. Even now, after the Earl had so pointedly given her and her children their *congé,* she found it hard to believe all her machinations had come to nothing.

But she had run out of options—unless her luck changed, and changed quickly. She had given the project her best shot and that shot had fallen far wide of the mark. So thinking, she at last reluctantly decided to return to her own highly mortgaged home and use the remainder of the winter to plan one last assault on the *haut ton* in the spring. Surely Helene's beauty was sufficient to snag some other lord—even a Sir or an Honorable would do if he were sufficiently plump in the pocket.

And so, her mind made up at last, Mrs. Anselm penned a short communiqué to her housekeeper apprising her of the family's intention to take up residence shortly after the holidays—a piece of information that would doubtless send that poor, beleaguered woman straight for the brandy decanter, as Mrs. Anselm was a most demanding mistress.

As Mrs. Anselm made her way down the stairs to the mail pouch that was kept on a table in the foyer, she heard Poole and one of the footmen in conversation. As was her custom, she immediately halted in her tracks and pricked up her ears to hear any gossip that might come her way—not that Poole was likely to say anything of importance, but lifelong habits die hard.

"This jist came special fer his lordship," the footman was telling Poole, waving a large, official-looking envelope beneath the butler's pug nose.

Poole extended one white-gloved hand and took the envelope, holding it as far from his eyes as possible as he read out the name scrawled on the flap just above the seal. "John Mortlock, Esquire, and Sons, Cambridge," he worked out painfully. "This be the letter his lordship has been pestering us about." He handed it back to the footman. "The Earl is out riding, Martin. Place this on the table beside the mail pouch so's as he sees it first thing when he comes in. Then," he finished stuffily, looking the lad Martin up and down, "go to your room and do something about your hair. You look like you combed it with a rake."

"Yes, sir!" Martin shot back smartly, retrieving the letter and doing an abrupt about-face in order to place it precisely in the center of the silver tray next to the mail pouch. Then he turned again, ran an assessing hand over his sandy locks, sighed, and made for the baize-covered door leading to the servants' quarters.

Blessing her good fortune, Mrs. Anselm acted swiftly before anyone else could wander into the foyer. Quick as a cat, she swooped down the steps, scooped up the letter, and retreated to the privacy of her chamber. She had no idea what she would find upon opening the letter (with a larcenous expertise acquired through long practice), but as she began to read, a slow smile fitted itself across her face and she was hard pressed not to jump up and do a sprightly jig at her good luck.

With the myopic vision of a mother intent on marrying off her beautiful but brainless daughter, she had not been able to see any reason for the Earl of Linton to choose that dark-haired nobody from the Colonies over her Helene. She, of course, excused any possible physical attraction Mannering might have for Alix with the same nonchalance with which she would dismiss Linton's small indiscretions after his marriage to her daughter. Men were inclined to indulge in these little adventures with women from the lower orders —as she obviously considered Alix, even if her grandfather was of noble blood—but she certainly couldn't understand why he felt he had to *marry* the chit.

Now she knew. Well, this letter would certainly put a whole new light on the subject—as Nicholas would surely realize once he read it. But before he reads it, she thought as she sat fanning herself with the heavy envelope, I shall have to find some way to get Helene back into his good graces. Then he will quite naturally turn to her in the midst of his rejoicing and the matter will be settled once and for all.

I shall produce the letter the night of the pantomime, she thought. Helene shall certainly be in her best looks then—in her new gown that so sets off her complexion. After dinner when she has wound Mannering around her little finger by way of her sweet singing and harp playing, I shall casually set this letter where he can find it. Yes, she told herself, nodding her head in satisfaction. That upstart heathen will not usurp my daughter in this house. This time I cannot fail!

Jeremy, Cuffy, and Billy felt their noses were put slightly out of joint by Nicholas's capture of the highwaymen (Alix having wisely given Mannering all the credit in her telling of the story), but they were sure their superb handling of the pantomime would serve to cast Mannering's feat quite nicely into the shade.

The boys had, they believed, come up with a true inspiration—they would hold the pantomime at Saxon Hall and fill the evening with an entire round of medieval celebration. Sir Alexander happily agreed to the scheme once Cuffy told the old gentleman that, as host, he would be crowned the Lord of Misrule and could then preside over the contents of the wassail bowl.

Alix also fell neatly into their plans, pointing out that, as they were all wearing costumes anyway, it would then be doubly easy to slip Reginald into the scene without detection. Alix was a bit distracted anyway, torn between elation over her newfound love and a nagging fear that Nicholas had somewhat compromised his principles in agreeing to marry her, and it was by and large left to the three boys to devise the evening's entertainment.

They did not stint. Indeed, they threw themselves into the project, as Linton was heard to mutter, with ten times the enthusiasm they brought to their studies—more's the pity.

They spent whole days closeted with Sir Alexander, plying him with gin and listening to his rollicking stories of long-ago Christmas celebrations. Soon they were as caught up in the spirit of the thing as was Sir Alexander—who found himself feeling at home to a peg in his role of Lord of Misrule.

Under Sir Alexander's direction, the trestle tables—having been designed so that each table top could be lifted off its trestles—were cleared away and temporarily stacked to one side in the Great Hall, while load after load of rushes were scattered on the cold stone floor "for atmosphere," or so said Sir Alexander. Harold's wigwam was banished for the duration.

Reginald, who had been keeping much to his room anyway, was then found to be annoyingly allergic to the rushes and was taken with sneezing fits each time he dared to enter the chamber. "At least we'll always be able to locate him when we want him," Alix laughed, handing the poor suffering soul one of her grandfather's large handkerchiefs. "Between keeping Reginald here out of sight until the proper moment and keeping the old man from swimming in the wassail bowl, we shall quite have our hands full!"

"Plenty of belly timber too, Alix," Billy put in, thinking of the fine menu that had been concocted. "Your grandfather's a real rum bluffer."

"Don't call him a good host until *after* the festivities," Alix warned. "I've been down to the kitchens myself several times in the last days, and let me tell you, some of Nutter's concoctions look pretty *strange*."

Nicholas remained aloof throughout a week of meetings and frenzied consultations, limiting himself to a few acid comments on the jumble of activities planned for the great evening, and mostly closeting himself in his study with his brandy decanter—when he wasn't prowling the halls berating the servants with questions as to when the post was due, that is. "Mustn't have liked that letter he got," Poole commented to Martin the footman. "Lord help us iffen another doesn't come soon to ease his gloom."

Inevitably, the night of the pantomime arrived with the boys nearly delirious with anticipation; Alix mentally figuring and refiguring her plans for the elopement; Nicholas still appearing to be a bit distracted; the Anselms muttering under their breath about the necessity of traveling to Saxon Hall in their finery; and Sir Alexander and Harold—who had been testing and retesting their recipe for punch—both wearing inane grins and giggling a lot.

The night air was crisp and cold, and the party from Linton Hall traveled the short distance with hot bricks at their toes, arriving at the castle at the same time as the other guests, drawn from the gentry in the nearby villages.

"It's nice to see Sir Alexander and the countryside hobnobbing together again after all this time," Nicholas commented, handing Helene down from the carriage. "He has little taste for society, you know."

Mrs. Anselm, who had not been delighted by the sad crush inside the carriage (so damaging to Helene's pretty costume), only replied acidly, "Silly me. I always thought it was the other way around."

The small party was greeted at the door by an ancient little man dressed in moldy green livery. After taking their names, he preceded them through the antechamber, stopping at the entrance of the Great Hall to stamp his staff smartly on the floor three times before announcing them in a quivering voice. Jeremy, complete in his guise of Lord Lollypop, which consisted of one of Nicholas's cast-off swallowtail jackets, a ludicrously bushy (and crooked) mustache, and a red velvet beret, hastened to greet them, pulling Mannering almost rudely into the room.

Even Nicholas had to admit the sight that greeted his eyes was most impressive. Flambeaux burned brightly from dozens of wall brackets, setting off the armaments and tapestries hanging on the walls to great advantage, while the immense yule log burning in the exact center of the room succeeded in keeping the great height of the vaulted ceiling cloaked in mysterious mist.

The Lord of Misrule could be seen at the opposite end of the chamber—sprawled on his throne like the reincarnation of Henry VIII, and already at least one or two sheets to the wind. Beside him, in full ceremonial splendor, sat Harold, looking just as kingly (and just as pie-eyed) as Sir Alexander.

Oh, thought Nicholas, I wager this could prove to be a most interesting evening! Then Cuffy and Billy joined the group and Nicholas knew he had made a sure bet. Cuffy, at his overdressed best, was Lord Flirt Away to the life—looking the complete dandy in his too-tight, padded jacket and enormous starched shirt points—the gilt quizzing glass he had stuck to his eye (the better to size up the damsels) giving him the appearance of some strange species of fish.

But it was Billy who fair stole the show as Spantu Long Tong Song. From the top of his flat straw hat to the curly tips of his embroidered felt slippers, he was every inch the Chinaman, although he would not answer as to just where his elaborate costume or the long stringy mustache and ratty-looking pigtail had come from. Jeremy might have given a good clue when he put a hand to his mouth and neighed, but Billy wasn't talking.

"Nick," Jeremy said then, noticing his brother's lack of costume. "You were supposed to be Lord Dashaway, dash it all! That is, I mean—where is your costume?"

"And where would you have me stick my quizzing glass, puppy—in my ear?" Nicholas responded with a smile that took the sting out of his words. "Besides, *brother*, do you actually mean to suggest that my patch is not sufficiently 'dashing'?"

All this byplay left the Anselms standing about entirely too long, at least to Mrs. Anselm's mind. "And what of our costumes, Jeremy?" she asked, with a pointed look in Helene's direction. The men all quickly agreed that the girl was Lady Languish to the life, raining down praise on her feathered headdress and oversized lace fan and courteously overlooking her sad eyes and the long sighs that gave real credence to her assumed title.

Helene had every right to feel overwhelmed. Her mother had given her strict instructions to play up to Lord Linton tonight and Helene's heart just wasn't in it. She missed her Reginald, that she did, and her several conversations with Alix about him had only brought that fact home to her with greater clarity. She didn't know what, as her mama had said, "ace" that lady had up her sleeve, but she did know that she may as well put paid to any grandiose ideas she might have been harboring that Mrs. Anselm would give up her scheming. Alix might be a valiant fighter on Helene's behalf, but although she might be able to bring the two lovers together, getting them married was nigh to impossible. Mama simply wouldn't allow it!

Summoning a weak smile in answer to the boys' praises, Helene leaned against her brother Rupert, who quickly shrugged her off, warning her not to crease his jacket. "Lord Dumble Dum Deary has no time for languishing females," he told her sharply.

"You're missing your pipe, Rupert," Jeremy, who had studied the drawings of the characters with some care, pointed out. When Rupert reluctantly produced a battered pipe from his pocket, holding the thing gingerly and eyeing it with some disgust, Jeremy told him to stick the thing in his mouth.

"Or any other appropriate place," Cuffy muttered under his breath before sending Mrs. Anselm a brilliant smile and flattering the woman with high praise on her incarnation of Mrs. Strut. "And surely you do appear ready for the promenade on Rotten Row, ma'am," he said with amazing sincerity, keeping to himself the notion that she looked much like Prinney's pet horse.

Taking the ladies' arms, Nicholas led them into a saunter about the large chamber, regaling them with the fact that the famed Hyde Park circuit was originally named the *Route de Roi*, but the English pronunciation had corrupted it into Rotten Row, a fact that may not have thrilled them, but at least kept them off the subject of Alix's noticeable absence from the scene.

As they walked about, their face masks raised to their eyes by means of thin gilt sticks, Nicholas bowed and waved to several acquaintances whose out-of-date, countrified evening dress made them appear as if they too were to be part of the pantomime. They at last approached the two thronelike chairs on the low dais and made their bows to the Lord of Misrule (who was just then nibbling on the tassel of his hat), complimenting him on the decorations.

"Nothing to it," Sir Alexander chirped happily. "But wait 'til you clap your eyes on the dinner, Linton. Nutter fair outdid himself there, I tell you." Turning to Mrs. Anselm he said, "You look a treat, Matilda, by Jupiter you do. Either that or I'm in my cups already. Must be that, eh, Harold?" he asked, peering intently at the Indian before looking back at the enraged features of Mrs. Anselm. "Really like that Indian, y'know. Doesn't talk the leg off a donkey, like some I could mention. You here to toast m'granddaughter and Mannering here, Matilda? Announcing their betrothal tonight, y'know. Damned decent of you to give in so gracefully, old girl. Didn't know you had it in you."

"It is never wise to count one's chickens before they are hatched, Sir Alexander," Mrs. Anselm replied through clenched teeth.

"Chickens, is it!" Sir Alexander shouted, highly amused. "And a good deal you'd be knowing about chickens, Matilda," he twitted her, looking Rupert up and down, "for Lord knows you ain't never raised no *roosters!*"

Just then Alix, who had taken an uncharacteristically long time over her toilette, appeared on the scene, saving Sir Alexander a thorough tongue-lashing at the hands of one highly insulted Mother Hen. Situating herself directly in front of Sir Alexander, Alix dropped into a deep curtsy and said, "Fanny Fandango regrets her tardiness, my lord, and presents her compliments."

My God, Nicholas grimaced painfully, eyeing Alix up and down, she'd tempt the saints themselves in that getup! Alix, once she had seen a drawing of Fanny Fandango, had entered heart and soul into the character, and the result was indeed breathtaking. Her gown, unearthed from heaven only knew where, was of deepest ruby red velvet, and done in the style of a Spanish dancer—ending well above ankles fetchingly bedecked in finely crossed black velvet ribbons hooked to a pair of soft black slippers. The off-the-shoulder neckline of her gown was as low as her hem was high, exposing a large expanse of creamy white skin, and her midnight black hair hung in several looped braids that caressed her neck and tempted Nicholas to unspeakable acts. When she rose to her full height, spinning round once and snapping her castanets beneath Mannering's nose, Sir Alexander roared in delight—as it is not often one can actually see beads of sweat appear upon a lordship's upper lip.

"Now, Linton?" the Lord of Misrule teased that poor harassed man unmercifully. "Shall I make the announcement now?"

After much ado the guests were finally seated along one side of the many trestle tables that flanked the two thronelike chairs where their host and his odd consort sprawled in regal grace. They were a colorful, festive sight, this group of fifty or more, and their conversation buzzed with the anticipation of what was to come next.

Suddenly the hoary vassel serving as hall marshall entered the chamber and ceremoniously banged his heavy staff, announcing the dinner as if it were an honored guest. After a slight pause Nutter appeared, attended by two other ancient servants carrying large wax candles. Nutter then bowed to his master and flung out one arm toward the kitchens. First to be carried into the chamber (on the outstretched arms of no less than four overaged waiters) was a tremendous silver platter upon which reposed an enormous pig's head elaborately decorated with rosemary—and with a lemon jammed in its mouth.

The pig's head was quickly followed by more silver platters carrying dishes such as pheasant pie, plum porridge, peacock pie, dozens of minor vegetable dishes, towering stacks of bread, and last but by no means least, a truly imposing sirloin of roast beef. From somewhere off in a dark corner a harper began twanging the song of the Roast Beef of Old England (a performance marked with more power than melody), and as the platters were laid about on the tables, the local parson rose to say grace.

Halfway through the long-winded invocation Sir Alexander stood up and bellowed, "If it was bawlin' I wanted, I'da gone to church, by Jupiter. This is a party, man," he admonished the cowering minister, "not a demned funeral. Now stow the blab and let's eat. Crikey, if my guts don't begin to think my throat's been cut!"

"Amen!" shouted Billy, earning himself a cuff on the ear from Mrs. Anselm, who had somehow been seated beside the youth. There was a short, uncomfortable silence while the parson raised his eyes seeking heavenly guidance, but as he saw only thin clouds of wood smoke above him, he at last merely shrugged his shoulders and sat down.

The feast had begun. Everyone fell to with a will, and it was not long before Nutter and his entourage were carrying in flaming puddings as a fitting close to a prime example of the Englishman's reknowned inclination to overindulge his belly.

After the tables were cleared and the cloths removed, Nutter carried in an outsized silver vessel of most rare and curious workmanship and placed it before the Lord of Misrule before half staggering back to the kitchens. Other servants then brought tray after tray of ingredients and stood ready to serve their master as he presided over the preparation of the wassail bowl.

With Harold hovering at his elbow, Sir Alexander poured bottle after bottle of the richest and raciest wines into the enormous bowl, then added several spiced apples that bobbed about on the surface of the mixture. Various other ingredients were added—a dash here and a cupful there—along with sugar, bits of toast, and a quantity of roasted crab.

Using a huge silver ladle, Sir Alexander stirred the concoction (causing Nicholas to turn to Alix and comment that he half expected the ladle to melt) and then poured out the first sampling into a silver goblet that he ceremoniously handed to Harold. The Indian lifted the goblet to his lips, sniffed delicately at the brew that by all rights should have curled his huge, hooked nose, and took a deep drink. Then he held out the goblet and said something in his own tongue that, to his awed listeners, sounded deep and rather profound.

"What did he say?" Cuffy asked Alix, leaning across Helene and Nicholas to ask his question.

"He said," she replied tongue in cheek, "that it is the drink that is bad, not the man. As an excuse, it's as good as any I've heard my grandfather spout. At least Harold doesn't try to justify his tippling by saying it's to ease his lumbago!"

Once the real, serious drinking had begun—the huge pitchers of nappy ale that had been consumed by all and sundry throughout the long meal not really counting—the noise and merriment in the huge chamber rose to near astonishing heights.

The actors in the pantomime put on a lively show that ended to loud applause when Billy tripped over his pointy slippers and nearly somersaulted into the fire, and they moved rapidly on to the presentation of some conundrums for their guests to puzzle out.

"If a single burner be taken from a chandelier, why should it then be brighter?" Cuffy asked the company.

"Because it's *lighter* by a lamp!" Mrs. Anselm trilled, clapping her hands at her own intelligence. Billy had been busy throughout the dinner refilling Mrs. Anselm's cup each time she took a sip, laboring under the idea that a tipsy Mrs. Anselm would be that much easier to deceive. From the way her headdress of ostrich feathers was hanging over her left eye, and taking in her slouched posture and asinine grin, it appeared that the dear lady was indeed rather mellow.

"Why is a wife like a joint of pork?" Jeremy queried when it was his turn.

Now it was Sir Alexander's turn to shout out an answer, which he did with some delight. "Because she's *a spare rib!*" he bellowed, and then he burped.

"Very good, oh Lord of Misrule," Alix teased, dropping her grandfather a curtsy. "But here is a real puzzler: Why, good sir, is an unbound book like a young maiden in bed?"

There was quiet in the hall for some moments as everyone tried to figure out Alix's conundrum. Then all at once someone in the crowd shouted out: "Because she's *done up in sheets!*" Everyone looked to see who had been the author of this wisdom, and all were astonished to see the red face of the local minister, as he stood beside one of the benches, his hands gripping the table top, looking like a sailor trying to maintain his balance on a storm-tossed ship. "Oh my," he whispered, aghast at himself. "Oh, my goodness!" Then, clapping one hand to his mouth as his rosy face took on a greenish cast, he turned and bolted from the room, the laughter of the rest of the company sending him on his way.

"My word, Alix," Nicholas whispered in her ear when she resumed her seat, "do you think the reverend is setting himself up as a wit?"

Alix could only giggle. "Oh, that poor, *poor* man. Nicholas, did you see his face? How will he ever be able to preach morality or temperance again!"

The organized portion of the festivities completed, the guests were now left to their own devices. They stepped admirably into the breach, singing, dancing to the badly played tunes the harper strummed on his ancient instrument, and telling ghost stories, each tale more chilling and more farfetched than the last.

Alix sat with her own little group, snickering and scoffing as Cuffy tried to frighten the women with one particularly outlandish tale. "Oh, Cuffy, what a hum!" She motioned to them all to draw nearer to her. "Now if it's a story you want—let me tell you a *real* tale."

They all cried out for her to tell her story, crowding about her while she smiled and rubbed her hands together in preparation of setting them all back on their heels. She told them about a fierce battle between two warring Indian tribes, graphically describing the punishments meted out to captured warriors and sundry methods of execution meant to make the hair on the backs of their heads stand up in dread.

"Then," she went on in a low voice, "they got together—after so many brave men had died, you know—and decided to forge a peace."

"That's it? It was all over just like that?" Jeremy asked, his voice full of disappointment.

"Not exactly, Jeremy, you bloodthirsty thing. You see, not too long after the peace was established, two braves from one of the tribes broke the treaty and were captured by the other tribe."

"Bet they burned them at the stake, huh?" Jeremy broke in again, his eyes aglow at the thought.

Alix shook her head. "So commonplace a punishment? Really, Jeremy, have you no imagination? The tribe did no such thing; they were far too civilized for that. No," she smiled, before dropping her bombshell. "They merely cut off all the warriors' fingers and thumbs before sending the two men back to their own tribe."

Hastily hiding his own fingers under his armpits, Billy breathed, "Whyever did they lop off their fambles?"

"It is simple really, Billy," she replied reasonably. "After the punishment was meted out, the two warriors were told," and here her voice became most mysterious, " 'We have agreed to hold the chain of peace and friendship with both hands. We have done so but you have not. Therefore, it seems you have no use for your fingers and we have rid you of these useless parts.' "

"I say," Cuffy exclaimed, seeming to be well pleased with the Indians' solution. "I'll bet that put an end to it!"

"Not really, Cuffy. The other tribe took umbrage at the punishment and a long war followed. But at least *my* story is true, which is more than I can say for that rapper you told about your Great-uncle Richard coming back as a malacca cane and going about your family home lifting up ladies' skirts."

Everybody laughed at Cuffy's expense and the small party split up, each after other amusement elsewhere in the chamber. Now was the time for Alix to seek out Helene and tell her that at last the time was at hand—that *this* definitely would be the night of her elopement. She couldn't have taken the chance of confirming this earlier, as the nervous Helene would have given the game away for sure, but as the clock was moving steadily toward twelve and the appearance of Reginald, the moment had come to make the first move.

Once she had pried Helene away from her mama—she had been serving as a supporting prop for that lady, who was now more than a little in her altitudes—she shoved the girl into the solar, where they could have a private chat.

"What is it, Alix?" Helene questioned in a shaky voice. "I know you said Reginald would be here tonight and I know you told me that you would arrange it so that we could be married, but I still cannot make myself believe any of that is true. Mama has been at me so about Nicholas all week, you know. She says it is now only a matter of time before an announcement of our engagement goes off to London, and try as I might to explain that I don't *love* Nicholas—that I shall never love Nicholas—she persists in assuring me that she holds the answer to all our problems right in the palm of her hand. Oh, Alix," the girl ended in a thin wail, "where is my Reginald? I vow I cannot exist without him much longer!"

Thinking to herself that for a shy, retiring sort of girl, the chit really could run on, Alix shushed Helene with a wave of her hand and pushed her down on the seat in the window embrasure. "It's true all right, you widgeon. Now shut up and listen," she ordered, showing scant regard for Helene's sensibilities. "Drat it all, I haven't gone through all this planning just for you to go all chicken-hearted on me. Your Reginald is safely tucked away upstairs . . ."

"He's *here!*" Helene shrieked. "My Reginald is *really here!* Oh, Alix, forgive me for doubting you. I've been trying and trying to believe what you told me last week, but it was all too wonderful to be real." She hopped to her feet and started for the door. "Where is he? I must fly to him at once!"

Alix grabbed the girl by the elbow and shoved her back down on the window seat. "Oh no, you don't. Now look here, Helene. We've got this thing planned down to the last detail—the boys and I. I won't have you go running through the place now calling for your Reggie at the top of your lungs and tipping our scheme. All I want to know from you is if you are truly game for an elopement to Gretna Green. If you haven't the backbone to go through with it, we'll call it a day right now and you can move yourself straight back under your mama's thumb.''

Then a strange thing happened. Helene sat up straight, her back in a defiant arch. Her rounded chin came up and a heretofore nonexistent gleam of determination glinted in her normally vague-looking blue eyes. "I would walk barefoot over hot coals to get to my Reginald!" she declared in a steely voice. "Just tell me what I am to do."

Alix stepped back and put her hands on her hips. "Well, I'll be switched! So there's a little of your mama in you after all." Then she sat down beside Helene and whispered confidentially. "Now this is what we intend to do . . ."

The Great Hall now resembled nothing less than the banqueting hall of Henry VIII after an especially rousing feast. Chewed joints of meat littered the ale-soaked rushes on the stone floor; bodies sprawled inelegantly on benches or propped up the walls; the tables were littered with overturned goblets and bits of gnawed fruit; and bursts of raucous song and ribald laughter issued by those of the guests still left standing mixed with the smoky atmosphere and floated away. It was midnight, and if the quality of the evening could be counted in the number of hangovers that would be nursed on the morrow, the party had to have been termed a rousing success.

When Alix and Helene reentered the chamber it took them some moments to search out the three boys—just then engaging in a valiant attempt to corner some local maidens under the kissing bunch of mistletoe.

"Well, aren't you fellows in high gig?" Alix teased as she stopped in front of the trio.

"Never say that, Alix," Jeremy grinned tipsily. "We ain't drunk, you know. Only tryin' to keep the party going, ain't we, fellas?"

"Quite right," Cuffy agreed, nodding his head vigorously and putting himself in danger of toppling over onto his face. "Now be a good girl, Fanny, and give us a kiss." He began walking toward her, his lips puckered.

Nicholas, who had been sitting on the dais beside Sir Alexander and wondering if Bedlam looked anything like the Great Hall, saw Cuffy and made to rise—he'd been itching to plant that cub a facer ever since that day in the woods anyway. But then a beefy hand clapped him on the shoulder and the Lord of Misrule was addressing him. "Now, Mannering? Should I make the announcement now? Soon won't be anybody left awake to hear me, you know. Harold here is already noddin' off."

It was while Nicholas was thus detained—for it would be no easy task to disengage himself from Sir Alexander's strong grasp without that woozy gentleman crashing to the floor once the support of Linton's shoulder was withdrawn—that a newcomer to the party descended the stairs from the upper floor and entered the hall.

Sir Alexander saw the woman first, peering intently at her through his liquor-blurred eyes. "Now who in Hades is that?" he asked, pointing in the woman's general direction. "Jars a memory, by Jupiter." He leaned farther front, causing Nicholas to brace his legs against one of the benches in order to keep them both upright. "Ugly bit of goods, ain't she? Still," he mused, shaking his great head, "those eyebrows sure look familiar." Then Sir Alexander's attention wandered and he poked his head in Nicholas's face—his breath hitting the Earl with enough power to fell an ox. "Now, Linton? Now?"

The woman Sir Alexander had seen had taken only a few timid steps into the chamber when she was quickly surrounded by the three boys. "Lady Lovewell!" Cuffy was the first to exclaim to the tall, angular-looking lady dressed in an ancient paniered gown, a concealing ribbed calash tied about her head. "It is a pity you missed the pantomime, for your ensemble is most ravishing."

"Wh-where is she?" Lady Lovewell stammered in a remarkably deep baritone. "Where's my Helene?"

"Stow the gab, cove," Billy admonished, sidling up to the tall figure. "Yer'll tip our lay else. The mort's here, all's bob."

"Huh?" was all Reginald Goodfellow (alias Lady Lovewell) could say before his elbows were taken and he was briskly frog-marched across the chamber to the antechamber, where Alix and Helene awaited them.

"Helene! My love! My darling girl!" Reginald exclaimed when he spied her out.

"Reginald! My dearest one! You really are here!" Helene returned breathlessly, and they launched themselves into each other's arms.

Alix stood back a bit and watched the two embrace. "Kind of makes you feel good inside, doesn't it?" she asked of no one in particular.

Cuffy looked at the odd sight before him—rather like watching Beauty with the Beast (in skirts). He folded his arms, lifted one hand to his chin, stepped back a pace, and commented meanly, "I don't know, Alix. Actually, it kind of makes me sick to my stomach. Don't know who we're serving the worst turn with this business—Mrs. Anselm, Helene, or Reggie."

Alix glowered at Cuffy's unromantic remark while Jeremy and Billy supported each other as they were overcome with a fit of the giggles and Helene and Reginald billed and cooed like a pair of out-of-tune turtle doves.

Then it was time to go. Alix was just beginning to direct the pair toward the door when Nicholas belatedly arrived on the scene—all his senses alive to any mischief. He had seen the small party leaving the chamber, and some sixth sense alerting him to the idea that something havey-cavey was about to occur, he had unceremoniously dumped Sir Alexander down on a nearby bench and gone off to investigate.

"What's going on here?" he asked as he took in the scene in front of him.

"Oh, oh," Billy blurted. "The cove is fly! We must brush!"

For once no one needed to wait for a translation of Billy's cant. In the twinkling of an eye the three boys had pushed

Helene and Lady Lovewell (who was having the devil of a time with his skirts) through the outer door, leaving Alix behind to face Nicholas with a brave grin and a small wave. "Hello, Nicholas," she cooed. "You aren't thinking of leaving yet, are you? It's still quite early."

"Stow it, Alix," he spat at her. "Who was that odd lady, and where are those three idiots going? Something's up, girl, and I mean to get to the bottom of it."

As Mannering began advancing on her, determination etched in every line of his face, Alix began to talk—and talk fast. "That lady was no lady," she said, grimacing as Nicholas responded with a shake of his head and an admonition to her not to be so cutting in her judgments.

"Only listen, Nick," she pressed on, holding him away from her with her outstretched hands. "That lady was Reginald Goodfellow—*the man Helene loves!*"

Nicholas shot a look toward the empty doorway where Reginald had just disappeared. "She picked that quiz over me?" he said in some amazement. "By God, I think I should be insulted!"

Alix giggled, relaxing a bit as she saw that Nicholas wasn't about to fly out the door and put a stop to the elopement—at least not yet. "You have every right to be insulted, love. The man's an absolute turnip-head, although he isn't a bad sort. Just the man for Helene, actually. They are on their way to Gretna, you understand."

Nicholas immediately climbed back on his high horse. "They're what!" he shouted, his words bouncing off the stone walls and echoing about their heads. "Have you completely lost your senses? Whose wild work is this?" He took a step toward the door, then whirled around to point a finger at Alix. "It can't have been the boys as they haven't the wit. It has to have been you. How very *enterprising* of you, Miss Saxon," he sneered. "Not content to singlehandedly destroy that girl's reputation, you have simultaneously put my brother and his friends in the position of having to meet Helene's brother on a field of honor."

"Oh, I seriously doubt that," came an amused voice from the doorway to the Great Hall. Rupert then sauntered into the room and, taking up Alix's limp hand, gave it a languid shake. "My compliments, ma'am. You have certainly tweaked Mama's nose with this one. I only wish I had thought of it."

"Why?" Alix shot back, for she did not like this oily creature even a little bit. "You wouldn't have had the backbone to get the thing done if you *had* thought of it." She smiled nastily. "Would you, Rupert, old sport?" Turning to Nicholas, she said, "Rupert's a pernicious little monster, you know, and loyalty is definitely not his strongest suit."

Rupert did not take offense at Alix's words, but only bowed again, saying, "You are an astute judge of character, ma'am, but you erred on one point. I am extremely loyal—to myself."

"You certainly are a cold fish," Nicholas said in disgust. "Don't you have the least feelings for your sister?"

"Why should I?" Rupert returned offhandedly. "She don't care a fig for me, you know."

"Now *that* I can understand," the Earl interposed before dismissing Rupert with a sneer and rounding once more on Alix (who had just then been trying to blend in with the ornate woodwork). "And as for you, you scapegrace," he grated, "I can only hope you don't live to regret your part in this night's work. Although I applaud your motives—if indeed they are as altruistic as you say—I heartily condemn your methods. Do you have any idea of the tragedy scene Mrs. Anselm is going to enact once she discovers that Helene has flown the coop?"

A purely delicious smile lit up Alix's face. "Oh, *yes,* Nick," she cooed. "I have a very clear picture of the scene in my mind." She held out her arm to Mannering. "Come, love, and we shall see if her reaction lives up to my expectations."

It took some little time to locate Mrs. Anselm—they at last found her half sliding under one of the tables, a small alcohol-spiced apple half stuck in her mouth. Alix leaned down to whisper something in the woman's ear.

"*What!*" Mrs. Anselm shrieked as she sat up with a jerk,

the apple dropping from her mouth. "My baby! Where is she? What have you done with my baby?"

It was Rupert who answered her. "Helene and Reginald are on their way to Gretna, Mama, and have been this last half hour or more."

The enraged woman whirled to poke an accusing finger in Alix's face. "This is your work, missy," she shouted as her ostrich-feather headdress slipped down to cover both her eyes. Shoving the thing back up high on her head, she went on hysterically, "And don't tell me my Helene went willingly, for I shall not credit a word of it. You've kidnapped her!"

All this fracas served to wake Sir Alexander from his happy slumbers, and he stood, wiped at his eyes, and called across the room to Nicholas, *"Now*, Linton? Is it now?"

"Oh, shut up!" Matilda Anselm screeched back at him. "I know what you're about, old man, and don't you think I don't. You mean to shackle your granddaughter to Mannering before he finds out he doesn't have to marry the chit. Well, sir, you shall not succeed. It is my Helene who will be Lady Linton—you mark my words!"

Rupert reached out and grabbed his mama's wrist before she could bolt across the room and take a swing at Sir Alexander. "Oh, cut line, Mama," he drawled. "You have lost. Helene has escaped you. Now stop making a cake of yourself and let's go home. You still have me, you know."

Mrs. Anselm looked up into her son's thin face, and her features assembled themselves into a sneer. "And what good are you, Rupert? Whatever good are you?"

Rupert only smiled. "Why, Mama, don't tell me you've forgotten that pretty little Miss Frobisher who took such a fancy to me last season? That sweet, pretty—*rich*—Miss Frobisher?"

Magically, Mrs. Anselm smiled. Giving her errant headdress one last shove, she slipped her hand through her son's arm and began to walk toward the door. "I hear the Frobishers have a magnificent mansion in Wimbledon. The city is so bare of company during the winter months, Rupert. I'm sure they'd be more than happy to have us visit with them for a while.''

Rupert patted his mama's hand. "Trust my mama to see the advantages of having a son such as me. You know I'd never forsake you.'' The smile on Rupert's face was nearly angelic. "Of course I shall be needing some additions to my wardrobe if I am going to pay my attentions to Miss Frobisher—some rather *extensive* additions, you understand.''

"Naturally, my pet,'' Mrs. Anselm assured him. "You shall be so handsome you shall have dear Miss Frobisher fair fainting with admiration.''

Alix folded her hands against her stomach and pulled a face. "I think I'm going to be sick. It's like Helene never existed! All she can think about now is how best to marry Rupert off to money.'' She shook her head. "And you want to know the worst of it, Nick? I think she'll find a way to do it.''

"I don't know, sweetings,'' Nicholas replied. "My blunt's on Rupert, personally.''

Then the three boys reentered the chamber and ran to join them. "Nick!'' Jeremy exclaimed, a huge smile creasing his face. "You'd never believe it! We just passed Mrs. Anselm outside and we told her how we had helped Helene and her Reggie on their way to Gretna and you know what? That daft woman didn't even turn a hair! We thought sure she'd try to murder us. Ain't any way of figuring out a woman, is there, Nick?''

Cuffy, who had been standing some ways off waiting to see which way the wind was blowing, now saw that Nicholas didn't appear ready to knock their heads together for their part in the elopement and decided it was safe to approach the man. "Before he climbed in the carriage, Rupert handed me this to give you, my lord,'' he said, holding out a large envelope. "He said he 'discovered it someplace' and thought you might want to have it. It does have your name on it. Wonder where he found it.''

Mannering took the envelope, quickly seeing that it must contain the information he had been waiting for. Now at last he would have his answer one way or another. Damn that

Matilda Anselm, he swore silently, somehow sure it had been she who had pilfered the letter in the first place. He made a quick wish that Rupert married a nabob's daughter and forced his mama to move to Bombay. Then, his anxiety warring with a reluctance to know once and for all that his lands really belonged to Sir Alexander, he moved closer to a brace of candles on one of the tables and began to read the letter.

" ' Dear Nick,' " he read soundlessly, his good eye rapidly skipping along the lines, " 'I have just finished checking out that document you sent me. It reminds me of the time Byron got his friend Scrope Davies into a muddle over just such a technicality. (You remember Scrope, don't you, Nick? George was always telling him he should marry so that he could raise a covey of little Scruples.) Anyway, Byron, being a minor, needed a guarantor in order to borrow money—a minor needs a guarantor for any monetary dealings, be they loans, wagers, etc. In Byron's case, Scrope went bail for George and nearly landed in the Fleet when our handsome bard took himself off to Italy. Your ancestor was, it seems, kinder to his friends. He didn't bother with a guarantor at all. Didn't have a valid document then either, because he was a minor at the time. I checked. Perhaps the whole thing was only meant as a joke between friends in the first place and never meant to be taken seriously. In any event, my dear friend, you may unpack—your estate is safe. Come up to Cambridge soon, chum, and we'll split a few bottles. Yrs., etc. John.' "

Although his hands were shaking, so great was his relief, Nicholas turned the paper closer to the candle so as to read an addendum his friend had scrawled at the bottom. " 'Marry the chit, Nick, and have done with it. You have my permission to name the first son after me in gratitude.' "

Throwing the paper high into the air, Nick let out a whoop that would have done any Lenape proud—succeeding in waking any revelers who had nodded off. Grabbing Alix about the waist with both hands, he then twirled the pseudo Fanny Fandango—*his* Fanny Fandango—about the large chamber, circling the blazing yule fire in an abandoned waltz that had the onlookers cheering and clapping their hands in encouragement.

Sir Alexander clumsily climbed up on one of the tables, an overflowing goblet in his hand. "Now, Linton?" he shouted above the din. "Is it *now?*"

Nick lifted the bemused Alix clear off the floor and into his arms, uncaring of her dangling bare ankles, and smiled down into her eyes. Not quite understanding just what had happened to make Nicholas look so suddenly happy, so *carefree,* but totally enraptured by the look on his dear face, she wrapped her arms around Nicholas's neck and smiled back at him.

As she was carried off toward the privacy of the antechamber, she turned her head to see her grandfather looking after her in some confusion. "Now, old man," she called to him over her shoulder. "Yes, dear, sweet, Grandfather—*now!*"

Epilogue

THEY were in the sweat house. It had become one of their favorite spots—long before Nicholas had had a chance to live out his fantasy with his adored wife, and certainly ever since. While Harold stood lookout at the top of the hill (his back discreetly turned), they spent many an afternoon between the squat hut, the stream, and one particularly comfortable bower beneath the trees.

It had been three months since their marriage—a marriage that had taken place on Alix's twenty-first birthday. It was her way of proving to Nicholas that she was wedding him because she wanted to, just as he was taking her to wife because he wanted to.

"We will be married," Alix had told her grandfather the night of the pantomime after the last of their happy guests had been dragged off to their carriages.

"O'course you will," Sir Alexander had replied, not understanding Alix's belated acceptance of what he had known all along to be an established fact.

"We're in love," Nicholas had explained while looking adoringly into Alix's bright eyes.

"Well, what is that to the point?" the old man had shot back before Harold took his arm and steered him away.

"Come with me, old one," Harold had said in perfect English. "Our work here is done."

Sir Alexander had halted in his tracks, suddenly very sober. *"English?* The savage speaks English?" he exclaimed in astonishment.

Still looking at Nicholas, Alix had replied, "He always did, Grandfather. Harold is a man of many talents. I do hope you've never insulted him when you thought he couldn't understand what you were saying. Indians have a fine way with revenge, you know. Now, Grandfather, as you love me, *palli aal.*"

At Sir Alexander's confused look, Harold had interpreted. "Alix says to bing avast, old man."

"Cant!" Sir Alexander had yelled. "By Jupiter, the man even spouts cant. *Nutter!* I need a drink!"

In the months that followed, Harold did not seek any revenge, the two old men content to sit in medieval splendor at Saxon Hall, drinking, playing at cards, and waiting impatiently for the Mannerings to produce a child or two for them to dandy on their knees and tell stories about the glories of another day.

Helene and her new husband had written to the Mannerings, thanking them profusely for all their help and telling them of their joy at being together at last—not to mention being shed of Helene's mama.

As for Mrs. Anselm, it appeared that she was finally to achieve her heart's desire, for just a week earlier Rupert's engagement to a Miss Cissy Frobisher had appeared in the London papers. One could only wonder at the tenacity of the woman, although Nicholas had said at the time that he'd bet a monkey to a pound note that the old dragon would get short shrift from her beloved son once the knot had been tied.

Jeremy and his chums were back at school but promised to be back at Linton Hall with the newlyweds at Eastertide "without fail," a thought that set Poole (and most of the villagers) to shaking in their boots.

"I know John Mortlock teased you about naming your first son after him, Nicholas," Alix was saying as she emerged now from the sweat house, a breechclout her only covering against the late winter chill, "but I'd really like to name this first one Charles—after Chas, you know."

Nicholas's head appeared at the door to the sweat house, followed closely by the rest of his nearly bare body. Straightening, he said, "Of course, sweetings. I think it would be very fitting if—*this first one!*—Alix, do you mean—"

Nodding her towel-wrapped head up and down she told him, "It is a most natural conclusion to what we have been doing, Nicholas, so you can stop looking as if Harold was about to come after you with his hatchet."

Barefoot, he walked slowly toward her, stopping scant inches away to lift his hands to loose the towel at her head and arrange her long black hair around her like a cloak. Their eyes met and held, their expressions suddenly intense, and he slipped his hand into hers and turned her toward the shoreline. Still looking at each other they waded into the stream—two glorious savages who knew they had somehow stumbled into Paradise.